Born in a London taxi in 1958, Charles Staunton emigrated to Sydney with his family in 1965. He joined NSW Police in 1978 but was drummed out in 1987 after refusing to grass on colleagues. Charles built a career as a private investigator and Mr Fix-It in Sydney and then a globetrotting money smuggler for the Pacific Mariner Cartel. In 1997 in Montreal, Charles was arrested by the American DEA for trafficking 25 tonnes of hashish worth over one billion dollars. He was sentenced to 10 years in prison but was released after serving a third of that and deported to Ireland. For the past decade he has travelled the world with a GT2 racing team and worked with security teams as a bodyguard for A-list celebrities. He has two sons, four grandkids, and lives in London.

THE GOOD BLOKE

AN INCREDIBLE TRUE STORY

CHARLES STAUNTON

MACMILLAN
Pan Macmillan Australia

Some of the people in this book have had their names changed to protect their identities.

First published 2019 in Macmillan by Pan Macmillan Australia Pty Ltd
1 Market Street, Sydney, New South Wales, Australia, 2000

Cataloguing-in-Publication entry is available
from the National Library of Australia
http://catalogue.nla.gov.au

Typeset in Fairfield LH by Midland Typesetters, Australia
Printed by McPherson's Printing Group

Aboriginal and Torres Strait Islander people should be aware that this book may contain images or names of people now deceased.

The paper in this book is FSC® certified.
FSC® promotes environmentally responsible,
socially beneficial and economically viable
management of the world's forests.

I'd like to dedicate this book to the wonderful women who have been part of my life and whose love and support have made me the man I am.

Contents

Prologue

THE END IS JUST THE BEGINNING

Montreal, Canada
23 January 1997

The sun was setting over a city camouflaged in a mantle of snow. I was staying in a discreet hotel in the very funky St Denis district. The room was nothing fancy. It had a good shower and a comfortable king-size bed. In my hands I held $10,000, just a tiny fraction of the millions I had collected, counted and couriered around the globe in my time working for the Pacific Mariners Cartel.

Suddenly, there was a knock at the door. It was an all-too-familiar loud knock.

'Police! Open up!'

Shit!

I was on the second floor and the windows didn't open wide enough to jump out. There was no escape. I had seconds to react before they forced their entry. I snapped into action.

I hid the $10,000, which consisted of only 10 notes, and an old-fashioned electric organiser with all my coded numbers under the mattress inside the nurse's fold at the end of the bed.

I approached the door with trepidation. As I turned the knob, they stormed in like the front row of a rugby team, pistols at the ready.

They knocked me to the ground. Amid shouts and scuffling, there were knees in my back, and I was handcuffed, real tight.

A man stood in front of me with a gun pointed at my chest. His pin-prick brown eyes pierced me like a knife through butter. Peering at his face, I realised I knew him. Or at least I thought I had. A traitor right under my nose. I was filled with rage.

You lying piece of shit! Why?

'Charles Staunton, you are under arrest for the importation of 25 tonne of hashish.'

I took a deep breath. I'd been in this situation before and had always been able to talk my way out of it. *Stay calm, Charlie. Watch for mistakes. All police make them and these guys will too.*

I glanced around and recognised members of the Royal Canadian Mounted Police (RCMP), but looking closer I noticed that some of the men were wearing Department of Drug Enforcement Administration (DEA) vests. A realisation dawned on me. *These men are American.*

Before I'd joined the Pacific Mariners Cartel, I'd done my homework. I knew the penalties for being involved in importing hash around the world. Short of the death penalty in South East Asia, America's sentences were among the worst. A cold curl of dread spread in my chest but I pushed it down, determined to stay cool.

A young officer in front of me trembled as he shoved a Glock in my face.

'Relax, young fellow, just relax. I'm not going anywhere,' I drawled.

A senior officer glared down at me. 'Oh yes, you are, Charlie,' he sneered. 'And it's going to be for a very long time.'

They hauled me to my feet and marched me outside to a waiting van. I took my last breath of freedom. A blast of sharp, cold air shocked my lungs.

As they slammed the door in my face, my sons' faces flashed through my mind.

I had a sinking feeling it was going to be a long time before I saw them again.

In the back of the police van, handcuffs digging into my wrists, a single thought bulleted through my brain: *How the fuck have I ended up here?*

1

COP THIS BLOKE

My name is Charlie Staunton. I'm a bloke.

For those of you people in the world who do not yet know what a bloke is, it is a kind of slang term for a man. In Australia, a bloke is the masculine archetype, associated with the country's national identity.

The Aussie bloke. Take that a step further and you have what was once commonplace, but is now an endangered species . . . *A good bloke*.

Here's how I see things.

I do not have a thousand morals. The Ten Commandments are a reference point, and thus my life is not complicated, no matter how hard I have tried to make it so. But the morals that I have, I will not sell or give up on.

I am a practising atheist, and I intend on living my hundred years enjoying my century, while not interfering with yours. If you need a hand, and you are a mate of mine, I'll be there for you. If you fuck with me, we are done. There's no need to bullshit me. I'm open to the truth, which I understand is subjective. But don't bullshit me. Life's too short.

I am not racist, sexist or homophobic. I am anti-violence. Having said that, I am not averse to stepping outside to settle our differences Marquis of Queensberry-style.

And if you're a good bloke, you'll understand what sportsmanship, and life, should be about. A sense of fair play. For me, it's not a prerequisite to be a law-abiding citizen to be a good bloke. It's about social qualities. It's about being reliable, trustworthy, loyal and true to your beliefs. It's about doing the right thing by others rather than bending the system to line your own pockets. It's about lending a hand when a mate is in trouble and, most importantly, it's about never, ever turning someone in. Even for your own benefit.

There are a lot of do-gooders ruining this world. They impose their high moral values without truly understanding the real-life impact of their actions. It's all very well to ban something, but until you've seen what affect that has on the street, you're only making things worse.

Money has never mattered to me. I've had plenty and I've had none. I am just as happy sitting in the back garden with a bottle of beer and a few mates as I am sitting at the Four Seasons with a supermodel. Every time I've made a quid I've given it away. You can't take it with you.

What I care about, what we all should care about, are my friends, my family and doing the right thing, be that legal or 'illegal'. I've met many a lawman I wouldn't call a good bloke and many of the best men I've ever met, society had consigned to the scrapheap. You've got to live by your code, your guts and your heart. That's what makes you a good bloke in my book.

*

My beginnings were ordinary. I was born in a taxi on the Fulham Palace Road in London, England, on 16 September 1958, to William and Winifred Staunton. My father was a bus driver on the London buses and Mum was the clippie (ticket puncher). They had each moved to London separately; Mum from Donegal and Dad from Wicklow. Just a pair of Irish Catholics who met on the buses.

I have five siblings: Ann, my older sister; Dermot, Kieron and Gerry, my younger brothers; and Rosaleen, my little sister. We were some of the first migrants to come to Australia on board an aircraft instead of a boat. We flew to Australia on an old prop aircraft, via sticky Bombay. We landed in Australia on my sister Ann's birthday, 16 October 1965.

I was seven. I do remember landing at Kingsford Smith Airport. It was pouring with rain. There was not a kangaroo in sight, nor an Aboriginal hurling a boomerang. I began to wonder if it had all been some ghastly mistake, that we had just flown around the world and ended up back in London.

During our first two months in this strange new world that somehow seemed familiar, we stayed with my father's brother Gerry and his wife Winnie. They lived in a terrace house in Newtown, an inner suburb of Sydney. Ann, Dermot and myself were quickly enrolled in the local Catholic school. On my first day, I was introduced to a Vegemite sandwich, and still to this day – half a century later – I regard it as one of the great pleasures in my life.

The first couple of months saw Mum and Dad trying to find work. Mum was pregnant with my little sister, but with her work ethic, that was never going to stop her looking for a job. Within a few months, we relocated to Smithfield, in the outer western suburbs of Sydney.

I started school at Our Lady of the Rosary, the nearest Catholic school. I spent 18 months there before I moved across the creek to Patrician Brothers College Fairfield – regarded to this day as one of the best rugby league schools in the country.

Six good years of my early teens were spent there before ultimately – as you do in life – the family moved on again. We went to Winston Hills, a newly built suburb near Parramatta in Sydney's west, into a very large, brand-new house. Mum and Dad had always worked hard. They both always had two jobs and grafted away. They taught us that an honest hard day's work is a prerequisite to a good life.

Moving again resulted in us changing schools, and I went to Parramatta Marist Brothers, which was not that far from home. By this time, I had my school certificate and the plans my mum had for me included doing the next two years of school, and gaining my higher school certificate.

I always had a job: first a paper run before and after school, and then a gig at the Sydney Cricket Ground selling confectionary on the famous hill. We got 10 per cent of the sale price and that was enormous money back then. I would get a train to Central Station and then walk up the hill to the cricket ground. Apart from the money, I got to see every sporting fixture that mattered in Sydney.

All the while Mum was planning my ultimate future goal: university. I, on the other hand, had a lot of different ideas, and they did not necessarily involve more school. But Mum and Dad were to be obeyed. There was no chance that any of us six children would be defying what they said.

Around August 1975, there was many a late-night discussion about me leaving school. Mum was having none of it, but she finally conceded that, if I were able to get a government job, I would be allowed to leave school. Still, in her mind, that was not going to happen. There were entrance exams for nearly all positions at the time, and dependent on your results, a long waiting time to start work. She was sure that I would – even if successful – still complete my higher school certificate.

The Commonwealth Bank was employing junior staff, and a chance came up for me to sit the entrance test. Knowing there was a very long waiting list for those jobs, Mum was happy for me to give it a go. So on a Saturday morning in early September 1975, I caught the train to Central from Parramatta, and went to the old Mark Foy's building (now the Downing Street Court complex) where I sat the test. It was all numerical, and for me, it was a piece of cake. I managed to complete it before any of the other 50 or so applicants, and wondered for a few seconds if I had got it all wrong, as there were some worried looks on the other faces around me.

That was on the Saturday. Less than a week later, I received a letter congratulating me on my success, and asking if I was able to start on 25 September 1975. Mum had some mixed feelings about it, and was certainly not happy that I was leaving school. But I'm guessing now that she was still somewhat proud that I had done so well. A deal was a deal, and I had just turned 17 years of age. So that was it. Goodbye to the old school!

I started on 25 September, at the head office of the Commonwealth Bank, in the Clearing Department on the third floor. I was pretty nervous, not really knowing what to expect. I had no idea if I was to be a teller, or what was going to happen.

As I got out of the lift on the third floor, I was thinking to myself, *Shit, there are a* lot *of girls here.*

Glass doors opened onto an area with a sign saying, 'Clearing Department'. I had with me a letter of introduction, and I could see a pretty young girl sitting behind the reception desk. I approached, handed her the letter and introduced myself with a smile.

At that moment, I heard the strange noise of machinery coming from behind me. I turned and saw a room half the size of a football field, an entire floor, full of beautiful young girls hard at work.

My first thought was, *Well, fuck me! I've just died and gone to heaven*. There were blondes, brunettes, redheads, tall, short, and they all seemed to be looking in my direction.

Just then, through the glass doors, out she came. The most beautiful woman I had ever seen. And nearly half a century later, Kim Ellen Harris still holds that title, although her name is now Kim Ellen Staunton.

The bank was brilliant. I was excited and exhilarated by a new-found sense of freedom. I enjoyed every minute of every day, and still today have the same good blokes as friends from the first day I started: Craig Horley, Bob Siemson and his brother Dave, and Harry Hiller (who would later be my best man).

We drove everywhere together, all having recently been released, to an extent, from the supervision of our parents and teachers. The girls at the bank were generally up for a bit of fun, and as there were only a few young blokes around it felt like I was living in a harem for the whole time that I was there. Kim was very prim and proper but nonetheless she hooked me up with most of the young girls there. It was a bit odd as she knew that she was the one I really wanted. I think she wanted to see what I was like without committing.

We all bought new cars, and immediately went in search of girls, beaches, rugby league and alcohol.

I had always enjoyed playing rugby league and the camaraderie of the team. I was playing on the weekends with Blacktown Patrician Brothers. The drinks at the pub afterwards weren't bad either!

It was a very good time for young blokes in Sydney back in the 1970s. Crime never entered our thought process. We had all seen our parents succeed. We all came from families where religion was the basis for the family moral code. Hard work was the only way to succeed in life. None of us had a problem with that and without exception I still believe that to this day. None of us knew any criminals. The only crimes any of us would ever even remotely consider committing were traffic offences, of which we committed plenty, and regularly.

By this time, I'd finally convinced Kim to go on a date with me. Pretty soon, we were smitten and I knew I'd found the woman who would one day be my wife.

As fun as it was, after a while the bank just wasn't cutting it for me. There wasn't enough excitement and I was on the lookout for more. In saying that, I did love my daily trip to the basement, which was the location, in what was almost a prison complex, of the bank's cash-counting room. It contained pallets of money, tens of millions in cash, and all within a hand's reach of you. Like many of my colleagues, I had many a fantasy of one day fleeing with the lot. There was only an old bloke on the gate, and he was the sum total of the security, him and his old Webley Scott pistol. If I could just . . .

Like many others, I had dreamt up a plan. I could get a truck and spray it to look like the security van that dropped off the millions that they had collected from all the branches in Sydney. There was a laneway at the rear of the bank and two huge cast-iron gates that opened onto a lift that dropped the van to the basement where the vault was situated. There was a very nice old man in the laneway at the top always drinking cups of tea. In my imaginary plan I would put something in his tea, as well as that of the old bloke downstairs, and once they were off to sleep, the three mates that I had hired to form my gang would come downstairs in the lift. We would load the van and be off before the old blokes woke up. Of course, I knew it would be a tad more complicated than that. But to be fair, not much more. In my life since then, I have met a few of the Great Train Robbers, and they would all have been part of my gang. Anyway, fortunately for me, the bank, and my imaginary accomplices, I picked up the *Daily Telegraph* instead.

2

WANTED BY POLICE

The ad read: *Join Now! The NSW Police force wants you.* I had felt for a while that I needed more from life than just a nine-to-five job. It's hard to know how long a job is going to fulfil and maybe exceed all your requirements. And one day, while rattling my way to work on the train, I saw that ad in the *Daily Telegraph*.

The salary alone was double what I was getting at the bank, and I thought, *That's for me. Some excitement for a change.* I could see myself as a lawman. I had always been interested in the law, and had I stayed at school, I felt sure that I would have gone on to university and become a lawyer.

I put the application in, and within weeks, received a letter asking me to attend the old Police Headquarters in College Street, Sydney, to sit the entrance exam. I went in to sit the test in early 1978. I was excited and curious as to what sort of exam it would be. I could not for the life of me work out why they included a spelling test. There were situation questions, and a few fluffy legal questions, but a spelling test? My concern was that my spelling was primarily phonetic. Suffice it to say, I passed (52 per cent), but got much better grades on the other situation questions.

I quickly got a congratulatory letter and resigned from the Commonwealth Bank on 14 April 1978.

After three days off, I started the next chapter of my life. On the morning of 17 April 1978, at the NSW Police Academy in Bourke Street, Redfern, I turned up smartly at 8am, complete with a new short haircut, as my hair had been quite long only the week before. I went to the office just under the archway, on the Bourke Street side. I handed my introductory letter to the administration clerk and was told to go and stand on the parade ground – a grassed area in the centre of the academy grounds, in front of the horse stables.

The mounted police were stationed at the academy, with all the stables lined up at the rear of the parade ground. Within minutes, some 150 new trainees were rolling in through the archway and gathering on the grass. It was 8.30am. Almost immediately there was an almighty roar from someone who could have been R. Lee Ermey, the drill sergeant from Kubrick's movie, *Full Metal Jacket*.

'Get into line, you fool!' It was the drill sergeant and his assistants. So began, just like in every Vietnam War movie you've ever seen, the bastardisation. The screams of, 'You big girl! You moron! How stupid are you?'

Our first inspection was really just a hail of abuse. 'Get a haircut. What are you . . . a fucking hippie? You're too fat! You're too skinny! Where's your mother?' A barrage of insults was spat at us. It was a cliché, a stereotype for army recruits and police trainees the world over.

The group of trainees were split into classes of about 25 each, and named Class A, B, C, etc. My class quickly became known as F troop, after the western comedy series at the time. The misfits.

As the weeks went by, the nine-week wonders – as we were known back then – formed friendships and relationships that remain to this day, in spite of the fact that we were nearly all sent to different stations in different parts of New South Wales. During the nine weeks, the training consisted of mainly book work, lectures and physical training including swimming.

There was one interesting diversion; a trip to the Sydney Morgue, just a few kilometres from the academy, at Glebe on the way to the western suburbs. There I saw for myself that which will be all of our futures; hundreds of bodies lying on silver benches, a name tag on the big toe of the right foot, all butt-naked.

Each body had a huge, roughly stitched scar from neck to navel, and a similar one around the skull. There they were: old, young, male, female; all very cold and very dead, lying side by side in a large cold room.

There were autopsies being conducted by the resident pathologists and their assistants, and the pungent smell that once sniffed will remain with you for the rest of your life. Death has its own obtrusive odour. Some of the recruits were physically shaken with more than one not able to hold down their cornflakes.

Much more my speed was a week spent at the Police Driver Training School, then based at St Ives, an affluent suburb on Sydney's North Shore. It was also a step away from the northern beaches. The five-day course was the fulfilment of every young bloke's racing dream, and on the Thursday of the week, we were to be tested.

It was a very enjoyable week, and on the Thursday, I passed my test, as had all bar two trainees in our class. After that, at 4pm, all the trainees headed straight to the Forrestville Hotel, the nearest pub to the driver training school, to celebrate our achievement. As we were F troop, we were the last class to pass our driving tests, and we were supposed to have our passing-out parade on the following Monday. It was all coming to fruition.

Well, maybe not yet. Around 10pm, after a good old drink at the pub, I drove home to Winston Hills a bit over 30 kilometres away. On the way home, I got stopped by – wait for it – the Forrestville highway patrol. The senior constable got out of his car and approached my door, looked down and saw my brand-new police hat on the passenger seat.

'G'day mate. Are you in the job?' he asked.

What a twit I was! I should have said, 'Yes.' Instead, I said, 'No, I'm at the academy. We pass out on Monday.'

'Where have you been?' he asked.

'At the driver training school, and then the Forrestville Hotel. We passed our test today, and went for a drink.'

'Ah, the Forry, eh. Who else was there?'

'Everyone!' I said, referring to my fellow trainees in F troop.

The senior constable frowned but then he tapped the duco on top of my car. 'Be careful, son. Get off home.'

I thought to myself, *Shit. That was lucky!* I was confused, though. Why did he let me go? If it had been my mates Craig or Harry, they would have been arrested. It wasn't even the drink-driving that bothered me, as everyone back then drank and drove. I questioned the fairness of it. Surely as a police officer I should be held to the same standard as the public, if not a higher standard? It didn't seem right.

I drove straight home, went to bed and turned up in the morning at the driver training school for a day of road driving and to pick up my certification. Then, over the PA system came an announcement: 'Trainee Staunton, report to the office immediately!'

I entered the boss's office with a vague feeling of dread, and, standing at attention, all in a line, were all the instructors. I was baffled. What were they doing here? They had nothing to do with the incident on Thursday night. None of them had even been at the pub.

The boss said in a loud voice, 'Which one of my instructors was with you on the piss last night while riding a police motorbike?'

They all rode police bikes to and from work each day.

Thinking quickly, I said 'None, sir.'

'You were pissed driving home last night, and you told the HWP officer that you were drinking with my staff.'

I denied that I had said anything like that. The HWP officer had misunderstood me. The boss told me to pack my bags and get back to the academy now, and report to Senior Sergeant Newman. As I walked out of the office, I walked past the line of instructors, all still standing at attention. The anger in their eyes was obvious.

On my way to my car, I had enough time to assure my classmates that they would be okay as I had not told the boss who was with me, and that he would not have any idea who could have been present the previous night. Two hours later I was back at the academy, and Senior Sergeant Frank Newman, F troop's class instructor, called me over.

'You have fucked it RIGHT up, Staunton, and I don't think you will be passing out on Monday. So, bring your uniform and kit back here on Monday. I will see what I can do, but it's not looking good.'

I shook as I got in my car and left for the day. What was going to happen? It wouldn't look good to anyone if I failed the entire training just because of something I'd said. It was to be a long, pensive weekend.

On Monday morning, I arrived with all my kit, wearing plain-clothes and without any expectations of going on with my police career. I saw Sergeant Newman. He had a look on his face that was not in any way encouraging to me. Then with a wry grin, he said, 'Get changed. I've gone in to bat for you, and you can pass out, but you are not certified to drive. You have to be re-tested at a future date, and you are being sent to Redfern Police Station as punishment.'

Thank fucking crikey. The thought of Redfern did not bother me at all. We had heard at the academy that Redfern was an all-action station. So I passed muster gratefully that day and was told to report to Redfern Police Station at 8am the next day.

The entire class was each given a .38 revolver and a pair of handcuffs, and this time, we all went to our separate homes to celebrate with family and friends.

I was now 19 years old. I had been brought up a good Catholic boy, and as with all of the new recruits, we were off to save the world. I was filled with hope and optimism about my new career. I was going to be the Commissioner of Police one day, I was sure of it.

*

Day one of my new life saving the world started at 8am at Redfern Police Station. Redfern is an inner suburb of Sydney, and home to a large Aboriginal population. Seven of the trainees out of my academy class were sent there, but only two from F troop.

We were all sent to the muster room. This is the first port of call for any policeman when he starts his shift. It's usually a hive of activity. The chief inspector of the station came down to the room and was introduced by the station sergeant. His name was Deck Heffernan, an old hardhead from the Kings Cross area, who wore the signs of a not-so-healthy lifestyle as brazenly as the pips on his shoulder. He was the fucking boss.

He had next to him a burly first class sergeant named Don Evendon, an ex-Australian Wallaby rugby player, and a pretty scary sort of character. The first words that came out of his mouth? 'Any of you blokes play rugby?'

A sudden hush fell over the seven of us, and Mick Sullivan – the other F trooper – dropped me right in up to my nostrils.

'Yes, Charlie does, and he's pretty good too.'

Fuck me dead, Mick!

Sergeant Evendon pointed at me. 'You! Upstairs. Now!'

I could have decked Mick Sullivan there and then. Within seconds, I was upstairs being grilled by Evendon and Jimmy Woods, the roster clerk. Then Chief Inspector Heffernan joined the party.

'We have a big game tomorrow.'

It was against North Sydney, at North Sydney Oval, the home of the Bears.

Heffernan shot questions at me. How fast could I run? What position did I play? Who had I played for previously? On and on he went. Then the decision was made, and

Heffernan said, 'Right. Be here tomorrow at noon, and you can get the bus across with the team. Bring your boots – that's all you'll need. Now, get back downstairs with the rest of them.'

I went downstairs, my mind racing. Over my shoulder, the station sergeant reminded me: 'Don't be late tomorrow. The bus won't wait for you.'

I wanted to find Mick Sullivan and belt the shit out of him. *What the fuck just happened?*

I thought the first week was induction. The rest of that day went as I believed the entire day should have, sorting out lockers, and a tour of the station and the local courthouse, which had direct access to the station.

I left there that day thinking to myself, *Have I come to the right place?* I mean, I was a 19-year-old bloke who thought he had just joined the New South Wales Police Force. Instead, I'd been shanghaied into a footy team! Totally bewildered, I met up with Kim that night and I was not happy. Sure, if I played well, it seemed quite obvious that having these senior blokes on side would be a plus, but something wasn't right and I was apprehensive.

3

HOW'S YOUR FORM?

Day two. Shortly after midday I arrived at the station, where I was met by Sergeant Ray Bourkes, a former St George first-grade rugby league player, and now the coach of the Redfern Police team. After a short introduction and some pleasantries, he said, 'You will be playing fullback today, and we shall see if you have what it takes.'

Well, I was as nervous as I'd ever been. As we barrelled across the Harbour Bridge to North Sydney, I was beset by worry and anxiety. It turned out I had nothing to worry about, not a jot.

The game kicked off; it was a windy day but all went well for me – it was just another game for another team. These blokes, on the other hand, were all older and a tad slower than me, thank fuck. Because when they hit you, you were hit, and I'll tell you that for free. These were big blokes who took the frustrations of their domestic and work situations out on the opposition.

The game was quickly over. We had won, and I was relieved, although still totally confused. *What do I do now? Do I have to go back to the station to be a policeman?* Not fucking likely, my son. Instead, it was off to the Crows Nest Hotel, just a mile from the ground. Both teams attended. There was a BBQ going, and beers aplenty, and everyone wanted to give the new boy a beer. You'll notice I didn't say 'buy', as for some reason unknown to me, police didn't pay for beer. And man, could they drink.

It was now about 7pm and the chief inspector – who had driven across the bridge in his unmarked police car – said, 'Young fellow, drive me back to the station, will you?'

He was, to say the least, well on his way, and I wasn't drunk, but certainly over the legal limit and still not technically insured to drive a police car. I said, 'Sir, I have had quite a few beers. And I am not a certified driver for police vehicles.'

'So what?' he retorted. 'I'm pissed. Let's go.'

He fell asleep in the car on the way back, and I woke him on arrival at Redfern.

'Good man,' he said. 'Training for you tomorrow, turn up about 3pm and we will sort your shifts.'

So, the first week in the force, you might say, was not exactly what I had expected. I certainly wasn't saving the world. In fact, I was barely doing any police work at all. It was confusing and I wondered what I'd got myself into.

Around this time, Kim resigned from the bank as well, and we decided to move in together. We rented a flat on Carrington Rd, Coogee, in Sydney's eastern suburbs. We could see the Pacific Ocean from our back window; the world seemed to have no end when you looked out at all that blue. It was our first home together, and a long way from the western suburbs where we had both been brought up.

Redfern was just six kilometres away, and easy to get to. Kim was working in the city at a print shop, so our commutes were short and simple. We had six of Sydney's best beaches within walking distance. We were young, and we had our freedom and independence. What could possibly go wrong?

*

On the weekend after my first week on the force, Kim and I visited our parents and friends in the western suburbs, and there was excitement at my parents' house. All our friends turned up to congratulate us both on the changes in our lives, and to find out all about them. What it was like to be a policeman? What was it like living together?

There was no chance I was going to tell my parents what was going on at the station. My mother would have rung the police commissioner the next day and had everyone sacked. Things were already tense between my mother and me. Her view was that by living together, Kim and I, as far as Catholic doctrine was concerned, were heading to purgatory; that we possessed the souls of sinners, and until we married, heaven was not on the agenda.

But my mates Craig, Harry, Bob, his brother Dave and Geoff, well, I could not wait to tell them all about the police force. It was as shocking to them as it was to me. It all sounded almost too outrageous to be true. The consensus was that the police were no different from us in that they loved a beer, a punt, and shagging any girl they could.

But it didn't take long before life took a turn. Kim and I seemed to visit the western suburbs less and less, and the friends in the force slowly took over our social time. I think it was mainly because I was doing shiftwork. We had both been nine-to-five prior to the force, and now our schedule was all over the place.

Week two, however, kicked off with me being introduced to my 'buddy'.

The powers that be in 1978 decided that the young trainees should be taken under the wing of a responsible senior member of the service. Meet Senior Constable Stan Preston. Sixteen stone, six foot three tall, of slovenly appearance, and a veteran of some 16 years. The last fucking thing he wanted was a buddy.

To be fair, nor did any of his contemporaries. The line of thought among the rank and file was, *This is a man's job and I am not a kindergarten teacher*.

It was completely obvious on our introduction that I was nothing but a bloody hindrance to him. I wasn't sure why, and thought to myself: *How can I get this bloke to accept me?*

It didn't start well, that's for sure. Our car was called over the police radio to a domestic situation in Waterloo, and I was full of excitement. At the academy, we'd been told that domestics were some of the most dangerous situations that a police officer can encounter, because there's usually very little information on what has happened and things can escalate very quickly.

He threw me the car keys.

'Have you got the bag?'

The bag was a case that contained things such as: an infringement notice book, street directory, accident information sheets, crime information sheets and other bits and bobs that you might need for any particular job.

'Yes, sir.'

He whipped around, snarling.

'Don't call me fuckin' "sir"!'

Another bit of bad news: I told him I wasn't certified to drive. He spun around again.

'I don't give a fuck. You're the boy; you're the fucking driver.'

So that was that. For the next six months, unlicensed and uninsured to drive a police car, I did exactly that.

The domestic was less than two kilometres from the station on Abercrombie Street, which I knew, thank god. So, I only had to find the number. I pulled up outside the house and jumped out of the car. There was a female voice screaming from inside, and as we approached, a lady in her early thirties, wearing what looked like a large t-shirt (as opposed to a dress) and nothing else, and I mean *nothing else*, came running down the footpath.

'He's inside,' she said, clearly distraught. She had a spot of blood just under her nostril, tears in her eyes, and bits and pieces of her body popping out everywhere. Then this very large, overweight bloke came running down the footpath, ranting at both her and us.

Stan stood there and screamed at the bloke, 'Hey, shut the fuck up!'

I was starting to panic. It looked like a possible blue between two men of nearly equal size. The bloke eyed Stan up, and approached like he was entering a boxing ring. The woman was screaming. I was frozen. Stan pushed both of his palms into the bloke's chest and he fell back onto the footpath.

'Calm down, mate,' said Stan, 'or you'll be coming with us.'

Firmly in control of the situation, Stan assisted him to his feet. The woman was still screaming and ranting. 'You bastard! You bloody bastard!'

Stan turned to her.

'Knock it off, or you'll be coming with us too.'

It transpired that they were both pissed. He had been flirting with the next-door neighbour, and she saw him at it. He denied it, and she whacked him again and again. He'd then given her a slap. The neighbour called the police, and here we were.

My assessment was that they were both pissed and had assaulted each other. I was sure he'd been at least flirting with the neighbour, but hey, they had both given each other as good as they'd got. What to do?

In any case, the decision was not mine to make. Stan said, 'Shut the fuck up, the pair of you, and get inside. And if I have to come back, you're both spending the night in the cells.'

The umpire's decision was made. Job done. As we were driving back to the station along Botany Road, there was a car swerving across lanes of traffic and hitting other cars, then bouncing back the other way. It must have hit four cars. Stan put on the siren and the blue light, and said, 'Get that cunt!'

The thrill of my first pursuit! It was short-lived, however, as the bloke pulled straight over. *Bummer.* I was disappointed, but I tried to be professional. *What happens now?*

Stan was already out of the car, walking over to the driver's side of the car. Then suddenly he shouted to me, 'Keep them back!', referring to the other drivers who had been hit by this driver and were by now pulling up behind our car.

What the fuck can I do? What's going on? I was a little bit lost, but hey, I thought, let's just improvise. I told two of the other drivers, 'Wait here, gentlemen, please. There seems to be an issue with the other driver.' They complied as Stan got the driver, put him in the back of our car and locked his car up.

He came over to me and said, 'Write down these blokes' numbers in your notebook.' I took their numbers and told them that we'd get back to them. Then we returned to the station with the offending driver.

Wow! I thought. *My first arrest.* Wrong again. It turned out that this bloke was Norm Nilson, the president of Souths Leagues Club – the licensed premises 300 metres from the station, and a known haunt for many of the police stationed at Redfern.

Stan sat with him in private for 15 minutes, then asked me for the keys to the car to drive Mr Nilson home.

'He'll buy us a beer next time we're at the club.'

That was all he said. I wasn't game to second-guess Stan's decision, as dodgy as it seemed. I just shook my head and went home.

I had to spend every shift for the next six weeks with this man, and starting the next day, we were rostered to work the night shift. That was an 11pm start, timed to begin just as Redfern came to life, so in spite of the first few weeks, I was genuinely excited about what might come our way. Well, I got that one wrong as well.

The first night I was told to relieve the station switchboard operator, common practice as he and the station sergeant needed a meal break. It was one of the old Sylvester switchboards with cords and plugs, quite simple to operate, really. A light came on, you flicked a switch and put the plug into the hole for the recipient.

I wasn't worried. All the reports and files were right in front of me, and I could read about anything that happened in the area of our patrol for as far back as I desired. So, as I was flicking through all the events that had been going on in our patrol, I looked up, and there was a lady standing at the counter. She was short, blonde, mid-thirties, slim, fair complexion, not the best sort in the world, but a long way from the worst. I stood.

'Yes, madam. Can I help you?'

She said, 'Just passing, wondered if anyone wants a blow job?'

'I'm sorry?' I stuttered. 'What was that?'

She repeated herself. 'Anyone want a blow job?'

I had to think for a second, not about her offer, but was this a joke? How should I react?

I rang the meal room, and in a muffled voice I asked the station sergeant what the go was.

'Oh, that'll be Norma. Send her up here.'

I turned back to the woman. 'Is your name Norma?'

She said, 'Yep. It sure is.'

'The sergeant said to go up to the meal room.'

She knew exactly where to go, and off she went. There were, I guess, six or seven officers in the meal room at the time, and one car on patrol. It must have been 2am when the station sergeant came downstairs.

'Go on, young fellow. Get up there and have a look.'

I sprinted up the stairs, not having a clue as to what I would witness. There on the table in the meal room was Norma: naked, legs in the air, flashing all her bits in any direction where there was a hint of interest, and masturbating with a police baton. The table she lay on was scattered with empty beer cans and there was the distinct smell of the old cooked onions that had stuck to the BBQ.

Norma disappeared into one of the interview rooms with a portly old senior constable, where I am sure she completed her intended mission for the evening, and not for the first time.

As the night progressed, and more beer was consumed, it was decided by a few of the older senior constables that we should head off to Moore Park, a large common that bordered Redfern's patrol area with Darlinghurst.

I was given the keys to a car, and two burly and intoxicated senior constables jumped in, and another car with two other constables followed. There were discussions in the car that 'we would teach them a lesson tonight'. So young, so ignorant I was. *Who are they talking about?* I wondered.

Moore Park is a large urban park, 280 acres of open space and playing fields, all within walking distance of the Police Academy and the Sydney Cricket Ground. I was told to stop the vehicle on South Dowling Street. I watched in the rear-view mirror as the other vehicle stopped behind me.

'Um, what are we doing here?' I asked.

'You'll see,' came the response.

We walked across the playing fields toward a toilet block in the centre of the park. I hung back as the four of them removed their truncheons (a small police-issue baton that slipped into the side of your trousers). Suddenly they ran screaming into the toilet block, waving their batons in the air, and almost immediately from the toilet block came running four mostly naked men holding bits and pieces of clothing and fleeing across the park in different directions.

The four constables all came back toward me, laughing and joking. I had no idea what had just taken place.

I said, 'What was that? Do we have to chase them? What did they do?'

One of the constables clapped me on the shoulder. 'Fucking poofters! That'll teach them.'

We drove back to the station, the constables in the back seat laughing and carrying on, as if they were all so very pleased with themselves. I, on the other hand, felt ashamed and solitary in my thoughts. If ever I'd wanted someone to talk to, it was that night.

I was alone in a situation where I felt very compromised by the actions of my colleagues. Without companion or partner to consider the matter with, I consoled myself with my own feelings and views, and vowed that if I were ever in that circumstance again, I would act.

On the way home that morning, I still couldn't grasp the reality of the night. *Where can I find the answers I need?* There was no way I could tell Kim about this, or my mates. What I really needed was to talk to someone else from F troop, to see for myself if it was just Redfern, or if it was everywhere.

I rang Gary Spencer, a fellow F trooper now stationed at Waverley, and he could not believe what I told him. He said that there was no way that the incidents that I described to him would happen at Waverley.

After this display of menace, I managed to avoid several of the police officers involved, and even though the activities that I witnessed surely happened again, I managed to avoid ever being present. In hindsight, though, this incident was one of the catalysts that saw my faith in the police force disintegrate.

My induction to Redfern was definitely not what the other six trainees endured. So, having already completed a night shift – unheard of for a policeman a mere two weeks into the job – and since I was on a first-name basis with the detectives on the first floor (as a result of half of them being in the rugby league team), I was taken down to the Courthouse Hotel.

The Courthouse was the local pub just a hundred metres from the station, in what was then a rough sort of area, and it was known as the 'coppers' pub'. It was part owned by Jack Gibson, arguably the greatest coach of any sport, let alone rugby league, in the world. And in a bloke's world, he was revered.

The terrace house next door was owned by the pub, or at least some close associate. A door had been installed in a common wall, and set up in the adjoining room was an SP (starting price) bookmaker named Barry. SP bookies were technically illegal at the time as you couldn't legally place a bet off the track except at the few government owned and operated TABs (where the tax could be collected). But so common and popular were the SP bookies that a blind eye was generally turned to their operations. The local SP was as much a part of the fabric of Australian life as beer and Vegemite.

I was introduced as the new young footy star at Redfern. Barry bought me a beer and said, 'You can get on here with me if you want, and we'll square up on payday.'

I had been a bit of a punter in the years prior. Harry Hiller and I went to Rosehill racecourse whenever the races were scheduled. Rosehill is a well-known track in the western suburbs, and while we were still at the Commonwealth Bank, the guy we all wanted to be was Mick 'The Whip' Elliott. Dashing good looks, a top footballer, surfer, and mad gambler, he had taught me all about betting. So, that was that.

I had been in the New South Wales Police Force for less than a month, and everything I had ever been taught in 19 years of a good Catholic upbringing, who to respect and what was right and what was wrong, was apparently not quite how life really worked.

At least during my time at Redfern I was re-rostered to attend the Police Driver Training School. It was a bit uncomfortable as a few of the instructors from my first visit were still there and remembered me. That said, they were fair and I passed. So at least I would no longer be breaking the law by driving a police vehicle.

The year flew by. Common sense saw me avoid any further incidents, and I was accepted as one of the boys at Redfern. I completed my probationary year, and was now a fully fledged constable. To top it off, we won the rugby league competition after Jack Gibson gave us a motivational half-time speech.

Shortly after, at the Cronulla Leagues Club, he told me that I was one of his best customers. We had a fundraiser the next week to raise money to purchase the following year's kit. So, of course we held it at the Courthouse Hotel. They chipped in with food and drinks, and it was a gambling night, as were most fundraisers back then. There were lots of local business people in attendance, and we raised a couple of thousand dollars.

At the end of the night, the money was counted – which included a few large cheques made out to the Redfern Police Rugby League team. I had had more than enough to drink and was somehow given the takings, I think because I was the last standing member of the team. I gave the bag with the money and the cheques to Barry the SP bookmaker for safekeeping, and he was to give it to one of the committee members on the following Monday.

Well, that Saturday, life was going on as normal at the pub, with the SP next door. Then, without warning, in stormed Beck's Raiders.

A recently appointed superintendent, Mervyn Lindsay Beck, had been given the task of cleaning up illegal gambling in New South Wales. As I mentioned, such gaming was rife to say the least. Every pub had an SP, and there were illegal casinos all over the place. Even though there was a Gaming Squad, there never seemed to be any arrests.

There was, I suppose, a touch of Eliott Ness in Beck. They were the Untouchables. So, they raided the terrace house next door to the Courthouse Hotel and Barry was nicked along with his two sidekicks. Beck's boys nabbed everything – including all the money.

There was just one small problem. Some of the money and the cheques they had were the Redfern Police Rugby League's funding for next year. Well, that wasn't Merv Beck's problem. Barry and the sidekicks were charged, and the money, reasonably suspected of being stolen, or otherwise unlawfully obtained, was seized.

Now, I was not privy to any of the proceedings that followed this embarrassing incident, but somehow Barry and the sidekicks were found not guilty, and the money was quickly returned to the Redfern Police Rugby League team's bank account.

Rumour had it that Merv Beck was not a happy man. I have always felt uncomfortable about the Merv Beck situation. Here was a very honest, hard-working policeman who did his job and did it well. Yet in the force he was regarded as a do-gooder and strangely not to be trusted. I found it difficult to find good role models.

It was a man's world back then in Sydney, and Australia generally. Attitudes were different. This was a time before HR departments and codes of conduct.

To be a 'real' man, you had to drink, smoke and bet and never show your feelings. You had to be 'strong' and never back down. In the police force this was doubly true. There was no recourse for anyone who wanted to question the status quo or report any of the wrongdoing. They would have been transferred to a desk job or to a station nobody wanted to work at, and that was the best-case scenario. I knew if I wanted to succeed, I had to toe the line even though I had serious doubts. All around me the police seemed to make their own rules and they never paid the price when they ended up in trouble. But they were meant to be the good guys . . . weren't they? Trying to work out who was 'good' and who was 'bad' was a bit of a quandary.

Only a few weeks later, two detectives were at the Courthouse Hotel and stayed for a lock-in. In the early hours of the morning, the detectives left the pub and walked, or staggered, down the road toward the railway station, about 500 metres away. On the way, they were confronted by a group of Aboriginal men, who were obviously as intoxicated as the two detectives.

The relationship between the police and the Aboriginal community had always been poor and when alcohol was added to the equation, it often became violent.

This occasion was no different. However, during this incident, the Aboriginal men properly flogged the two detectives, both of them ending up in hospital with multiple injuries. Now, in a normal world there should have been a report, and that would have been the end of the matter, especially as the two detectives who were known drunkards at times, and big-mouthed to boot, more than likely started the altercation.

But Redfern was far from a normal world and when Deck Heffernan, the boss, heard the version put forward by the two detectives, he ordered all rest days cancelled and every available officer at the station was to turn up in plain-clothes the next day. There was a meeting in the muster room at 6pm. Heffernan came down and ordered that every Aboriginal person seen walking the streets of Redfern was to be arrested. They were to be charged with using unseemly words (now this would be known as offensive behaviour), resisting arrest and assaulting police.

I could not believe what I was hearing. I thought the two detectives thoroughly deserved what they'd got. I witnessed some disgraceful behaviour that night, and I knew that it was time to leave Redfern.

I had just turned 21 when an opportunity came up for me to transfer to Maroubra Police Station. It was a new station, about the same distance away from where Kim and I lived as Redfern was. The main difference was that it was a beach suburb, with an Aboriginal community at La Perouse that would often kick off.

It was a much healthier, nicer place to work. The police stationed there had a more finely tuned moral compass, they had a good football team and a good bloke and mate of mine, Peter O'Brian, was there. As a bonus, the South Sydney and Australian Rugby League legend, Rupert 'Jack' Rayner, was the boss. He ran his division, his football team and his punting with equal vigour.

As for me, I had learned some major life lessons at Redfern, but it was time to move on. Across the board, Redfern was a punishment station for police who, for whatever reason, needed more supervision and discipline – of which they received neither. If you put all the rotten eggs in the one box, you just had a box of bad yolks. Sadly, that was Redfern.

I had witnessed criminal behaviour at Redfern. The police were a law unto themselves. The rule of law just didn't apply to them. They could do what they wanted, when they wanted. I never saw or heard about anyone being paid a bribe or of a financial gain being made, but then I was very new and knew nothing about what went on behind those closed doors.

Maroubra was a totally different story. The scenery was far more appealing, aesthetically speaking (the girls were generally topless on the beaches), and the police seemed to me to have a relaxed, surfer mentality. The football team was doing okay, and Kim and I were about to marry.

Just after moving to Maroubra, I met a very good bloke by the name of Laurie Jones. Laurie was a second-class sergeant, and had been around the block more than once in his life. He was usually a supervisor on a shift, and enjoyed nothing more than getting in a car with a couple of young blokes and 'sharing his wisdom', as he called it. Laurie gave me two bits of advice that I have never forgotten.

The first: 'It's better to be king of the shit, than shit among the kings.'

The second: 'If you have $5,000 in your pocket, there is nothing in the world that you can't do.'

Halfway through the football season, we were playing Campsie Police away, and Peter O'Brian broke his leg, and it was a bad break. After he left hospital, I took him to Mum's at Winston Hills where he spent the next two months recovering.

Mum was a nurse at the time, and she always loved helping. Peter, forever well-mannered and a good Catholic boy, was temporarily adopted. When Peter was finally back to health and back to work, it was around the time that the Rev Fred Nile (a New South Wales politician and ordained Christian minister – you could say he is an Australian version of Billy Graham) had decided that it was improper and offensive for women to show their breasts in public, and going topless on our beaches was made illegal.

Peter and I got the job of beach patrol, a sort of 'thank you' from boss of the district Jack Raynor. We really should've been thanking Rev Nile! We were 'forced' to walk the beaches, telling all the topless girls that what they were doing was now illegal, and that they could be arrested. And we needed their name and number. *Really! And this is an ACTUAL job? Well, I'm having some of this. Did I remember to say 'Thank you, Reverend'?* This went on for the entire summer. Er, and did I say, 'Thank you, again, Rev'?

I was still betting with Barry at the Courthouse Hotel when my mother found out – and I'm still not sure how she did – and she was having none of me gambling. She rang Jack Raynor and verballed me. She said that I was tipping off the local SP bookmakers as to when they were to be raided. Well, even though the accusation was untrue, the verbal worked.

I was standing in front of my boss 15 minutes later, and he absolutely gave it to me. A non-stop rant. 'How the fuck do you know? *I* don't know when they're going to be raided! SP bookmakers are the worst way to gamble, you can't win!' On and on and on he went.

Then came the clincher: 'If you continue betting with them, I will get rid of you.'

Yes, sir!

At this point, I was enjoying being a police officer. Yes, I broke the law, but I wasn't bent. I was a straight cop. I wasn't corrupt or on the take and I wasn't violent. I believed in fairness and justice for the people I dealt with. I wasn't vengeful and I didn't see myself as better than everyone else just because I was a cop. I didn't take advantage of my power the way other cops did. I did indulge in some of the harmless perks, like betting, but I had morals and I stuck to what I believed was right. All was well, and I was back on track: the commissioner's job was there in my future.

4

HERE'S YOUR CHANGE

It was around this time that Kim and I wanted to buy our first house. Dad had us planning to move back out to the suburbs.

He was working for Neeta Homes, a building company in the western suburbs that catered primarily for young couples building their first homes, and he could get us a deal. It was never going to be our first choice, but as each day passed it was looking more and more like the best option in the ever-expanding Sydney metropolitan area.

If moving away from Maroubra was going to be the case, I knew I was going to have to get a transfer out to somewhere in the western suburbs. As Sydney expanded west toward the Blue Mountains, some 80 kilometres from the coast, the opportunity to be stationed out that way was diminishing with the build of each new house.

I made an application to be transferred to the Modus Operandi Unit. The Modus Operandi Unit analysed crime trends and patterns to identify offenders. They were based at the CIB (Criminal Investigation Branch) building in the city, just up the hill from the Downing Street Courts. The job was a way of eventually being transferred out to the suburbs where Kim and I wanted to live. The CIB building had 20-odd floors, and each squad had its own floor. The unit was a hive of activity from dawn till dusk.

I paid attention at the Modus Operandi Unit and became an avid reader of methods, crimes and police procedures. It occurred to me that there are not very many bright criminals. They all seemed to make silly mistakes. They wanted to tell someone what they were doing, as if to seek approval. After a time, I surmised that tattoos are a bad idea, as are telephones in general, not to mention being a poor driver.

And then, let's say you actually pulled off a job and got away with your goods, valuables or money, you'd then be faced with the biggest problem of all. What to do with all the money? I can't say I've met many bright sparks among the criminal class, but reading up on all the ins and outs sure was interesting.

*

Just as my professional career had finally turned a corner, good things were happening at home, too. Kim and I at last moved to Parramatta, 30 kilometres west of Sydney, where we rented a flat on the river and had easy access to the station. We were married on 30 August 1980 in a small ceremony in a registry office and had a gala feast on her parents' rose farm. They had bought it a few years earlier at Rouse Hill, then a semi-rural area, 40 kilometres west of Sydney.

My mother cried for the whole day, as we had not married in a church – so eternal damnation was surely still on the cards for Kim and me.

As we were leaving the wedding reception, Kim's dad Bernie, now my father-in-law, asked me, 'Are you all right for money?'

I said, 'Yes. All good.'

Little did I know that he had robbed the local building society the day before. Or that for the past two years he had robbed pretty much one a month.

Bernard Frederick Harris was the father of the most beautiful woman in the world, who was now my wife. A nicer man you were unlikely to meet. He protected his family, worked extremely hard, had some good ideas and went with them. He was a grafter who had opinions on good and bad, legal and not so legal.

He built a four-bedroom home on five acres of land at Rouse Hill, in a semi-rural area of the north-western suburbs, and started a rose farm. Bernie worked hard, and did all the labour himself, and you could see the pressure he was under. The farm had a natural dam, but alas, there was no town water. The local council said it was supposed to be coming, but then, so was Christmas.

There was an extended dry period, and the dam had long since dried up, which meant Bernie had to purchase tankers of water to keep his roses alive. Then, as now, it was an expensive fix. He had a wife who worked as hard as he did and four children still at home.

Not long after our wedding, we were delighted to announce that Kim was pregnant. Everyone was thrilled, including Bernie.

One afternoon, close to the due date, Kim rang me at work, in floods of tears. I immediately thought something was wrong with the pregnancy, but no, she was weeping for her beloved father. He had been arrested.

'Don't worry, darling,' I said. 'He's probably had a few beers and been caught drink driving. It will all be okay, don't worry.'

I got the train home, and Kim greeted me at the door with more tears and the news: 'They say he has been robbing banks.'

I roared with laughter. 'Don't be silly. Where is he?' She said he was at Chatswood Police Station and gave me the contact name. I immediately rang Chatswood Police. 'Can I speak with Detective Sergeant Alan West, please?'

They put me through. I introduced myself and he knew who I was.

'G'day, mate. Got some bad news. We've just arrested Bernie for a stick-up, and we are going to charge him with at least twenty more.'

'Fuck off!' was my first response. 'You're not loading my father-in-law. I'll be there in 40 minutes!'

Loading is where a person is charged with extra crimes on top of the main crime they are alleged to have committed. My immediate thought was that they were trying to clear unsolved hold-ups by putting them on Bernie. I got in the car and floored it across to Chatswood. I stormed upstairs to the detective's office.

'Where's Alan West?'

He came over and introduced himself. I had seen him around but had never met him. He was a good man, an honest cop, and a decent bloke. He took me to his office.

'Look here,' he said.

He pointed at 50 pictures on a whiteboard. They were all of Bernie at different locations with a sawn-off rifle, entering and leaving different banks, smiling in nearly all of them.

Instantly, my mind went back to Bernie's lounge room a year earlier. We had been visiting their farm and I was lying on his lounge, in my uniform. The six o'clock news was on the television, and the presenter showed a fuzzy photo, taken with a video camera, from a recent robbery. It wasn't the clearest shot (they never were back then), but you could see a man walking out of a bank with a cash bag of money, holding a rifle, with a grin on his face.

I said to Bernie, without flinching, 'Shit, that bloke looks like you.'

His reply: 'It does, too!'

'Sydney's gentleman robber', they called him. The man would say, 'please', and 'thank you', and even 'goodbye'. Once when a teller got upset, he said, 'Look, don't worry, I'll come back next week,' and left, only to go back the next week, true to his word.

I remember lying there on his sofa laughing, saying, 'You had better be careful next time you go to the bank, Bernie. They will grab you.'

It had never even occurred to me that it could possibly actually be Bernie. Alan West had to bring my thoughts back to the present.

'Look, Charlie. It's not a fit-up,' Alan said, meaning the charges were for real and not an attempt to frame Bernie. 'He's gone. He has not said a word, and asked us to call you. You can see him if you like, and then we are going to charge him. Needless to say, bail is a no-go. He will be at Central Court tomorrow morning.'

I went into the interview room where Bernie was being held. Surprisingly, he seemed calmer than me. I think he thought his arrest was a blessing; he was glad it was all over, and was up for the consequences. He knew that I would do whatever needed to be done to sort his family matters out.

I was at a loss for words. I asked him if he had made any statements and he shook his head. I told him to say nothing and that I would get him a lawyer and I would see him soon. He could see I was disappointed in him and that probably made him feel worse.

Still, I was in shock and I can tell you, it was a bloody long drive home that night. The end result was that Bernie was charged with 27 armed robberies. He was refused bail, and Kim and I moved out to Rouse Hill. She was now days away from giving birth and suddenly, I'd inherited an instant family.

It didn't take long before everyone I worked with knew about Bernie and there was many a joke that I knew where all the money was hidden. Sadly, there was none left, but I was grateful as that would have put me in a much more complicated situation.

Kim had two sisters and two brothers between the ages of nine and 17, a mother with a mortgage, and five acres of roses without town water. It's amazing what you can do under pressure. I had to make a decision about Bernie. I decided to support my father-in-law.

The sawn-off rifle he had presented to the staff at the banks and building societies was a relic and not actually able to fire a projectile of any kind. The only person ever likely to be physically hurt was him, and there was every chance that had he been caught at the scene, he would have been the one getting shot.

Not in any way was I ever going to condone Bernie's actions, but when I heard that the gun was found at the bottom of the dried-up dam, I began to understand his answer to the crisis that he'd found himself in. My response was the same: 'I'm gonna need more money!'

So, I started working seven days a week; five shifts in the police, and as many doors around the clubs as I could. Back then, you were not allowed to have a second job in the force, but nearly everyone did, usually at the local discotheque where they paid cash. There were good reasons that the licensees were happy to employ coppers: any problems, and your doorman would ring the station and there would be an immediate response to sort out a blue of any kind. I was working long days and double shifts, but it was exciting, and it paid well.

In the midst of that crazy time, Danial, my eldest son, was born, and that was probably the most magnificent thing I had ever watched.

There was, however, still the problem of Bernie in Parramatta Gaol. I learned quickly that if you murdered someone, there was a presumption of bail, but armed robbery . . . there was no presumption of bail. So it fell to me to prove that Bernie was the exception to the rule.

I have often thought that Bernie's arrest was the catalyst in what has been a very interesting life on the fringes of the legal profession. I went to court cases, hundreds of them. I watched, and I paid attention, and I learned how lawyers and the judiciary interacted.

I was, in a sense, the lone juror, and decided in my own mind on the guilt or innocence, although none of these cases had anything to do with me. I just saw mistakes made on both sides and questioned the veracity of both on occasion.

I observed the legal system from a surprisingly objective point of view. I watched the results. I saw who got the lenient sentences and who got life. I noticed who the good lawyers and counsel were, and noted the ones I'd rather avoid.

Here's something I'll tell you for free. To this day, without exception, if your lawyer is no good, you are totally fucked. It was around this time that I first saw Christopher Murphy. A criminal lawyer based in Sydney, he was hated by nearly every police officer in the country, let alone Sydney, and for good reason. Murphy was the enemy of every police officer who had ever verballed or loaded a defendant, and there were plenty of them.

Verballing comes from the time before interviews were recorded, where an officer would type up the content of an interview. 'Verballing' is where the officer tells the interviewee what they have done and types it up, regardless of what the interviewee actually says or has done.

Once I saw Murphy defending a client at Central Local Court in the heart of Sydney. A detective was called to the witness box, and Mr Murphy viciously harangued him, alleging that the detective had verballed his client. The ashen-faced detective left the witness box some time later, both he and his partner calling Mr Murphy 'the biggest cunt in the world'. They were saying, in effect, that he was no better than them.

Both detectives were clearly shaken, and you could tell they never wanted to go through that again. 'What a prick,' they both kept muttering as they were leaving the courthouse. I watched Christopher Murphy walk out of the court with a victorious look on his face, and I saw the unexpected joy on the face of the now-free client. I felt conflicted. It seemed to me that the better man had won. *I'm a policeman, though. Why do I feel pleased that the bad guy got away?*

The whole situation was indeed life-changing for me; it was the first time I considered that perhaps the bad guy may not in fact always be the bad guy. I saw too that the application of the law could be like a game; and like most sports, the better prepared you are, the higher your rate of success. Real justice doesn't always get a look-in.

However, I knew that the offences I had witnessed were summary matters, that is, less serious offences garnering shorter sentences. *Could the same tactics apply to others in direr situations?*

What I needed to do was head up to the district courts to see what happened to people who are found guilty of indictable matters (more serious cases that go to a trial with a judge and jury). If you plead, generally, you're quids in with regards to sentencing. If you don't plead, and you go down, you can expect a good deal more time.

References and referees can show mitigation (extenuating circumstances), and you can reduce your sentence dramatically. I went to the Darlinghurst District Court, which was the closest court that dealt with indictable matters. Here, if you were convicted, you were very unlikely to be going home that year, or possibly for the next decade.

In this court, there again was Christopher Murphy, except this time, he was instructing a barrister by the name of Patrick Costello (known as the Counsellor). My lord, what a dynamic duo. Like Batman and Robin, fighting for good over evil. And there *were* times where that was definitely true. I watched the two interact, and indeed, they could have been enemies at times, but they were a team, and a formidable one at that.

As the days went by, I attended so many sentencing matters that I thought, *At this rate there will be no room in*

New South Wales prisons for any more offenders. Not at the rate they were locking them up. Again, as I watched, I saw very similar charges get different results, and I paid attention to how exactly that was achieved.

Lessons learned, it was soon time for Bernie to plead guilty to all 27 robberies. With my acquired knowledge of the system, I got the referees together: I was one, the local federal MP another, family and friends, and get this: his bank manager!

Bingo! Bernie got 12 years with a seven-year non-parole period, of which he only had to do a third. There was also a prison strike coming up, and you got three days' remission for each day of the strike. The result: Bernie did 26 months in the laundry at Parramatta Gaol. Whether you believe it or not, it was the right result for a very good bloke. Had I not known Bernie it would have been difficult to support him after what he had done. But I did know him, he was family, and I loved him, so it was a no-brainer.

Now it was time for me to sort a few things out. I quite grudgingly put in an application to join the Highway Patrol. I mean, *no one* wants to volunteer to be a highway patrolman. But it was the only way I could possibly be transferred to an area closer to home. I was in need of every possible hour of every day to pay the bills. Sadly, in week five, I had an argument with the boss's secretary. She went to him crying and mentioned our little chat. The result of this was that he informed me that I would be stationed at North Sydney until Hell froze over. Fuck me. I was screwed.

The following weekend while on patrol in the Mosman area, a beautiful part of Sydney's North Shore, a call came over the radio around sunset saying that there was a pursuit of a vehicle and it was heading our way, then further information that the vehicle had crashed, and the offender had decamped down an embankment onto a boat on the foreshore of Sydney Harbour.

Just at that moment, the clouds ruptured, and the rain slammed down. My offsider and I arrived minutes later at the scene. After slipping our way down a steep incline, we saw seven or eight police, pistols drawn and pointed at the offender, who was wielding a machete on a boat, screaming that he would kill anyone that approached.

At the top of the slippery incline were the inspector and detective sergeant in charge of the district on a portable radio, calling to launch OPV (Offshore Police Vessel) *Nemesis* of the Water Police to attend the scene. I thought to myself, *This all seems a bit bloody ridiculous*. I put on my raincoat, which in hindsight meant no one knew my rank.

I was clearly the most junior member of the force at the scene. I shuffled down the embankment further, made my way past the police that surrounded the boat, and said to old mate with the machete, 'Hey, I'm coming on board.'

'I'll fucking do ya!'

'Oh mate, relax, will you, buddy?' I said, and approached the mooring rope attached to the bow of the boat. I eventually balanced my way on board. I was calm, and the offender waving the machete was out of striking distance, trying to keep one eye on shore and one on me. I noticed a case of Victoria Bitter on the deck.

'Come on, mate. What do you say? Let's have a beer,' I said, pointing to the case. He turned and took a can from the case and as he approached me, I came from the ground with a clenched fist, and with precision, produced one of the best uppercuts of all time, landing square on his chin and lifting him off the deck of the boat and straight into Sydney Harbour.

The machete went flying with him, and then to my total amazement, all the police surrounding the boat on the shore jumped into the harbour as well, guns and all. I balanced my way back along the mooring rope, walked past the fracas now taking place in the harbour, slid my way back nonchalantly up the hill past the inspector and the detective sergeant, who were both clapping.

'All correct, sir,' I said, and got back in the car to continue patrol.

Some two hours later, a call came over the police radio: 'The highway patrol vehicle with Constable Staunton to attend North Sydney Police Station immediately.'

This was not the highway patrol station, but the district head station. My driver at the time said, 'I think you may be in the shit, Charlie, but it was bloody funny!'

We were not too far from the station, and acknowledged that we would attend immediately. On arrival, the desk sergeant winked at me. 'Well done, mate! The boss wants you in his office at the top of the stairs. Turn left.'

I walked up the stairs, and there in the office was the chief inspector of the district.

'Sit down, young fellow. Firstly, I want to say thank you. What occurred today was the best piece of police work I have seen in a decade. I have recommended you for a commendation, for bravery and good police work. You will write up a report of today's incident and submit it here to North Sydney and I shall take care of the rest. Now, is there anything I can do for you?'

'Well, sir, it's funny you mention that . . .'

I asked him politely how long it took for Hell to freeze over, and explained my version of the events of the previous week. He nodded. 'Might have frozen already, son.'

With that, we shook hands, and I left his office. Hell *had* frozen over, and I was transferred to Penrith the next week. Kim was overjoyed. We had our own new home built, albeit not in our preferred location. There was, nonetheless, a sense of new beginnings.

Bernie was doing well, and my new extended family were getting by. Danial, our son, was getting bigger with each passing day, and Penrith was a station of really good blokes with a good football team.

I spoke too soon. People always complain about highway patrolmen and people like my new boss were the reason.

Sergeant First Class John Dickinson, otherwise known as my new boss, preferred to book people rather than give them warnings. His philosophy? Numbers, numbers and then more numbers.

In every HWP station there was what was called a day book where each officer had to complete his numbers at the end of the shift, for example, the number of speeding, parking, infringement notices issued, arrests, etc. There was also a box for cautions issued. Cautions were frowned upon by Sergeant Dickinson, but for me, they were the obvious thing to do.

I had paid attention to the course at North Sydney. I believed that if you stopped someone and pointed out to them that they were probably doing something really stupid, and indicated to them the possible ramifications of their actions, it was a win-win situation. The end result: drivers would be more receptive to the idea that they should slow down, and that perhaps not all highway patrolmen were the pricks they thought they were.

It was always going to be a short-term stay for me at Penrith. Even though it was very close to our new house, and the general duty police were a fantastic group of men, I really didn't like highway patrol duties. It was time to go.

5

MEETING BILL

An opportunity came up for a transfer to Parramatta, halfway between Penrith and the city. I had been to school there, knew lots of people in the community, and my own family were still living in the area. Plus I was an avid Parramatta Eels supporter.

There was a general duties vacancy. I applied, and the transfer was approved. It was next to no time before I knew everyone.

One evening there was a call to Spurway Street, Ermington, a modest suburb of working class people about four kilometres east of Parramatta on the way into the city. This was my introduction to Bill Bayeh. Only a few months older than me, Bill was a Lebanese migrant, good-looking, tall, slim, olive complexion, dark hair and possessed of a unique charm.

He was poorly educated, but street smart. Well liked, but known in his community as a bit of a scammer, he was also illiterate (a later diagnosis revealed he was dyslexic).

On our first meeting, I answered a call to attend a domestic. A tall, very attractive blonde lady with whom Bill had a casual relationship was outside his house, screaming that he was a lying bastard, and that he had been shagging someone else. The story was never confirmed, but was more than likely true. And she was not happy. She wanted him charged with *anything*. She wanted revenge and would have said absolutely anything for that to happen.

Instead, I persuaded her to get a cab home, and happily, she took my advice. Bill's parting words to me were, 'Thank you, my friend. Thank you.'

Not a week went by before Bill – and 20 other Lebanese migrants – were transported from an illegal card game in Granville, a neighbouring suburb, and part of Parramatta's jurisdiction. Once again, Beck's Raiders had struck and wanted them all charged with illegal gaming offences. Bill approached me in the charge room, and with a big smile said, 'Hello, my friend.'

I had only met the man once for 10 minutes.

'Can we sort this shit out? Have these blokes [Beck's Raiders] got nothing better to do? These guys are all family men, no criminals here. They all need bail. They have to work tomorrow.'

There was never going to be a problem. At this time, the early 1980s, you could give any name you wanted, pay $50 for bail, and a $2 recognizance fee, whereby you would agree to appear at the local court a week later. Of course, no one ever turned up and that was that.

Beck's Raiders got their numbers, and everyone was happy. To this day, I still have friends who were arrested in that group of gamblers. I would see Bill around the Parramatta area every month or so for the next few years. He seemed harmless, always charming. He was the younger brother of Louis Bayeh – who at the time also lived in Ermington, just a kilometre from Bill's place.

Louis was a Kings Cross identity – why, I was never sure. Much thicker set than Bill and nowhere near as charming, Louis was always seen being driven in a Mercedes around Parramatta, usually in the early hours of the morning, stopping at a late-night café for coffee with characters of dubious appearance, and always with a much shorter, very wild-looking young Lebanese man by the name of Sam Ibrahim. Now there was a fearless criminal.

From the first time I met Sam, he seemed to take pride in the fact that I told him (more than 30 years ago now), 'Sam, you are a hoodlum.'

Sam could fight. Lightning fast, with exceptionally large hands, he could swing a leg higher than seemed humanly possible. And if it connected with your head, you most assuredly would be unconscious for some time. He was loyal, and if you were on Sam's side, no matter what, you had little to fear. If you crossed Sam or went anywhere near the Bayeh or Ibrahim families . . . Good luck to you.

It was then, on the horizon, that I met Sam's younger brother John, a much quieter young man, but you could see the difference between him and the rest – he was on a mission.

The Ibrahims and their mother had migrated to Australia from war-torn Lebanon back in the 1970s, arriving in Sydney and settling in Merrylands, a neighbouring suburb of Parramatta. Sam was the eldest of five children. Both the Bayehs and Ibrahims had their limited educations in the same turf as me.

There was a strange respect between myself, the Bayehs and Ibrahims. All the way back to the 1980s, we had no dealings other than the day-to-day life in the district. Just a respectful nod from opposing members of the community.

How funny life can be. No one knows what the future holds in store. I certainly had no idea how close John and I would become over time.

Parramatta was a social station, and the general duties staff – of which I was just one of many – were busy all the time. We had detectives, highway patrol, a district court, a scientific section and a cell complex that had a constant trail of prisoners up and down the sealed corridors to the busy courts.

In addition, there was the newly built Westmead hospital, the largest hospital in the southern hemisphere, and the rugby league team, who were champions at the time, with their new stadium. To top it all off, we had the largest Westfield shopping centre in Australia at that time.

The whole district was a hive of activity, 24/7. A new squad had just been created – the Tactical Response Group, known as the TRG. There were about 50 initially, and over the next few years, it grew to nearly a hundred. All young and very fit, they were the pride of the force at the time, the real tough guys.

They had smart-looking uniforms for tactical purposes, and were trained in the use of more advanced firearms. When shit went down, the first responders were always the TRG. When a siege situation happened, the TRG were the first called, and held what was called 'the inner perimeter' until the arrival of SWAT, the Special Weapons and Tactics team who would then take up the inner perimeter for negotiations, and, if it came down to it, a full assault.

I was in the fourth group to be trained for the TRG. An intense course, it was very physically demanding. There were no women in the TRG; it was a squad for men. There were quite a few women joining the force at that time, but the TRG was considered a man's job, and in the early 1980s, this wasn't questioned. Each division in Sydney had at least one team, and each team consisted of four officers. At our stations, we had a room that contained all our equipment – shields, helmets, shotguns, bullet-proof vests and the like. We trained regularly in our teams, and the whole squad would meet at least once a month in the city for training and testing.

The first real test for us was what became known as the Father's Day Massacre, on 2 September 1984. This was an out-and-out gun battle between rival motorcycle gang members. The shootout had its roots in an intense rivalry that had developed after a group of Comanchero bikies broke away from the club and formed the first Bandidos Motorcycle Club in Australia. It was believed that the split was caused by a domestic situation involving a matter of honour over a woman. The Comancheros set up their clubhouse in Harris Park, the next suburb over from Parramatta.

Parramatta was just 10 kilometres from the scene of the bloodbath, and home to most of the Bandidos. The community was shocked that this had happened. The Bandidos were a common sight around the area, and certainly known to most of the Parramatta Police Rugby League team. There was many a pre-season trial game played against Bandidos members – these games were always no holds barred – followed by beers later at any one of a number of local hotels.

Seven people were killed at the Milperra Hotel that Sunday, some of them innocent bystanders, with a further

28 injured. This event was the catalyst for some very significant changes to gun laws in Australia, and I have often thought that America should have paid attention to how we handled those changes.

In the aftermath, 43 people were charged with seven counts of murder, under the doctrine of 'common purpose' (whereby all the participants in a criminal enterprise are held responsible for everything that results from that enterprise). What was about to unfold was the longest joint criminal trial in the history of New South Wales.

A total of 58 policemen provided security, consisting of armed members of the TRG. It was a logistical nightmare. The Bandidos were being housed at Parklea Prison and the Comancheros were at another prison. The newly built Penrith police station and courthouse complex became the venue for the trial. All participants had to be in the court at 10am. There were 43 defendants, 58 immediate police, 40 court staff, and 25 lawyers and barristers. Add to this a total of 1,500 jurors for the selection process. You work it out! Bloody chaos.

Shortly before the court proceedings were to start, numerous logistics commanders were assessing and assigning personnel to various tasks. They required prison van drivers to pick up the bikies from prison. If possible, all police were to be TRG-trained. To be assigned, a knowledge of the parties involved was obviously a bonus, and a relationship with the legal profession an even bigger bonus. Christopher Murphy was the supreme commander for the defence of half of those charged, and was disliked by most police.

It was pointed out that a young constable first class by the name of Charles Staunton, previously stationed at Penrith, may just have a role to play. I had been licensed as a prison van driver a year earlier, had completed my TRG course, knew nearly all the Bandidos, some of the Comancheros, and had a relationship with Christopher Murphy, albeit only at the Rosehill racetrack when the races were on.

Murphy's brother, Vince, was a bagman for a rails bookmaker. I would not go as far as to say we were friends, but we certainly had a respect for each other, and frankly, I really liked the bloke. Therefore, it was decided I was to be stationed at the trial for its duration. The overtime that could be earned was a huge bonus for any of the police participants.

It was certainly entertaining from the spectator's viewpoint. For the duration of the committal, I sat in court all day looking attentive, the more boring moments broken up by an earpiece and a small transistor radio. I could listen to all the horse racing, every day. I am sure everyone knew when I had backed a winner, judging by my facial expressions.

The proceedings went on for more than two years, and the tension and the grind of the daily routines certainly got to all involved. Personalities were at loggerheads every day, and I found myself constantly being the intermediary between the various factions. The fun was gone. Time to move on.

The jury finally delivered 63 murder convictions, 147 manslaughter convictions and 31 for affray. In all, 16 Bandidos received sentences of seven years each for manslaughter. Operationally speaking, the commanders running the show clearly deserved any commendations that came their way. And as for me, it was time for a little trip to Bathurst.

*

The Australian Motorcycle Grand Prix was held at Bathurst each year. Bathurst is a country town in western New South Wales, some 200 kilometres north-west of Sydney, just over the other side of the Blue Mountains. As with many large events, sporting or community, there was a need for a police presence, for control and general public order.

Bathurst had two annual events, the Motorcycle Grand Prix and the Bathurst 1000, both held on the Mount Panorama circuit. Both required some major, well-thought-out policing.

At Easter in 1985, the bikie court case was coming to an end, and a week away with my TRG team to Bathurst was just the type of diversion we all needed. Pretty much the entire TRG Unit was sent to Bathurst each year, especially to the bike race.

The car race, held in October, is a much more family-oriented event. The bike race, though, was a totally different scene, from a police perspective. It is Australia's premier bike race, but it was also Australia's premier battle between the police and public, with several hundred injuries and arrests every year in those days. And, to be fair, the police loved it . . . as did the troublemakers.

There are differences between bikers and bikies. In America as well as Australia, Motorcycle Associations (MCs) consider bikies outlaws because they do not adhere to Australian Motorcycle Associate (AMA) rules. Instead, bikies have their own outlaw culture and rules. The US Department of Justice as well as its Australian counterparts consider Outlaw Motorcycle Gangs (OMGs) to be organisations whose members use their motorcycle clubs as conduits for criminal enterprise. The crowd heading for Bathurst wasn't made up of bikies, but rather bikers and motorsport fans. But this mob would surely be raising hell.

From the TRG perspective, the trip to Bathurst was a chance for the teams to have a week away from the tedium of normal police work. All TRG police performed general duties for most of their daily routines, and this was a bonding week, a training week, a big drink and a punch-up.

By this time, 1985, I was a seasoned 26-year-old copper, and this was my third stint in Bathurst, but my first time as a member of the TRG. We set off from Parramatta, west along the Great Western Highway. It's just one road, up over the Blue Mountains; a three-hour trip in a mini-bus.

There were three TRG teams of four. While we were there, we stayed at St Stanislaus' College, a Catholic boys' boarding school (the students were on holiday for the duration of our stay). Our first report for duty wasn't until 3pm the following day so on arrival we signed in, got our beds, got dressed and headed for one of the many clubs and pubs in the town.

The town of Bathurst opens its doors and hearts to the contingency of police that arrive twice a year, and ladies from towns far and wide flock there.

There was a pub in the centre of town called The Tavern, with a disco on, and it looked like the late-night place to go that particular year. There was a queue to get in, and as I was waiting at the entrance, I heard a doorman telling the punters that there was a $2 cover charge.

The guy in front of me got to the doorman and pulled out his wallet, showing him a police warrant card (ID), and said, 'Police,' to which the doorman said, 'Marty, how are you?' The policeman, who I had never seen before, was of the opinion that he did not have to pay. The doorman, who stood a good six inches above the policeman, said, 'Mate, it's $2 in, or that's the exit over there.'

With that, the policeman took his exit. I was next in the queue and handed the doorman $2. 'G'day mate, what a prick that bloke was. Charlie's my name.'

He shook my hand firmly and looking me straight in the eyes, said, 'Marty Clapp is my name. Nice to meet you, Charlie.'

It was at that moment that I met a true friend, the best bloke and friend I have met in life.

Well, after a huge night, it was time to sharpen the mind, run off the hangover, and prepare for the almost-certain melee that awaited us, come the following night. There were about 80 of us, well drilled, and up for whatever came our way. Or so we thought!

In 1979, a compound had been established at the top of the mountain. It was smack-bang in the middle of the bikers' camping ground and twenty metres from the toilet block and public telephones. It consisted of one small brick police station, fitted with bulletproof glass; and a four-metre-high, cyclone-mesh fence, ribboned with barbed wire. The grounds were large enough to hold half a dozen vehicles, and the 80 of us.

At 5pm, we were given our orders, kitted up in riot gear and bused up the mountain past a number of designated random breath testing stations, six along the road in to the track. Something for motorcyclists to negotiate en route to the camping grounds.

As we passed each one, we got the acknowledgements and nods from the highway patrol and general duties traffic police. Noted and appreciated. We were the troops heading to war, and everyone in Bathurst knew it.

On our approach up the dirt road for the last kilometre, it was becoming obvious that it was going to be a wild night. The crowds were gathering, and the alcohol was flowing.

There were no limitations on the amount of alcohol sold or consumed, and it was a surprisingly warm, humid evening so it seemed everyone had started early.

There were nearly 15,000 people already there, and more arriving every hour. As the sun set, the pre-riot entertainment was already in full swing. The smell of hundreds of campfires burning, large numbers of people forming 'bullrings' surrounding riders who were displaying their skills at doing 'doughnuts'.

There was also the traditional ritual of soaking toilet paper rolls in petrol, lighting them, and then hurling them in the air. There were drag races illuminated by the embers of the campfires, a chaotic carnival atmosphere, and the continuous roar of the motorcycles. There was a tension in the air unmatched by anything except perhaps the moments before a Grand Final.

It was 8pm, and the scene was being set inside the barbed-wire fence. Here we were, the agents of the state, the notorious TRG, equipped with riot shields, extended batons and helmets.

Outside was a crowd of nearly 20,000 people, each equipped with bricks, empty beer bottles filled with petrol, stones and whatever else could be used as a projectile. The superintendent Nev Tamlyn approached the crowd through the gates of the compound, with a loud hailer, and read out the riot act.

'Disperse now or be arrested!'

In response came a roar of mocking laughter, and a rhythmic chant of, 'Bullshit! Bullshit!' Then, over the top of a wall of people, came the first of many Molotov cocktails, and then an explosion as the Channel Seven news crew's vehicle was set alight. Burning people scattered left and right, with some bystanders caught up in the affray.

We were given the order to move toward the crowd, hitting our batons on the sides of our shields, which made a loud thudding noise. In the eerie noise of riot, it was not unlike a scene from the classic movie *Zulu Dawn*. The next five hours saw a pitched battle, as old as time itself.

We would charge, striking the crowd with our batons, then retreat. Several of us were struck with Molotov cocktails, myself included. The fear and panic that comes with rolling in the dirt trying to extinguish yourself is a truly terrifying experience. We had extinguishers on hand, and designated police for this precise role. I was alight for only seconds, but that did not in any way diminish the abject fear of burning to death.

The night seemed endless. There were a progression of disturbances, each unveiling another strange scenario. There was one explosion after another, one brick or some other object flying over the crowd, a constant barrage of rocks, beer bottles and cans full of piss. There was many a 30-metre retreat on both sides, but not much further. Police were regularly falling to the ground, accompanied by a huge roar from the crowd that became ominously louder when one of us was hit with a Molotov cocktail.

What did I learn from this battle in Bathurst against people, who at any other time, I might nod to in the street? For one, there is a certain resoluteness among fighting men in the midst of battle, as though the trepidation ignites an inner skill to summon the ability to conquer. It is the will to power, to win against overwhelming odds.

We, the Tactical Response Group, had it that night, and we had it in abundance. As the battle continued through the night, a fog came with the cold night air, the alcohol took its toll, and the resignation of the dwindling crowd became apparent. Slowly but surely, shortly after 3am, they were finally done. We had endured their onslaught – and as we had been taught, 100 trained men will always beat a mob, no matter their number.

There continued to be a large number of arrests made during the rest of the night for varying offences, some serious, some less so. The injuries on both sides were appreciable. I had six stitches on the inside of my lip, and my right thigh muscle was torn in two.

At Bathurst District Hospital, there was an endless queue, some unable to even walk, burns and plenty of broken bones. A designated ward was assigned to those wounded police, to avoid further confrontations with the bikers. We were quickly attended to and ready to go. However, it was sunrise before any of us that were discharged left. Like the other police I was patched up and sent to have further treatment upon my return to Sydney.

We went back to the college, and as the talk turned serious about incidents the night before, officers made notes of particular arrests and the offenders that had got away. There was a sense that revenge was required; a squaring up. In any situation like the previous night, there may be thousands of people, mostly just drunken motorsport fans. They have no desire whatsoever to hurt or maim a policeman. Fuelled by alcohol, they just want to be part of the action, spectators, so to speak, but not participants.

There are only a hundred, perhaps two hundred, who have a real hatred of the police. Incited by the multitudes, they make themselves known, as they did on that night. They were looking at a group of 100 police, they didn't know any of them, and had no specific targets. On the other hand, in a crowd of thousands, they stood out like dogs' balls. They were the ones with the Molotov in their throwing hand, clearly visible by the lit bottle in their grasp.

We were in town. We were incandescent. We had been patched up and we were heading back up the mountain, some on crutches, some covered in bandages and all in pain. We were on our way. *And YOU LOT are all fucked.*

It was a jolly successful Sunday rounding up what we described as the 'escapees'. A few painkiller injections and more than a few beers compensated for the pain. It was a great Easter Sunday in Bathurst in 1985. Monday morning, not too early, with all our physical injuries and the odd hangover, we drove back across the Blue Mountains to Parramatta. Every member of the TRG was commended for bravery on that memorable night on the mountain.

Over the next few days, a number of us were off on sick report, mainly due to not being able to walk without the aid of crutches. Everyone had to attend Police Headquarters in the city to see the government medical officer and have their injuries recorded. The stitches in my mouth healed quickly, as did most of the minor head wounds, but my thigh was another story.

I fronted Dr Vain, the police medical officer, who offered me early retirement. 'That will never heal,' he said.

Come on, Doc! I'm 26 years old and you want to make me a pensioner. I don't think so!

He was basically right, though; years of physiotherapy and occasional painkillers later, it has still never fully repaired. The constant pain has dissipated over the years. But hey-ho! That's life. I've never been a person who can sit still, and in my working life, I never had a day off sick. My logic is that if you're sick, don't sit around moaning about it – get on with something, and lose the thought altogether. Work is the best distraction.

Parramatta was becoming a busier place to work. Apartments were being erected at pace. The population was increasing, and Kim and I were contemplating our own addition to the population. We'd been discussing having another child and we had sold our house and were renting a house in Northmead, the adjoining suburb to Parramatta, where Danial had just started school. I knew everyone in the area, and everyone knew me.

I was always rostered to work at the races at Rosehill when they were on. I had credit with the on-course bookmakers, probably not a good thing, but I managed it. We had a wonderful social life. There were so many good blokes stationed at Parramatta. I had just been selected in the New South Wales rugby league representative team to tour New Zealand.

Things were very good and I thought that life was moving along quite smoothly. But you know, surprise, surprise! I was wrong.

Out of nowhere, I got a call to the roster room one morning and was informed that I was to be transferred to Darlinghurst, Kings Cross patrol. Amazed, not to mention furious, I demanded: 'Why?'

I was told there was a new policy, and that constables who have been in the western suburbs for certain periods were being swapped with personnel of the same rank from the city stations. There was an ounce of truth about the statement, but there was another reason I had been chosen: I had recently given character evidence for a friend of mine in the district court at his sentencing. When the superintendent of our district found this out, he berated me for doing so. All police have to get permission from the officer in charge of their station to give character evidence in a court matter.

Well, had I gone down that route, then my mate would have been left hanging. So as annoyed as I was, I had no right of appeal, and as we say in the business, I just had to cop it sweet.

6

GET ON THE CROSS

Darlinghurst in the 1980s was the centre of all the dirty work in Sydney.

Darlinghurst is also the name of the police station that encompasses the patrol of Kings Cross. The Cross was the home of Sydney's nightlife: clubs, bars, illegal casinos, brothels, prostitutes walking the streets, heroin dealers on every corner, and addicts shooting up in alleyways. When the sun falls, Kings Cross rises to bright lights and a night economy as busy and shady as any in the world.

It was a place where a crime was committed every second of every day. That said, if you were a person who lived or worked there, it didn't feel that way. Everyone knew what the pecking order was and what everyone else did. Everyone had a nickname usually associated with their nationality or size. So for a participant in this life, a crime was only a crime if you did something other than your normal illegal activity.

There was no shortage of excitement or inducements for any person wearing a police uniform. From my first shift, I could see the doormen and the street grafters on Darlinghurst Road, the main thoroughfare of the Cross, eyeing me up and down as I walked or drove past.

'My friend, my friend,' they beckoned to me. 'How are you? Anytime you want, you can come in no problem! Just ask for me.'

'Come past after work and I'll buy you a drink.'

I often thought that it would not take much to find out who was and was not on the take back then, as every spruiker and club owner would say, Sergeant Brown or Inspector Bloggs is a good friend of mine, which meant they were being looked after in some way. For me, it was best just to stay clear, and I made the decision as soon as I arrived. *It will be a long time before any of you lot are friends of mine*.

Very few people there were Australian, by birth at least, so it was a truly multicultural and cosmopolitan Golden Mile. But I had little in common with anyone. The whole world of the Cross seemed like a scammer's paradise, all cash, cash and more cash, generated more by illegal means than legal ones. It had been going on forever and I was a nobody, and certainly not going to change things.

The powers that be were, at the time, happy with the status quo, and so was I. Anyone who thought that they were going to in any way affect another's income would be quickly put back in the pecking order.

I made another conscious decision: I don't live here, I don't socialise here and they will never be a part of my inner sanctum. I have one role here: if you break a law in this district and I am called to arbitrate, I will. Because then you have come into my world.

Certainly, there were nice people there. At the time I thought they just lived by a different moral code from mine. As you will soon see, that was presumptuous of me. There were, however, similarities in the morals we lived by even then; for example, for all of us a rat was a rat, and sexual offenders were the lowest of the low.

Darlinghurst was different from a policing aspect as well; there was not the harmony that existed within other stations between the different sections. The detectives' office was a closed shop from the perspective of the general duties staff, and Liquor Licensing was just not available to anyone.

Welcome to the world of corruption.

Here I was, having just turned 27, when I had my epiphany. The Japanese call it 'satori', literally, the kick in the eye.

I drove home that night after the revelation, feeling like an idiot. Corruption in liquor licensing had been all around me my whole career and I'd never noticed. Police got free drinks at every station where I'd worked. Some clubs would stay open after closing just to have a lock-in with the afternoon shift, who would not arrive until midnight.

At Christmas, every pub and club in every district would drop off cases of beer to the local stations or they'd be collected by the licensing sergeant, then divided up just before Christmas. It was always pointed out who the alcohol had come from.

There was money to be made from controlled substances, like liquor, so invariably that meant that if you wished to sell the controlled substances, you required a licence to do so. And where did you get the licence? From the police, of course. To my logic, corruption all started right there. If you were dependent on a policeman to make your living, in that he was the administrator on behalf of the government body who controlled your livelihood, you would pay for that service. Now there were statutes that told you how much it should cost and it was usually quite a small amount of money. But if your business was, as they all were, a hugely profitable cash cow and there was some technical reason, or even a small statute within the act, that could prevent you from gaining the licence that would allow you to be a very rich man, then what would you do?

The bloke who would allow you to become that very rich man earned a meagre wage, had a mortgage, three children all at school, and a wife who did not work. What do you think was the next step in the process? The rules of the licence were stringent as generally they had been made by people who had never been to establishments that require such regulations.

These places were visited on a daily basis by detectives, since these types of premises were also frequented by people who were not nine-to-five workers in society. Permitting criminals on the premises was a breach of the licence. What do you think happened next?

Then just to complicate things, some save-the-world evangelist policeman turned up to a licensed premise and witnessed numerous breaches of the liquor act, and god forbid, was going to cause the cash cow to stop milking. Bless him! But good luck to ya, son. Because that was an extremely unlikely scenario.

I realised that the corruption around liquor licensing was so deep and dirty, it wasn't worth getting into. It had been going on since time immemorial, and it certainly wasn't going to be stopped by one single bloke – yours truly.

After the epiphany, I resolved to extricate myself from involvement in anything at Darlinghurst other than the general duties, the football club, the Tactical Response Group, and my life outside Darlinghurst.

7

THE MELBOURNE CUP AND THE MISSING SCOTCH

The Melbourne Cup is the race that stops the nation. It was for some time the richest horse race handicap in the world.

On this particular Tuesday in November 1986, I was on the 7am start morning shift at Darlinghurst with my newly appointed 'buddy', a young probationary constable who I had to look after for the next six weeks. I was supposed to teach her the ropes.

Kirsty McGrigor was a 21-year-old from the northern beaches. She was so innocent. It was a pleasure to have her around. But it was Melbourne Cup day, and as in every Melbourne Cup, there are 20-odd horses, of which 10 just can't win. While on the way home the day before, I'd boxed 10 horses in a trifecta, covering all combinations to run in the first three in the correct order, and that cost $720.

On arrival in the morning I mentioned to all the general duty staff that for $72 each, we could have a brilliant chance of landing the trifecta.

In Australia every person wagers on the race, on their lucky numbers or their mother's name: anything resembling any association with any aspect of their lives, but generally, they have no bloody idea. I convinced nine others at the station to participate for $72, and a 10 per cent share.

So being overconfident, I went across the road to the nearest betting shop and took the same combination again, so I would have 110 per cent should it win. A few minutes after 3pm on the first Tuesday in November, At Talak ran first, Rising Fear second, and Sea Legend third.

We won the trifecta! You fucking beauty!

It paid more than $13,000, and I had 110 per cent and the other nine at the station each got over $1,300. So, I raced across the road and picked up nearly $27,000. Four of the nine had already gone home, not knowing of their win. The rest of us went to the Forrester's Hotel just a few kilometres from the station. It was normally a detectives' haunt, as it was a bit more up-market than the typical pub in the area. It was my shout and it was known at the station. As the night went on, a number of detectives arrived and heard the story, and a plan was soon concocted by them that, seeing my state of inebriation, perhaps we should all play in a pool competition for $100 a game. Seeing as I had more than $20,000 in cash in my pockets, I agreed, much to the consternation of some of the general duty staff. The games began.

I fleeced them all, not losing a game and adding further winnings to my pockets, about $1,500. My youth had been spent at the Savoy snooker room in Fairfield where the York brothers taught me everything. And I can say it gave me more pleasure to get their $1,500 than the first $15,000. It was great timing, as Kim was six months pregnant then and that nice little bonus came in handy.

The next few months were testing, and poor Kim did not enjoy the long hot summer, but eventually on Valentine's Day, 1987, Kim gave birth to our son Timothy. He was a fine healthy baby, and we were elated.

Darlinghurst was about to close, and we were all being transferred less than a mile away to the newly completed Sydney Police Centre near Whitlam Square.

With Kim being pregnant, I had not worked a night shift for a few months and on Thursday, 19 March 1987, at 11pm, I was rostered with Constable Michelle Summerville, and was looking forward to it. I liked Michelle. She was petite but a real terrier.

Shortly after clocking on, there was a call to Wylde Street, Potts Point, a block of flats halfway down Macleay St, just up from the Cross. Allegedly someone was trying to break in. We arrived at 11.30pm, and after speaking to the complainant, she pointed out a 22-year-old man in the area, and said that he was the person who was trying to get into her apartment and that he had damaged the door in doing so.

As we approached, he started ranting and then he struck Michelle. I grabbed him and a struggle ensued. It was on, he and I, toe to toe. I landed a right to his forehead, and he promptly hit the ground. We cuffed him and arrested him, but I managed to break my hand in the process.

We took him back to the station, where he was charged, and then I went to St Vincent's casualty and had the hand X-rayed. I was told that I had broken the fifth metacarpal in the right hand, commonly called a 'boxer's' fracture. Bloody painful, it was, and other than ice and strapping, it's usually a four-month healing process. The doctor advised me to take a few weeks off. The staff strapped me up, gave me some painkillers and I went back to work an hour later.

The next few nights were uncomfortable to say the least. On the following Wednesday night, the twenty-fifth, I was rostered to work with Graham Goodwin. He was a good young bloke from the western suburbs who was about the same age as my younger brothers. In fact, they had mates in common.

At 2.08 am on Thursday, 26 March 1987, I was called to an address in Rushcutters Bay. The building was a Liquorland, owned by Coles Myer. Unbeknown to me at that moment, my life was about to change forever.

Together with Graham Goodwin, I drove to the takeaway liquor shop on the one-way section of Bayswater Road at the foot of Kings Cross, and the gateway to the eastern suburbs. At the scene, the front glass doors were smashed. A witness gave me a registration number of a black BMW sedan which had been reported stolen earlier that day, and said that there were a number of occupants in the car who appeared to be young Aboriginal men.

The vehicle was owned by Grundy Television and reported stolen by a lady named Kerrie-Anne Kennerley, Australia's most respected variety TV host. It was her work car.

Prior to starting my shift, I had, as usual, perused the daily synopsis reports. They told you about local crime activities in surrounding districts as well as your own. I recalled that there had been a number of similar break and enters in the area, and the offending vehicles were often located in and around the Aboriginal community in Redfern, an area that I was very familiar with. I said to Graham, 'Let's head over to Redfern. These blokes will end up there, I'm certain of it.'

He quietly said, 'That's not our patrol area.'

'Yeah, well. It's not far out and if we get into any strife, I'll wear it.' And off we went, softly slipping into one of the very narrow streets in Chippendale. We had to be discreet because if the local community found us there, things would kick off for sure and certain. We sat waiting for nearly 20 minutes and over the radio came a pursuit call; the BMW was being chased on the north side of the harbour.

Graham was less enthused now, as that was miles away and he thought it unlikely that they would end up anywhere near us. Then the pursuit was called off; the driver had eluded the pursuers. Graham wanted to return to our patrol. I was not so sure and was prepared to wait a little while longer. Within minutes, the black BMW appeared, turning the corner of Cleveland Street.

Graham put the flashing blue light on and we were off. They immediately stopped and decamped into the back streets of Chippendale, and were gone in a nanosecond.

Feeling quite smug at my decision, we approached the vehicle and searched it, advising the police radio of the find. A search revealed that in the boot of the vehicle were six dozen bottles of various brands of whisky.

A number of other cars attended the scene and searched the area with what was never going to be success. I contacted the station to arrange a tow. The vehicle was to be taken back to the police centre for fingerprinting. I would bring the Scotch back to the station to be booked up as 'found property'.

It must have been 5am when we returned to the Sydney Police Centre. The car was parked in the secure parking area. I drove our old paddy wagon, the name given to the old Ford F100s, into the charge dock area, and unloaded the Scotch.

What happened next was the only real regrettable moment of my life. With his offsider looking on, the station sergeant on duty said, 'I'll take charge of that. You don't need to book it up, it didn't come from Liquorland. I'll take it. It'll just be a drama for you, and it'll eventually be auctioned off in a year's time, so don't book it up.'

What he meant was that the whisky hadn't been purchased from a shop or been reported stolen, so it would have to be booked up as found property and then sold at auction after lengthy inquiries to try to find the owner. I knew the blokes just wanted it for themselves.

I was not happy being put in that situation. Firstly, there was no benefit in it for me. Secondly, I hated whisky. Third, I did not like the person in charge, or his offsider. Most importantly, it was wrong and a cheap, pathetic dereliction of all that I stood for. But in the end, it was just easier to let them have it than have a file hanging around for the next 12 months, and in the scheme of things, it should have been a non-event. So I said, 'Fuck it. Do what you want then,' and I went to book the car in and make out the report.

I had no idea that my police career was about to end.

8

INTERNAL AND EXTERNAL PRESSURE

By the time I had finished the paperwork, it was 7.30am, and we had handed over to the morning shift. I was already pissed off at myself, but in the scheme of things, it was just another day at the office.

Traditionally, on Thursday morning after the completion of a night shift, the entire shift went for a drink at whatever pub in the area was an early opener. You had four days off before your next shift, and, as with jet lag after a long-haul flight, there was no point going home and going to bed. You would have a drink, then at about 10am, you'd make your weary way home. It seemed the best way to adjust one's body clock.

I arrived at the Moore Park View Hotel in Waterloo at 8am. Waterloo is not three kilometres from the Sydney Police Centre and the venue for our night shift's early morning drink. I was the last person to arrive as I'd had to finalise the paperwork.

At the side of the pub, there was a driveway, primarily for the brewery trucks to park and offload. For us, it was a car park where we parked our private vehicles. It was peak hour and there was nowhere else to park. As I was the last to arrive, I boxed everyone else in, but this wasn't a problem as everyone knew it was my vehicle and I'd move it if necessary.

There was a lot of discussion about the impending twenty-first birthday of a young policewoman on the shift named Carla Tomadini, and most of us were attending on the following Saturday night. I stayed possibly an hour, had a few beers and then drove home.

Kim was up and caring for our newborn son Timothy, and Danial was at school. The day passed normally, and I had an early night. I was asleep in bed when Kim came into the room whispering, 'Charlie, Charlie, wake up, there are some police here.' Half asleep, I rose from bed, put some clothes on and came out to the lounge room.

There in front of me were two suited, plain-clothes policemen, both with their warrant cards in the open position and a piece of paper that they handed to me. They introduced themselves as detective inspectors from the Police Internal Security Unit.

Still waking up, I shook the cobwebs from my head and asked what they wanted. I started to read the piece of paper that they handed me. It was an occupier's notice, part of a search warrant, stating that they were looking for Scotch.

My mind started racing. Quite obviously it had to be something to do with the Scotch that I had not booked up the night before, but why were they at my place? I was nervous but not overly concerned. As they searched, Kim tried to be as obstructive as possible. I gave her a wink and an assuring smile to ease her protective nature. I felt somewhat humbled and proud of my wife with this innate gesture of love.

The search continued and just as they appeared to be finishing up, one of the inspectors asked where my car was. I pointed to a blue sedan. He asked me to open the boot, and I did so. We were all surprised to find a box containing 12 bottles of Scotch and two grey blankets in the boot.

The inspector said, 'What is this?'

I said, 'I have never seen this before.'

'Are they prisoners' blankets?' he asked.

'I don't know.'

The other inspector then removed the box of Scotch and the two blankets from the boot and put them in the boot of their car.

The senior inspector said, 'You have to come with us now to Police Headquarters.'

'Am I under arrest?' I asked, cautiously.

'No,' he said.

'Then I am not going.'

'You are now directed to come with me.'

It is an offence under the Police Regulations Act to disobey a direction from a senior officer, and I knew that. I assured a very emotional Kim that everything would be all right. I gave her a kiss and left with the two inspectors. The more junior officer drove the three of us back to Police Headquarters in Sydney, a drive that took just over half an hour, but seemed to take a week. My head was spinning. What the fuck had happened, and how did the Scotch end up in the boot of my car?

On arrival at headquarters, we parked in the basement. The whole atmosphere was unsettling. Neither of them said a word as we entered the lift and rose to one of the higher floors. As we exited the lift, I could see several of the police who had been on my night shift being interviewed by officers whom I assumed were from the Police Internal Security Unit.

Then from around the corner came a very disheartening face – none other than Sergeant John Dickinson from the Highway Patrol at Penrith. My first thought was, ooh, maybe he was in trouble for something as well. Hardly. He was now Inspector John Dickinson, Internal Security Unit. *Shit!*

I was taken to an office out of view from any of the others and the senior inspector said that he was going to interview me regarding the theft of a quantity of Scotch stolen from Liquorland the previous night. He sat at the typewriter and cautioned me that I did not have to say anything.

There was a pause. I knew my rights and I wasn't going to say shit. I didn't trust these pricks as far as I could throw them. Someone had put the Scotch in my boot and was trying to frame me. If I stayed silent, they couldn't verbal me so I kept my mouth shut.

He cautioned me again.

Silence. More silence.

'I take it by your silence that you are not going to answer any questions in relation to this matter.'

I maintained my silence. He then handed me a copy of what he had typed and said, 'Just sign here.'

He was trying to verbal me, trying to get me to sign a confession of sorts, and I was having none of it. I did not sign it, and with that, I stood up, took a copy of what he had typed and walked out the door, all the while the senior inspector advising me that I was now suspended until further notice and angrily watching me walk away.

As I approached the lifts, I turned and yelled to the other police: 'Once you have been cautioned, get out of here.'

I then caught the lift and left the building.

Police Headquarters is a five-minute walk from the police centre, so I headed over there straight away.

The new night shift had just started, and as soon as I walked into the building, I was hurried away by a few of the police on the shift to the meal room, and quizzed as to what had gone on. Internal security had been there all day, and the rumours were rife.

I gleaned from the conversations that someone had contacted internal security, and told them that I had stolen the Scotch that was found in the back of the BMW. Logically, this meant that someone on our shift the night before must be the informant. I went to the station office and removed all the address cards from the staff that had worked the night before. I then caught a taxi to their addresses and arranged a meeting at Coogee Beach at 7am.

Some turned up with records of interview, while some had not yet been visited by internal security. There was a conspicuous absentee: a young constable who had been on the shift that night, but not at the rendezvous. He had not attended the pub at the completion of the shift, nor was he invited to Carla's party that coming Saturday night. This was it. I knew it was him.

There was, however, one person at the rendezvous who could speak with him, and I told him to do just that and get this young constable to come and see me. I found out what had happened to the Scotch, and just shook my head in disbelief. The station sergeant had divided it up between the guys on the shift. To this day I don't know how some of it made its way into my car. My contact told me that the young constable said he had reported that I had brought the Scotch back to the station but not booked it in. He assumed that I had kept some and was sure that if they came to my house they would find it. I don't know if he even knew that the others had shared it out.

Later that day, it was confirmed that he was the informant and that he'd been granted leave of absence, and would not be returning to Sydney Police Centre.

I didn't need any more information. I had copies of all the records of interviews, with the exception of the informant's. I had people who would keep me updated and it was now a waiting game.

Over the next few days, I did more than just ponder my future. I had an enormous sense of regret, not guilt, primarily for succumbing to peer-group pressure and not booking in the Scotch. It had never happened before and never has since. Two days later, Kim and I and the younger staff on the night shift all attended Carla's twenty-first birthday party.

I needed space, because Kim was distraught and angry over what had happened. She was a second backbone for me; whatever I needed or wanted her to do, there would be no questions asked. She was there for me. There was talk of revenge against the informant, and even more talk of his illegal activities, since it was common knowledge that he was far from a saint. I decided that I needed more information as to what on earth he had told them. I figured the best source to glean this from was internal security themselves.

I concocted a plan. I knew my stuff. Under Section 5 of the Listening Devices Act of 1984, I knew I could record a conversation if I was doing so to defend myself. So I went to an electronics shop in Parramatta and purchased a micro-cassette recorder and some mini-tapes and headed to the offices of internal security, a building hidden away in the city and locked up like Fort Knox. I had tested the recorder and had a backup cassette. I pressed the intercom and was greeted by an inspector at the door. He asked what I wanted, and I said that I wished to assist them with their inquiries.

He ordered me to piss off, and that I had been given an opportunity to assist them on the night. 'And you didn't say a fucking word.'

With a smile, I said, 'But sir, I am only here to try and help you with your inquiries.'

'Fuck off,' came the retort.

I left, got down to the street and pulled out my recorder. It was all there. Every word, crystal clear. I had it on tape from a member of their own unit that I had not said a word. They couldn't verbal me now. Having that tape now made me feel secure in knowing that things were not likely to get worse. I went home and told Kim that I needed to get away and make a plan. It was obvious to us both that things were going to change in the very near future.

My life was now in turmoil. I had always been a straight policeman. Sure, I had broken a hundred laws, but I had never been a crooked cop. My dream of being the Commissioner of Police was now rapidly fading, and it was because of the thing that I hated most about the police. I felt they took the easy way out most of the time. The loyalty they spoke of was only loyalty when things were going well – when their necks were on the line they backtracked at speed, scared of losing their jobs. The Tactical Response Group were different – they would take a bullet for you no matter what – but I'd had enough. Things were going to change.

9

ANOTHER BATHURST, A DIFFERENT BATTLE

Coincidently, the Bathurst bike races happened to be on the next weekend, and had I not been suspended, I would have been attending. I had a very good friend called Terry Walkinshaw who owned the Kelso Hotel. (Kelso is a small town just near Bathurst.) I rang him, and he said he had a spare room at his pub, and that I was welcome to it for the weekend, or however long I needed.

The only police I could trust and seek counsel from were the members of the Tactical Response Group and they would all be there, away from the prying eyes and ears of Sydney. I packed a bag and drove to Bathurst. Word had spread around Sydney about the situation I had found myself in and Kim was being bombarded with calls from friends and acquaintances, offering help and advice. I needed to think and have some distractions, and a riot at Bathurst seemed, strangely, to be just the place.

I arrived late on the Thursday night before the race weekend, and had a long chat with Terry, who I had known for a few years. We had met at a motor-vehicle collision when I was stationed at Parramatta a few years prior and I had booked him for negligent driving as a result of that collision. He had been on his way to Hawkesbury Races, where a horse that he owned was running and he was sure it was going to win.

I issued him with an infringement notice for negligent driving. His only concern had been whether he could possibly get to the races in time to back his horse? I thought it would be difficult, bearing in mind the time of day. But my old football coach from Penrith, Senior Constable Geary (or 'Dollar' as he was affectionately known), was stationed at Windsor (the nearest station to the race track) and he was always rostered to work at the races.

Back in the day, of course, there were no mobile phones. So I walked across the road into the petrol station and asked if I could use their phone and naturally, they obliged. I had an account with several on-course bookmakers and I rang directory assistance and got the number of the office at the admin office at the track and rang them.

'Can you find Senior Constable Geary?' I asked, saying that it was an urgent police matter. Fifteen minutes later, she came back saying that he had not responded. I was tempted to ring the police radio section and have them contact him, but decided that it may cause questions to be asked.

So, the next best thing. I rang my SP bookmaker and had him put $500 on Terry's horse Meadow Minstrel at 9/1. I asked Terry if he wanted to back it with my SP, and he declined, saying that he believed that he would make it just in time to back the horse himself. Terry left and headed off to the track. I thought he would never get there in time. I continued my patrol and listened to the race on the radio. Meadow Minstrel won, and I picked up $5,000.

Later that night, I rang Terry at his pub in Kelso. His first words to me were, 'You fucking cunt. I give you the winner and you win $5,000, and then you book me for neg driving, and I might lose my licence. I missed the race, you fucking cunt!'

There was a pause in the conversation, then he said, 'Would you and your offsider like to come up to Bathurst for the weekend? Bring your birds and you can stay at the pub. We have pretty good rooms, and it's my shout.'

How can you refuse an offer like that? The four of us headed to Bathurst that weekend. And many a weekend after that. Terry Walkinshaw is a very good bloke and a life-long friend of mine. Terry knew a lot of police, and by the time I arrived at the hotel, he already knew of my situation.

He listened hard, and said that if I was out of the police he would always have a job for me in Bathurst. Over the weekend, a number of police came to see me at the hotel, offering advice and help. The general perception was that it did not seem that bad a situation.

Everyone hated the Internal Security Unit; they were not real detectives, just plain-clothes policemen who thought they were better than the rest of us. They did not even have a complainant, or an owner for the Scotch, and they had no witnesses.

Well, other than the informant, who had been on shift that night but had seen nothing, and had, at best, inadmissible hearsay evidence. I had said nothing. And with the tape recording, they could not verbal me. Everyone in Bathurst thought I was going to be okay, and that I should look after myself and forget the rest. I spent the weekend searching my soul for answers.

Come Monday morning, my mind was made up. I felt that I could beat the charges, but what about everyone else on the shift? There were others who were under scrutiny because they'd also been found with some of the Scotch after it had been divided up, and I knew that they didn't have my resources and know-how to get out of trouble. Ultimately, too, while I was innocent of stealing the Scotch, I felt the situation was my fault because I hadn't booked it up as I should have done. I rang the Police Internal Security Unit from Terry's hotel and asked them to meet me at Parramatta Police Station later that afternoon. I told them I intended to make a full confession. I arrived at Parramatta Police Station just after 1pm.

I knew everyone at Parramatta. They also had heard on the grapevine about my situation, and upon hearing that I was about to confess, no one supported the idea. Voices were raised and the constant rhetoric of 'Fuck the rest of them, Charlie. Take care of yourself.' But I knew what I had to do. I wasn't going to let other cops go down for my mistake. I should've signed the Scotch in properly in the first place. It was one thing for the informant to get his revenge on me; I knew I could take the heat. But to put others in jeopardy? I knew I couldn't stand for it.

The internal security officers arrived, and, after introducing themselves to the station staff, they were then roundly ignored by everyone for the next three hours. Strangely, I felt quite proud. Every time they asked for something, or where something was, they were totally ignored.

We sat down in an interview room and I gave an extensive statement outlining my guilt, and vindicating everyone else. They were not happy; they knew they were all guilty and that I was going to get them off. 'Bullshit' was the response to my statements.

I felt a sadness that my body had never known. I had to leave immediately and find some fresh air, as my eyes were filling with tears and crying would have been utterly embarrassing for me.

I felt, however, a sense of real pride in my actions, and as though a weight had been lifted off me. I was certain I had done the right thing. I drove home, which was only minutes away, and told Kim what I had done. She was upset but could see in my eyes that it was not a time to berate me, but a time to console me.

The phone did not stop ringing that night, or for days to come. I had arranged for my statement to be made available to the lawyers who represented the other police that were on the shift the night of the incident. All charges against the other police were withdrawn, and I was subpoenaed to appear at the Downing Street Court Complex in three weeks. I was charged with 'stealing by finding'.

For the next two weeks, I pondered who I should retain as a lawyer to represent me at the impending sentencing. After careful consideration I retained Tony Bellanto, QC. While I was stationed at Parramatta, I had seen Bellanto several times in the Parramatta District Court, and he was marvellous with juries.

He spoke with conviction and sincerity, and I wanted him to put my case forward. The day went well, the magistrate accepted my plea of guilty and, after numerous referees had given character evidence on my behalf, he dismissed the charge under section 556a. Section 556a is a form of discretion whereby there are grounds not to convict an offender if the court is satisfied that it is inexpedient to punish them and not convicting them reduces the likelihood of the offender offending again. No conviction was recorded against me.

That did not sit well with the two inspectors or the rest of the Internal Security Unit. They knew I had taken the fall for everyone else and that it would look pretty pathetic that they had only been able to get me. I felt they wanted a result, so they charged me again, this time with stealing two prisoners' blankets, the property of the New South Wales Police Department, the value being recorded at $11.56.

As unbelievable as it sounds, a month later I had another hearing. This was at the Downing Centre again, with the Internal Security Unit gunning for me. I once more retained Tony Bellanto, QC to represent me. My instructions to him were quite simple: they were trying to fit me up. Revenge was their motive because I had outwitted them.

He could not believe the pettiness of the allegation, and felt sure that after speaking with the prosecution services that he would be able to have the charge withdrawn. He was somewhat dumbfounded when informed by the prosecutor that there was no way they would be withdrawing their case.

The case commenced with the first internal security officer in the witness box. And wouldn't you know it, it was old mate from internal security who featured on my tape! He sat in the box and lied and lied, and then he lied some more. At this point, I realised it was time to play my ace. I had been sitting on my recording until the time was right. It was such potent evidence that I hadn't wanted to use it until absolutely necessary. Hearing the inspector spin such porkies made me hot under the collar. Tony became somewhat annoyed at me for interjecting, as I was trying to tell him about the tape recording that I had made. I think he thought I was making it up. He asked the magistrate for an adjournment.

Reluctantly, the magistrate allowed us the adjournment, much to the indignation of the prosecutor and the internal security. We walked back to Tony's office, not far from the Downing Centre, and I told him of the secret recording and that I had a copy of it in my suit pocket. I had brought it with me as I'd had a sneaking suspicion that I'd need it. I did not have the recorder, but told him what was said on the recording. He ducked out to an electronics store near his chambers and purchased a recorder.

After hearing the tape, a smile came over his face. 'My God,' was his response.

We went back to chambers, and he listened over and over to the tape and I assured him that his witness in the box was in fact the voice on the tape. We knew that the recording was legal and admissible. We had him! Together, we quickly marched back to the Downing Centre. He sought out the prosecutor and duly played him the tape. The prosecutor then summonsed his witness to his office and played him the tape.

Let me tell you this for nothing: You will never in your life see a look of fury as that projected at me by internal security. With that, the prosecutor advised the magistrate that he was withdrawing the charge against me. Of course, the magistrate wanted to know why, and so was reluctantly told. Not impressed to say the least, the magistrate forwarded the court papers to the Attorney General, with the view that internal security should be charged with perjury.

The charges against me were immediately dismissed and the prosecutor personally gave me a genuine apology. As he stormed off, leaving two chastened internal security inspectors behind, I walked past them both, with a wink and a smile. I walked out of Downing Centre with Tony Bellanto, QC, feeling a good six inches taller.

Just when I thought it was all over and I could start moving forward, the other shoe dropped. I was at home a few days later and I got a call from the chief superintendent of the metropolitan area. He was requesting that I attend Police Headquarters the following morning, as he wished to interview me on behalf of a request by the Attorney General of New South Wales to investigate an allegation of perjury by members of the Internal Security Unit, in a matter involving me over allegedly stolen blankets. I told him that I would. That night at home I kept wondering over and over if I would be able to stay in the Police Force, and it kept coming back to me that it was very unlikely. I thought, *Shall I let internal security have it?*

The following day I walked into Police Headquarters and was shown to the chief superintendent's office. After introductions, he asked me to take a seat. 'Mr Staunton, before we start, can I ask if you are recording this conversation?'

'Yes, sir, I am.'

'Are you aware that it is an offence to do so?'

'With respect, sir, I think that you might find that Section 5 of the Listening Devices Act of 1984 allows me to do just that, if I am using it to defend myself.'

'Do you think that you need to defend yourself here?' he asked.

'Well, the last time I spoke with a commissioned officer trying to assist him, he verballed me. So, what can I say?'

With that, we both smiled, and he then asked me if I would be prepared to assist him in the investigation of a complaint, made by the magistrate in my court case, regarding the perjury by the Internal Security Police.

'No! Sir, I am not prepared to assist you.'

A look of astonishment crept over his face, and that of his typist. 'But why, after what they tried to do?'

'Sir, we all know what really happened over the last month. There are no winners here.'

I then stood turned and walked out the door and entered the lift. As I walked out the door of Police Headquarters, it dawned on me. It had been 10 years almost to the day since I sat my entrance exam in this very same building.

I still have a lot of friends who are either serving and retired members of the New South Wales Police Force but I have never seen nor spoken to any of the police officers that worked that fateful night shift ever again.

On the whole, I loved most of my decade in the New South Wales Police Force. I did a good job, I learned a lot, made lifelong friends, and met a lot of good blokes. They did, however, break more laws than any of my friends outside the force.

10

ON THE STREET

1989

A new day, a new life, entirely.

What was to come?

There were calls daily from police offering support and assistance with possible employment opportunities. But I had decided the police force was no longer for me. I was cutting my ties with all but my mates. Because I'd taken the fall for them, I now had nothing to fear. It was a liberating feeling.

There was some urgency in starting a new career, as Kim had just given birth to Timothy, Danial was at school and both of us were still in our twenties. First things first, though, I still had to pay the bills. A call came from a sergeant at Darlinghurst saying that Baron's, a bar/restaurant in Kellett Street, Kings Cross, was looking for a doorman/host for night shifts, and that the money was very good.

I went over there as soon as I could, and met the two Austrian owners, Bernie Rosenburg and Joseph Zangerl. They had worked in the Cross for an eternity, and were shrewd operators who ran a tight ship and had a very successful little business. They had heard about my situation, and were not in the least concerned about my recent history. I looked smart, and could handle myself and look after their interests. I had been given excellent references by every police officer they knew, and that was good enough for them.

Generally speaking, other than fast food outlets, the Cross did not open her doors for business until the sun went down. The nights were late, never ending before sunrise. It was a very sociable place to work.

Police would call past every night to see me, and to make it visible to all and sundry that this was a sanctioned bar in the area. By that, I mean Kings Cross was unlike any other suburb in Sydney. Every transaction was paid in cash. The Taxman was Enemy Number One, with second place going to the Licensing Police, who, it must be said, had a lot in common with the Taxman.

With few exceptions, staff were paid in cash. On every corner there was a dodgy character with a bargain, or someone trying to sell you any type of drug that might take your fancy, and between the pair, many a woman offering you her services. The streets were overflowing with punters who had come from far and wide to gratify their desires and to be parted from their hard-earned.

Baron's was a late-night safe haven, usually the last port of call for the sober staff around the Cross and the eastern suburbs. My nights usually started around 10pm. Bernie and Joseph had always maintained a qualified chef to be on hand, as it was a condition of this and every bar's licence that a meal had to be served. Bernie and Joseph were both restauranteurs, and proud of that fact, although the bar accounted for 90 per cent of their revenue.

Very few bars had kitchens, let alone chefs. A few years prior, after a court case, some establishment found out that if its customers had 'the intention of dining', then they could partake of alcohol as long as they still maintained that intention. There was no such thing as a nightclub per se. They were all restaurants, at least according to their liquor licences.

But it became much easier and cheaper to employ a doorman, who would ask everyone entering the premises if they had the intention of dining, accompanied by a wink. A menu of sorts would be available, and in clear view, and there was usually a member of staff working who was practised in the art of putting a plate of spaghetti bolognaise in a microwave oven.

Thus, every bar and nightclub in the area was quasi-legal.

I started working two nights a week, and it wasn't long before I was working six nights a week. Bernie and Joseph both realised that with me on the door the clientele were better behaved, and it saved them the aggro they had endured for a decade.

Bernie told me I more than paid for my own wages. If I needed a day off for some particular reason, there were very few people that I could call on. However, one of those was Felix Lyle.

Felix and I had worked the door together at Annabelle's nightclub in Bondi Junction, when I was working extra shifts while still in the police force. He had an exceptionally courteous manner, and if it came to a blue, he was the man to side with. His brother Daryl was a policeman whom I had known through the service and was then stationed at the coroner's court.

Felix's son and my eldest son Danial were mates as children. Bernie and Joseph liked Felix, as did most of the police who patrolled the area. He was known for not calling them and they were never required at Baron's.

Not long after I started there, in the early hours one morning, Tongan Sam, a giant of a man, who back then was known for causing carnage, especially when intoxicated, rocked up. Sam was six foot four tall, weighed 16 stone and all of that was rock-hard muscle. Even his hands were twice the size of any other man's.

I could see right away he was the worse for wear, and thought it prudent I tell him that we were closing. In a flash, he threw a right hook that hit me on the forehead, knocking me back some five metres into the hallway of the entrance. I thought I had been hit by a truck as hundreds of silver stars flashed through my vision.

I shook my head a few times and got my balance back. I lunged forward, getting both of my arms around his waist, and thrusted Sam toward the open doorway and, fortunately for me, he was caught off balance and he stumbled back out onto the footpath. I slammed the door behind him.

He banged and screamed at the door for a minute, and then wandered off down Kellett Street. There was no need for any further action, and he was spoken to by two detectives the following night and advised that he was no longer welcome back in Baron's.

It was just a week or so later that Sam started working for John Ibrahim, and to this day he occupies the role of John's personal bodyguard and friend.

Lots of celebrities would turn up at Baron's. It was a cool bar that had a piano for anyone to use, the only stipulation being that you could actually play a piano. Many an ivory tinkler was gonged not long after touching the keys.

One Thursday night, Kerry Packer turned up at the door and introduced himself, a formality which was hardly necessary, he being the richest man in Australia, and the man that changed the international cricket world forever.

He told me he was there to attend a private function at 8pm, the booking made in another name. It turned out that he had his polo team in town, and had booked the function room for a show for the players in his team.

The door was closed behind him, with instructions that they not be disturbed. An hour later, Mr Packer popped his head out of the function room and remembering my name, said, 'Excuse me, Charlie? Could I trouble you to organise 10 taxis to be parked out the front at 9.30pm?'

He handed me a piece of paper with the destination address. I said, 'Certainly, Mr Packer.'

At 9pm, I walked the 40 metres to Darlinghurst Road, and hailed the first ten taxis in the endless queue of vacant cabs that filled the streets at that time of the evening. Telling them that they could start their meters, I told them their destination. At 9.30pm, on the dot, the polo team walked out of the function room and jumped in their taxis and left.

Mr Packer walked out, shook my hand and thanked me and the bar staff, and was taken away by his driver. The next night, a very short man, impeccably dressed, came to the door soon after I started work, and asked if I was Charlie.

'Yes, that's me. Can I help you?'

He handed me an envelope, saying it was with the compliments and regards of Mr Packer, have a good night, and walked away. I opened the envelope full of $100 bills. A good bloke and a class act, Kerry Packer.

It was around this time that Kim and I separated. It was a difficult period for us as a family. We had been through a lot together. There was no woman I loved more dearly than Kim, but our relationship just wasn't able to hold together and sadly we parted ways.

Not long after, while I was still coming to grips with all the changes in my life, I was standing at the door when the phone rang at Baron's reception desk. 'Hello, mate! It's Jeff.'

That would be Jeff 'the Hit Man' Harding, Australia's up-and-coming light heavyweight boxer. He was seven years younger than me, and after turning professional in 1986, had been fighting around the local circuit for two years. He'd previously had only 14 fights and was undefeated. I had been to the last three. He was brutal. He tended to lead with his forehead, and the more he got hit, the more he came after his opponent. His were always good fights to attend.

Jeff looked a bit like Matt Damon but was taller and had a pugilist's nose. He was a quiet man, a charmer with a great sense of humour and perfect manners. He loved a drink and was often being chased down by his trainers to get him to bed. He had champion written all over him.

He asked if I was coming to his fight on Saturday night. I thought about it for a minute. 'Sure, why not? I can get Felix to cover for me.'

I asked where the fight was, and he said, 'Atlantic City.'

I asked him if that was a new satellite city in the Newcastle area.

'No, Atlantic City, New Jersey. In the US.'

'Sure thing, mate. Stop mucking around. Where is it again?'

'The Trump Convention Centre, Atlantic City, New Jersey.'

Jeff went on to explain that Donny 'the Golden Boy' Lalonde and Dennis Andries were scheduled to fight for the vacated light heavyweight title formerly held by Sugar Ray Leonard. But then Lalonde had seen God or something, and no longer had the desire to hit people. As a consequence, Hit Man had moved up the rankings, and was now a contender.

Well, it all sounded too far-fetched to believe. I asked him for the number he was at, and he gave me a number which I rang. The lady at the other end of the line said, 'Trump Convention Centre, can I help you?'

I asked the receptionist for Mr Jeff Harding's room, and she put me through. Well, that was it. I was on the flight on Thursday and sat next to Ray Connelly, who was arguably the face of boxing in Australia, the whole way.

On arrival, we shared a twin room. Atlantic City and its iconic boardwalk on the Atlantic coast were very new to me. It was sort of like a mini Las Vegas, with numerous casinos and hotels on the boardwalk. Atlantic City itself was lavish but only a few miles inland and the land turned to swamp.

We all went to the boys' club for Jeff's last hit-out, and when he was finished, Jeff Fenech, Australia's triple world champion, asked me if I would like to run with him back to the convention centre along the boardwalk.

I accepted the offer and off we went. It wasn't that hard – turn right, and in a mile, you would be in the Atlantic Ocean. What I hadn't noticed was that Jeff was wearing his gold bracelet, which had three gold gloves on it – one for each of his world titles. I hadn't noticed, but the people sitting outside of their houses in the narrow streets sure had.

Let's just say, it was a very quick trip back to the convention centre. I had no desire to make any headlines as Jeff had made a few while out with a few of the boys a day or two before, when there was a punch-up in one of the other casinos.

In the days preceding the fight, the build-up was amazing; there were the boxers of history, now retired, all over the boardwalk. There was another world title fight on the day before Jeff's, and Bill Mordey, Jeff's promoter, had looked after all of us very well with regards to tickets. Jeff always insisted that his mates were taken care of. It was a pugilist's dream weekend.

On the day of the fight we were positioned around the ring so that the support could be heard from all sides. Jeff Fenech sat next to Mike Tyson and Donald Trump. Joe DiMaggio, the legendary baseball player, was there, along with numerous other celebrities of the day. What a fight that was. Two of the fittest athletes on the planet stood toe to toe for twelve rounds of boxing at its best. You can see it on YouTube these days. It was the fight of the year, and rightly so, with the excitement culminating in the later stages of the last round.

Jeff was behind on points but from somewhere produced the strength and power to stop Andries in the last seconds of the twelfth and final round. Well, it kicked off then.

The euphoria at ringside was palpable. There was a standing ovation from the crowd around the convention centre, and the media, predictably, went apeshit. We all headed for the dressing room. Between the lads thumping each other on the back, and the media, the whole thing was a scramble.

As I was trying to get to the dressing rooms after the fight, down the hall came Donald Trump with that familiar grin from ear to ear. He had an entourage; everyone wanted a piece of him. I was just standing there with a few of the security guards and he walked up to me, stuck his hand out and said, 'Donald Trump. You Australians are a hard lot.'

He looked me in the eye, and I shook his hand. 'Charlie Staunton, nice to meet you.' Whether you like the man or loathe him, what an autobiography his would be if he told the truth, lock, stock and barrel. I'm pretty sure he took the time to shake the hand of every Australian who was at the fight. Jeff, on the other hand, had to receive medical treatment and stitches.

Meanwhile I had to get to Clearwater Beach in Tampa, Florida. I had a friend, Heather, who had worked at Baron's as a barmaid and was now working at a bar down there. She had invited me down. Atlantic City was great – the glitz and glamour, the rich and famous – but ultimately that wasn't me. I'd had a terrific time because there were some great blokes there, but now, I was off.

I thought, what a perfect time to see America! A journey of 1,700 kilometres would pretty much cover the entire east coast. I could get a Greyhound bus, see the country, and stop off here and there.

What was I thinking? A bus from Atlantic City, New Jersey, to Clearwater Beach, Tampa, Florida involves two days of freeways and bus stations. Let's just call that a learning process. Never to be repeated.

The Fourth of July celebrations were imminent. The St Petersburg Pier on Tampa Bay was not too shabby a celebration at all. I stayed nearly two weeks, and Heather was wonderful and looked after me, showing me around a nice part of the world.

Crocodile Dundee had just been released, and Paul Hogan, without knowing it, surely gave every young Aussie bloke who travelled America back then a much better chance of pulling a bird. It was a lot of fun being a young, blond Aussie in the States at that time. But all good things must come to an end.

I went to London to see my relatives and took a quick trip to the All England Lawn Tennis Club, Wimbledon, and then it was back to Sydney. It was an anti-climax in many ways. Nothing much had really changed, other than a few waitresses at Baron's, but everyone wanted to hear the stories about the madness and brilliance of America.

11

WHAT MATES DO

I settled back into Sydney working at Baron's. Marty Clapp, the doorman I had met a few years before in Bathurst, had just bought the Manzil Room, the most iconic late-night music venue in Australia. He had renamed it Springfield's and it was the private club for the music industry. Springfield's would usually close at around 5am and the staff would then come for a drink at Baron's, as we would finish closer to 7am.

It was not really my scene, though Marty tried on numerous occasions to get me to come over for a drink. I didn't care for the Springfield's crowd. Springfield's was only 200 metres away from Baron's, and it was off the main drag. It could hold 400 people at a pinch, although it was only licenced to hold 150. If you were not part of the music industry, there was little or no chance of you being allowed to enter.

Marty and I had lots in common. We both worked in the hospitality industry, both worked nights, we both loved footy, both had two children, and had pretty much the same moral compass. Our kids got on well. When we had sports days for the staff, all the families would turn up for a BBQ and a game of baseball.

Put it this way – if he had a problem, then I had a problem and vice versa.

Once again, I took a late-night call at Baron's.

'Charlie, it's Marty here. I'm in trouble. Can you come and pick me up?'

'Sure, mate. What's up?'

'I think it's bad. But I'm not sure.'

It was starting to sound mysterious. Marty asked that I get a car that no one would associate with him, and meet him outside a house where we both knew the owner. It had nothing to do with the lady who owned the house, it was just a location that we both knew, and he didn't want to mention his actual location over the phone.

He told me when I got near, to flash the headlights on and off, and he would appear out of the bushes. Right . . . Mr Mystery. I can tell you, it sounded intriguing to say the least, so with that I rang Felix and asked him to come in and work for a few hours. Then I proceeded up to the main drag, Darlinghurst Road, where I walked down and saw Billy Bayeh outside a café. He was always about looking for an earn or a young lady. I told him that I needed a car that no one knew.

He walked directly into the café, and came out with the keys to a gold Mercedes.

'Here, no problem, my friend. Take it for as long as you want.'

I had no idea who owned the car, and that person had no idea who I was, and apart from the colour, it was perfect.

I headed off over the Harbour Bridge; the pick-up location was at least an hour's drive. The traffic was not so bad until I got within a few miles of my destination.

I was heading to a place called Church Point, a suburb in the Northern Beaches region of Sydney about 30 kilometres north of the Cross, a very expensive and beautiful part of Sydney. There were perhaps a thousand residents in total. There was one road in, and one road out, and the only other way was by boat.

As I was about to take the turn-off to Church Point, I saw in front of me a police roadblock, and there were search teams checking each and every car. As I approached, a young police officer neared my window, and I recognised him.

'G'day mate!' I said. 'What's happening?'

'Hello, Charlie, long time. How's it going?' Looking at my Mercedes, he said that I must be doing well.

'Yeah, not bad. What's going on here?'

He told me that the 'Gatekeepers' were in the area looking for somebody. 'Gatekeeper' was a derogatory term used by the New South Wales Police when speaking about the Australian Federal Police (the nickname implies that the AFP are only good for looking after gates at the airports). Apparently, they had lost some bloke up in the bush earlier in the day and were looking under every rock and tree to find him.

I asked what this person had done, and the cop was unaware. I told him that I was off to shag a girl just a mile down the road and that then I had to get back to work.

'No worries at all. When you've finished, just slip down past the queue on the other side. I'll tell the boys that it's you.'

'Thanks, buddy.'

I eased up the hill to Church Point, and the street where Marty should have been was pitch black. As arranged, I flashed the lights several times. Out of the bush darted Marty, somewhat dishevelled, but not injured. We drove to a driveway nearby, and he gave me his version of what had happened. He had turned up at a pre-arranged meeting for what's called 'a show of money'. If someone wishes to purchase something (usually illegal), they produce a bag of cash to show the vendor that they do, in fact, have access to the funds to purchase said product.

Oh, dear. It's an old chestnut, a sting operation, used pretty much only by police. So, Marty had turned up to meet these alleged tough guys and show them half a million and change in cash, on behalf of someone else.

As soon as he showed them the cash, out of the bush came all the Gatekeepers, pistols at the ready and ordering Marty to the ground. Well, that was never going to happen.

Instead, Marty dropped the bag and was off charging at the opposition, and barrelling them into the bush one after the other. It was extremely dense bushland all around the area and after knocking more than a few out of the way, he managed to find a hollow. He covered himself in some bush as camouflage, and waited hours until darkness. Then he rang me, and well, there we were.

Well, I can tell you, I was furious that he had done something so stupid as get involved in a show of money, and then even more furious that he had done it without seeking my advice. But that was a conversation for another day. The immediate problem was getting back through the roadblock and then finding somewhere to hide him. I put him in the boot of the car, in which he could barely fit. Thank god I hadn't turned up in something smaller.

As I approach the roadblock I moved to the left and started moving down the nearside lane. I wound the window down and honked the horn at the police who were searching the other vehicles, and with a wave, they passed me on through, with the comment that it was 'a quickie', referring to my imaginary sexual encounter.

On the way back to the city, I grilled Marty as to what his involvement was, who owned the money and who, if any, were the other participants. He wasn't talking, even to me.

I accepted that, and decided my concern was where to hide Marty. I was living with an old F trooper from the academy, who just happened to be Detective Sergeant Gary Spencer in the Drug Squad, who I knew would be at home fast asleep in bed.

I drove to the house, told Marty to get some sleep as he would need to have his wits about him over the coming days, and I then drove to his house in nearby Vaucluse, knowing full well that the AFP would be there searching. I rang John Ibrahim, as he had a clear view of Springfield's from his club, the Tunnel, which was just 100 metres down the road.

I asked him if there was anything happening. He told me that the streets were full of feds, and that they seemed to be focusing on Marty's place. He said he would get the boys to sniff around and try to glean any information that may be helpful.

I rang Bill to see if he needed the car back, he said that he did not, and nor did the bloke that owned it. He was also advising me of an extra police presence, and as with John, would rally the troops of the Cross to assist. There is a difference when criminals surveil police than when police surveil criminals: the police stand out, while the criminals are at home.

I arrived at Marty's house and there were about a dozen or so police searching the house. I introduced myself to the officer in charge, who surprisingly to me was aware of my existence. I asked how long they would be, then went to comfort Philippa, Marty's wife, and their children. They had two friends staying with them at the time, and there was a tension in the air inside the house.

Then a younger officer came out from a room with a joint of marijuana. You would have thought he had just won the bloody lottery.

The officer in charge had told me to hand Marty in. He was sure that I knew his whereabouts, and that the operation was the biggest of its kind, and involved the importation of a large commercial quantity of cocaine. I actually felt relieved when he told me, as the whole thing was not possible. They definitely had the wrong bloke.

But always the one to take advantage of a situation, and with the young bloke still holding the joint, I told them that if in fact what they were saying was true, why confuse the issue with a shitty little joint? I suggested that the item should be flushed down the toilet. The officer in charge then took the joint and gave it to another officer, and he flushed it down the toilet. Illegal, but common sense.

I hurried the search team along, and soon afterwards they left, advising me to bring Marty in for questioning. Like that was ever going to happen.

There was work that needed to be done, and time was of the essence. I dropped the car off to Bill Bayeh and thanked him. Both he and John had kept me updated during the night with reports of the police surveillance. Some helpful defence evidence was obtained including photos and vehicle registration numbers; police are not used to being surveilled themselves.

I had closed Springfield's and collected the night's takings, then slipped out the back door where a vehicle and driver were arranged to take me home and get Marty. John also came through with some info that the police were sitting outside Springfield's waiting for me to leave.

There was a back lane behind my place, so I jumped the back fence, grabbed Marty and we were off. Thanking the driver, I tipped him and the lads for the information.

Marty had to be secure and there was no need for anyone to know where he would be. I had earlier spoken to Ross Seymour, a friend of both of ours who was living in a rented house in Lavender Bay, a beautiful harbourside suburb on Sydney's North Shore, just a stone's throw from the Harbour Bridge.

Ross was legendary around the Cross, and in the music industry, having managed the Sydney Cove Tavern for years, as well as other music venues. He was known as a good-time party man. He was prepared to hide Marty indefinitely. So, with Marty as secure as possible, now came the laborious task of getting to the bottom of what was going on.

The first part was not that difficult. There had been two other arrests in relation to the same matter. I then contacted a lawyer, who in turn contacted the lawyers of the others that had been arrested. They then produced the facts as being alleged by the Australian Federal Police.

It was going to be alleged that Marty and others were attempting to import large amounts of cocaine in an ongoing deal. Marty's role was to show that the funds were obtainable, and that he would be the bag man, so to speak. That was the Australian Police version.

It seemed that two American DEA agents had come to Australia after allegedly being given a tip from a reliable informant that there was a gang in Australia that wanted multiple kilograms of cocaine in Sydney to supply the ever-growing need for that product.

After getting the whole brief, it was blatantly obvious that the Australian Federal Police, in collusion with the American DEA, were breaking the law. It was going to be my job to prove just that.

The next month became a game of hide and seek between me and the Australian Federal Police. I needed to speak with Marty in person after uncovering different aspects of the brief. The feds knew that I was aware of his location and followed me unsuccessfully for more than two months. I also needed to obtain more information on the two DEA agents, who were now having the most wonderful holiday in Sydney, all at the expense of the Australian taxpayer.

In Sydney, as with most cities, there are places where police are known to meet and socialise after work, and George Street in Sydney had a number of bars known to be frequented by the AFP. It didn't take long before I found out where the two DEA agents, together with some of their Australian counterparts, were drinking.

I employed the services of a very attractive lady friend of mine, who was a professional escort. She was a regular around the city hotspots and often came to Baron's for a drink after a job. She was always quite open about her vocation, about the good clients and the thugs. She never named them.

It was always 'the client'. I liked her discretion. One night the year before, I had saved her when she was accosted on the street. Some jerk grabbed her arse as she was leaving and attacked her after she fought back. I grabbed the baseball bat that was always behind the bar and made him apologise. She and I had been friends ever since, because she liked the fact that I declined the reward she offered.

I pointed out the two police that I wanted her to befriend. She came back the next day, with information that would almost, but not quite, prove that Marty and his co-accused were not guilty. She had taken the younger DEA agent home, and in short order, gleaned all the information I required. She also commented on the fact that the younger policeman was a very good shag.

She had his phone number, which was a fantastic asset. Nearly two months had passed, and Marty was becoming agitated. He was not happy. He was a family man, and desperate to be reunited with his wife and kids.

I had secured his legal team. Solicitor Greg Goold at Watsons, a very good bloke and a friend of mine, had just gone into a partnership with Chris Watson. He had previously had his own company in Bondi Junction.

I had filled Greg in on the whole story, and the fact that Marty wanted to hand himself in and make a bail application. Given the circumstances, it was never going to be easy, and he was aware that he may be locked up for a few months while waiting to be listed at the Supreme Court for such a hearing.

We were confident that he would make bail, but there is no sure thing when the stakes are so high. I brought Marty to see Greg and his legal team and after a lengthy consultation, they handed him in. Bail was refused and he was sent to Parramatta Gaol, where he would wait until he was listed at the Supreme Court for the appeal.

I visited him regularly at the gaol and he asked me if I would leave Baron's, and move across to Springfield's to assist there and continue on his brief. Working on his brief was never going to be a problem, but the Springfield's crowd did not appeal to me as much. I was a squarehead to them, and they were all a bit weird for me. But that said, I accepted and I moved across the road, handing my job at Baron's to Felix Lyle.

As I saw it, my first duty at Springfield's was to open the doors and let the punters in. Marty had made it somewhat exclusive, and in my view, he was going to need a lot more money to fund his defence. That sort of exclusivity would not pay the bills.

Almost overnight, the place was heaving. There was now a cover charge, and if you had any association with the music industry, you were more than welcome. Over a month passed, and Marty's hearing was set at the Supreme Court. It was there we found out who would be prosecuting. Elizabeth Fullerton, a formidable opponent, was someone I had met previously in the company of Greg Goold, Marty's lawyer.

She had only just been appointed to the Commonwealth Director of Public Prosecutions as an in-house counsel. Unluckily for Marty, she was now the enemy. Marty was granted bail and there was not likely to be a committal hearing for some time.

The longer things dragged on, the more information could be obtained for the defence and even though it was a very bad situation, things were actually getting better every day.

There were legal arguments to and fro, from Marty's team to the DPP, and much ado about nothing. It just seemed to drag on and on.

A date was eventually found for his committal hearing, and it was to be heard at Central Local Court in the middle of the Sydney CBD. The two American DEA agents had arrived and were so full of themselves it made me want to vomit. Together with the Federal Police, they were certain that Marty would be committed for trial.

Marty had secured Patrick Costello, 'the Counsellor' as he was affectionately known, and who I had been aware of for years after watching him and Christopher Murphy demolish many a prosecution. There could not be two more different opponents at the table than Elizabeth and Patrick. If nothing else, it was going to be fiery.

I had spoken to Patrick about an idea that kept cropping up in my head. The feds had found no drugs; that was a fact. If Marty and his co-accused had conspired, it must have been with the two DEA agents. They – the DEA – had no right to come to Australia and sell cocaine, or any other drug.

Off my own bat, I went to the desk at Central Local Court and politely asked the clerk at the court to issue me with two subpoenas where I was the complainant and named the two DEA agents as the respondents. The charge was conspiracy to import a large commercial quantity of cocaine, for which he charged me the standard fee of $26 each.

Shortly after leaving the police and teaming up with a variety of lawyers, I had obtained a Private Investigator's Licence which allowed me to perform a number of tasks such as serving official documents and swearing affidavits. So I met the two DEA agents at the steps of the courthouse, and duly served them, advising them that they were to appear at Central Court the following week, charged with supplying a large commercial quantity of cocaine. They both laughed at me, took the subpoenas and walked off down the street. I, on the other hand, could not wait until the first of them was called to the witness box.

I sought out Patrick Costello, and told him what I had just done. I had advised the court that the subpoenas had been duly served. The clerk shook his head at me with the usual, 'Charlie, Charlie, what have you done?'

'If you want to see something funny, be in court number two this afternoon,' I said.

Patrick was amused; he too could not wait. Just after the lunch adjournment, the first DEA agent took the box and gave his name, rank and occupation and was administered the oath. Springheeled Patrick Costello jumped to his feet, hands raised, flapping papers to and fro through the air.

'Your Worship! Your Worship! No, stop this man, Your Worship!'

The magistrate was looking highly unimpressed with these antics. Peering over his spectacles, he said, 'Yes, Mr Costello, what is it this time?'

'Your Worship, at this point, I think that the witness should be cautioned.'

'And why is that, Mr Costello?'

'Well, Your Worship, this witness has been charged with a criminal offence that makes him a possible co-accused of my client, and I feel that he should be rightly cautioned.'

The magistrate was totally confused, and called in the clerk of the court who showed him my subpoena. Elizabeth Fullerton, taken by surprise as much as the magistrate, objected, saying that it was a ruse and nothing more. After seeing the smile on my face, and noticing that I was the informant of the allegation, she was furious.

The magistrate, on the other hand, noted her objection and duly cautioned the DEA agent that he was not obliged to say anything, as anything he did say, could be used in evidence against him at the pending hearing with regard to my subpoena. He then advised him to seek legal advice.

The DEA agent arrogantly drawled, 'I'm the goddam police!'

'In America you may be, but here, you are just a witness.'

Elizabeth was fuming, and said that she would advise the witness. To her disgust, which was directed primarily at me, she was informed by the magistrate that there was, in his opinion, a conflict of interest, to say the least. With that, the DEA agent was sent marching down the street to Daking House to the Legal Aid Office.

The matter was then adjourned, until he had been advised as to his legal position. I was more than confident that he and his buddy would be on the plane back to the USA post-haste. The next day at the resumption, he was called back to the witness box, and surprisingly could not recall what his evidence had actually been. He and his buddy returned to the States and were never seen again.

That pretty much started a new career for me there and then. It seemed that it was hard to keep a result like that quiet. And the work started pouring in, everyone wanted an investigator, especially one who had police connections and who could be trusted.

Most people thought that if you paid a policeman, you could get off a criminal charge. Well, that was not how I operated. I could look at a brief and see where the police had made mistakes or lied. There was no way I was ever going to pay a policeman to sort something out for me, let alone someone else. I hadn't been a corrupt cop and I sure as hell wasn't going to be a corrupt PI. But what I could offer seemed to help a lot of people out. I'd found a new niche. Between Springfield's and my PI business, I was doing very well for myself. My life seemed to have settled down again after my tumultuous departure from the police, and I was glad of it.

12

SPRINGFIELD'S ROCK AND ROLL

1993

Meanwhile, back at Springfield's, things were starting to go rather well. I was learning constantly, but I became aware that I was naïve when it came to drugs. They had never been a part of my life, and now I was meeting people every day who took them socially. My only previous experiences had been with addicts.

It seemed that everyone in Kings Cross took cocaine. Then it seemed that every professional person took cocaine as well, and then I began to question who other than me *didn't* take cocaine. At first I just thought some people could drink a lot more than me before falling over. And then there were the smokers: they always looked very chilled, like they were about to fall asleep, especially the ones who had done skunk. I eventually realised that this horrible form of marijuana several times more powerful than your normal weed was something to stay well clear of. The only person I saw regularly who smoked marijuana was John Ibrahim, and he was always calm as opposed to his brother, Sam, who took cocaine and was always hyper.

The punters at the venues all over Kings Cross seemed to be able to self-medicate when it came to drugs. No one had a problem getting anything they wanted. It didn't bother me in the slightest, as they were generally all well behaved. Drunks from the suburbs were the real problem.

I was getting used to the music-industry people, too, and they were getting used to me. Marty had introduced me to all the stars in the industry, and that has resulted in many life-long friendships.

Through Marty I met a bloke by the name of Steve Hands. Steve was working for Warner Records. He had started his career with EMI in England in 1969 and joined Warner Records in 1972. He was instrumental in bringing Cold Chisel, arguably Australia's premier rock band, to public attention.

Steve knew everyone in the music industry. When I met him, he was head of marketing and promotions, working with international artists, and they all loved him. It was on a Wednesday night at around 9pm that I got a call from him. He asked me to come down to the Park Hyatt, a very fancy hotel in Circular Quay, a mere 500 metres from the Harbour Bridge.

'I have someone that would like to meet you,' he said.

Earlier that day, I had bought my first Porsche and thought, *Why not?* I can race down Macleay Street, and I'll be there in 15 minutes, knowing full well that Steve would not waste my time.

On arrival, the security guard at the front door knew me as he was an old highway patrolman stationed at Parramatta when I had been there on general duties. He saw the Porsche with me inside.

'Go, Charlie! Life is obviously better outside of the coppers, and your name is on the door! Nice one, Charlie!'

He pointed me in the direction of the function room where I was expected. I turned the corner and saw Steve immediately as he was taller than most and stood out in a packed room, one that was obviously a well-to-do after party. With that big broad smile, he came over and thanked me for coming, adding that he wanted me to meet someone. He ushered me across the room. 'Charlie, this is Paul and Linda McCartney.'

Then he went straight back to Paul, saying, 'This is the man I was telling you about.'

I was embarrassed. What could he have *possibly* told them about me that required me to come down to a party at this time of night? I smiled, trying to catch Steve's eye, to ask what he had told them, but was unable to. Eventually, he left me with Paul and Linda, and the conversation flowed easily all night.

It's very rare in life that three people hit it off as well as the three of us did that night. They were on tour with Wings, Paul's band, and they also introduced me to Hamish Stuart, the legendary Scottish guitarist from the Average White Band. After a very special evening for me, Paul suggested that I come to the concert the following night, which just happened to be at the Parramatta Football Stadium.

I said I would love to, as that's where I had been stationed as a policeman. He asked how many tickets I wanted, and I said that two would be plenty. He was having none of that, and said that I should invite all of my friends and family, and that however many I wanted would be available.

Linda was so insistent that, again, I was embarrassed. Steve had just returned to the table and jumped in at that point and said that he would sort out however many I wanted, and would add my guest list to the promotion list. I finally collared Steve on the way out of the hotel, and asked him, 'Why me?'

He said that real people love to meet real people. That a conversation had come up about illegal activities and that he had told them about me, and they said that I sounded like a person you need to know if you were in trouble. He said he would ring me as I was just up the road. I thanked him for a wonderful evening and went home.

I had been busy in the weeks prior with a number of criminal matters, and the following morning I went to Watsons Solicitors. I had been suggesting to a number of people in and around Kings Cross that Greg Goold and Watsons were good lawyers and that they specialised in criminal matters.

I had an appointment with both of the junior lawyers. Martin Richie was a South African bloke, mid-thirties, very bright and charming. The other, Paul Hardin, also mid-thirties, had been trained by Christopher Murphy and had obviously paid attention. Very sharp, and also charming, he also happened to be the son of Bruce Hardin, a very good bloke, and a well-known Sydney identity who has been mentioned in police despatches more than a few times, and just happens to be one of my best mates.

I had no formal arrangement with Greg Goold, or Watsons, but referrals went both ways and it seemed to produce an abundance of work, resulting in me spending more and more time at their offices. After our meeting that morning, I told all the staff in the office that they could have a ticket plus one to the Paul McCartney gig at Parramatta that night if they were inclined to go.

I rang Mum and Dad and my siblings and made them the same offer. At the time, there was a commercial solicitor at Watsons by the name of Elouise Stark. I quite fancied her. Elouise, on the other hand, was having none of me. She was a corporate lawyer, and didn't want to have anything to do with criminal law, and was certainly not interested in dating someone like me.

I was, as she perceived, the 'Wild Colonial Boy' as in the Clancy Brothers and Tom Makem song, whereas she was British and straight as an arrow.

I had a plan: I asked all the staff. They were more than happy to go. I walked into Elouise's office, and asked her if she would be interested in going to a concert with me that evening. She declined, almost before I had finished asking her.

'That's too bad. The bloke's a mate of mine, and he's English. I thought you might have heard of him. Paul McCartney is his name, and his new band is playing at the Parramatta Football Stadium tonight. I know quite a few people there, and it will be a grand night for sure.'

'Paul McCartney is a friend of yours?' she asked, disbelievingly.

'Yes,' I said. It almost sounded plausible.

'No, I don't think so. I am quite busy.'

Not to be discouraged, I went downstairs to see Martin Richie, and told him to get straight upstairs and convince her that, in fact, Paul and Linda McCartney, were indeed *very good friends of mine*. More than an exaggeration, to say the least!

Martin, being the smooth operator in court, as well as in real life, soon had his colleague convinced, and she reluctantly accepted. I told her that I would pick her up at the office at 6.30pm. I turned up at the office at exactly 6.30pm in my newly purchased Porsche.

She came downstairs and saw the car, believing that I had borrowed someone else's ride to take her. There was not much said on the way to Parramatta. I knew the area like the back of my hand and I knew that parking was always going to be a drama. The stadium on O'Connell Street had none but there was a spot on the footpath right outside the ground. I drove up onto the footpath, and Elouise was disgusted.

'You can't park here; this is not right!' She pointed to a policeman walking up to the car, and, looking as disgusted as she was, he approached and I opened the door. He was one of the Parramatta boys. He could see it was me, and said, 'Hello, Charlie. How are you?'

'Great, old mate. Listen, can I park here? I'll leave the keys with you.'

'No worries, Charlie. You keep them. I'll tell all the boys it's yours.' Elouise and I got out of the car parked on the footpath. We both walked to the promotion ticket office, and together with Mum, Dad, all the staff from Watsons, and my family, I collected the tickets and handed them out, briefly introducing Elouise to my family as I did so.

There were two 'AAA' (Access All Areas) passes for Elouise and I, and the other tickets were in the first half-dozen rows. My colleagues and I certainly all felt quite special.

Nearly all the security working at the concert that night were off-duty police, so as we walked around the grounds, everyone that looked even vaguely official offered me a nod of the head. 'Hey, Charlie!'

I could see by the look on Elouise's face that she was reassessing her opinion of me. And the *coup d'état*? Elouise and I were in the pit in front of the stage, and the smoke machines were in full billow, so you knew that the show was about to commence, and then amid the haze of the smoke being expelled from the smoke machines, on a moving crane came Paul, Linda and Hamish.

All three looked to their right and saw me with a big grin on my face, and in unison, they gave me a nod and a wave. 'Hey Charlie! Make sure you come backstage!'

Well, that was it. Elouise was finally convinced that perhaps I might not be such a Wild Colonial Boy after all. I felt reasonably sure that after dropping her home that evening there was a chance of a second date. I rang Steve the next day and thanked him for sorting out what was a fabulous show and evening, and he said that it was a pleasure and quizzed me as to why we had not gone backstage to see Paul and Linda as they had thought I was going to.

I explained that there were so many hangers-on backstage, and that their night would have been very late, and a little tedious. I had been to so many gigs, and found that after a performance, most artists would rather sit down, have a beer and relax.

He reminded me that Joe Cocker was in town, and we'd had a huge night out a few years before, and that we should all catch up then, and he would let me know. I assured him that

I would be up for that. The following day, the talk around the Watsons' office was all about the previous night, and whether Elouise and I would see each other again. This time, I got an unequivocal 'yes'.

*

I'd made a name for myself and business was booming. One of my clients was Ronald Geoff Montgomery (often called Monty), an American citizen who lived in Lima, Peru. Monty was also a client of Watsons, as I had referred him to them. I had met him before his arrest in Kings Cross, and he had asked to meet with me again. He wanted to find out if he was being sought by the police and was prepared to pay for the information.

I told him if you needed to ask the question, then the police were after you. And in which case, best you return home before they arrested you. Long gone were the days when you could or would speak to a policeman and pay for such information. Now it would involve using a computer, and then questions would be asked.

Monty was only a few years older than I, and a few inches shorter. He had a sense of humour that endeared him to you. He enjoyed the night life, and all the vices that came with that lifestyle. He was a timber merchant, and would bring wood up the Amazon River to Lima, and he was in Australia looking for buyers. I told him in no uncertain terms that he should leave Australia as soon as he could.

Monty sent his wife and children home to Peru, and he stayed for what was only to be another month. Unfortunately for him, he was arrested in the eastern suburbs and charged with possessing a kilogram of cocaine. The arrest was complicated, in that while his rented apartment was being searched, a man by the name of Robert Stalder came strolling up the stairs supposedly to see someone.

Stalder was confronted by an Australian Federal Police Drug Task Force member, and an altercation took place. Stalder received a punctured lung, numerous broken bones and other injuries. He was arrested and conveyed to Prince Henry Hospital where he was placed in a secure wing and treated by hospital staff.

Unfortunately for Stalder, he died two days later. The post-mortem revealed that he had actually died from a heroin overdose, not his injuries, but how could that be when he was in hospital? I was employed to ascertain the truth.

Monty was of the opinion that Stalder had been brutally bashed by the arresting police, and he believed that the actual cause of his death was more than suspicious. The line of questioning ran like this: firstly, who had visited Stalder in his secure ward?

Secondly, how was it possible for Stalder to obtain heroin in that secure ward? On the face of it, something was not right.

Monty's case would not be for some time but the inquest was imminent. I liked Monty. He was a straight shooter. He had no money, no family or friends, and the only person left in Australia that he knew was me. His wife and two children were back in Peru and she had no idea about the timber business and his situation was getting grimmer by the day.

He asked me if I could help, both financially and personally. I made the decision that I would. I had met the detective sergeant in charge and did not trust him or believe him. So, I was in.

Over the next few years, I supported Monty's family by sending them money, and by putting funds into his prison account. He would, in turn, offer my services to other inmates in the prison, and with their lawyers, I would work on the cases where necessary.

The inquest into Stalder's death was full of excitement and intrigue, allegations to and fro. The arresting police glared at me throughout the proceedings.

I really liked Coroner Derek Hand. He was a good bloke, and he gave me the nod, and the Australian Federal Police were not happy about it.

Two facts were not in dispute. Stalder was dead and the cause of his death was an overdose of heroin. But there were lots of questions that needed answers. In a nutshell, it was akin to having a second chance at a trial as many of the primary issues were the same. By the inquest's completion I had successfully found a whole new team of Australian Federal Police who disliked me intensely.

I was not spending much time at Springfield's other than socially. I was spending more time with Elouise, but then within months she told me that she was returning to England as her family business in Hartley Wintney, Hampshire, was undergoing changes and she would have to return to supervise.

I was extremely busy with work. It seemed that the police in New South Wales were working overtime; people were being arrested at a rate that kept Watsons and me extremely busy. Before I could blink Elouise was gone and I ploughed into the work. We wrote to each other lots and spoke on the phone. But I really missed her, I was in love and within a few months I was back in London.

Royal Ascot, the biggest horse race event on the English calendar, was taking place the weekend that I arrived. Elouise and some friends had tickets, and there was a spare for me. I was so pleased to be back. When I was in Elouise's company, it was as if my soul was being cleansed. Her intellectual stimulation invigorated my mind. She took me shopping that day and I bought the compulsory blue blazer and pair of chinos, and we were off.

I hadn't heard of a single horse that was running that day, but as luck would have it, I backed every winner and won thousands. With the proceeds, Elouise and I were off to Paris. Her family business was to do with fine wines, and she spoke near-fluent French and knew every vineyard in the Côtes du Rhône Appellation in France.

I had a bag of cash, it was summer, and our trip would end in Marseilles, some weeks later. As we travelled through the French countryside on our way to Monte Carlo, we were very fortunate to secure a stay at Le Montrachet, a large stately house set behind the chestnut trees of the square in a peaceful village just outside Beaune, in the heart of the vineyards. The hotel was a perfect setting, and with the assistance of world-renowned Burgundy expert and resident sommelier Jean-Claude Wallerand, we were somewhere south of heaven.

We stayed and tasted some of the finest wines on the planet. A few days later, we continued south to Monte Carlo, where we stayed in a very nice hotel on the beach. Then it was on through Saint-Tropez and Cannes to the French Riviera, where it was hard not to fall in love with the cobblestones and panoramic coastline in and around Cassis.

The weeks passed, and we ended our stay in Marseilles, and flew back to London. I had to make a tough decision, and I did just that, though not without real sadness in my heart.

Reluctantly, I flew back to Sydney.

13

ATM COCAINE

When I landed after a month's absence, there was a noticeable change in the Kings Cross area. There were drug distribution centres popping up all along Darlinghurst Road, the main drag through the area. Just as there are holes in the wall for cash machines, it seemed the same was now true for drugs.

It had developed almost overnight, and rivalries between vendors were becoming obvious. As I knew the whole area, I had my own database of intelligence, stored only in my head. It was comprehensive and invaluable when coming to the defence of a number of clients. My main client was my friend Bill Bayeh.

I had met Bill a decade before while stationed at Parramatta. Bill was a grafter, a lousy punter, and was constantly borrowing money. When it came to punting, he stood no chance. He would have been better off buying lottery tickets.

Suddenly, quite literally overnight, that all changed – with the exception of him being a terrible punter.

Somehow, Bill managed to obtain the leases on a few premises along Darlinghurst Road. Some very dodgy staff were employed. And Bill was no longer borrowing money from anyone; in fact, it was the exact opposite, he was now paying for everyone and everything.

Bill kept his affairs to himself, and the people that he was dealing with were unknown to me, and that suited me and many others. Ignorance is bliss, and all that. He was, however, concerned about being framed by the police.

His fears were somewhat justified. He had been arrested a few years earlier by the Drug Squad at a hotel in Bondi near the beach. The allegation was that the police had received information that Bill was at the hotel, and that he was in possession of cocaine. The Drug Squad duly kicked the door in, searched the room and in their version of events, found an ounce of cocaine in a plastic bag under the pillow where Bill was sleeping.

According to Bill, they indeed kicked the door in, searched the room and found a bag of white powder, but that it was not in fact under the pillow as stated by them, but was inside the leg of the bed that had a cap on it. I believed Bill, and you may well ask, 'What's the difference?'

There was a big difference when it came to defending him. The police were lying about the facts of the case. It became my first job defending for Bill. And there were many more to come.

Elouise rang about a month later and asked if it would be possible to get tickets for Madonna. She was playing at Wembley Stadium in London, and the show had been sold out for quite a while.

I rang Steve Hands, as Madonna was with Warner Music at the time, and he got me four AAA passes to her concert the following Sunday. I rang Elouise, and told her that I was unable to get the tickets and although she was disappointed, she said not to worry. I then rang her flatmate Carol Grey, and told her that I had four tickets, and that there was one for her and their girlfriend Miranda as well.

I asked her not to tell Elouise, but that I would turn up on Friday and deliver them myself. I booked a ticket that day, and flew to London on the Thursday, landing at 6am on Friday. I got a cab from the airport to their house, Kimbolton Cottage, a fairy-tale, freestanding cottage smack bang in the middle of Knightsbridge. It was almost as if they had forgotten to pull it down, and just built department stores around it.

I got there at 7.30am, and tapped on the door. Carol, very excited and pleased to see me, sent me to Elouise's bedroom, where I tapped her on the shoulder. She was very pleased to see me, too.

We spent the weekend racing around London, and went to the show on Sunday evening. On the Monday morning, the girls dropped me back at Heathrow, and I flew back to Sydney.

Bill rang me with bad news. John Ibrahim had been arrested, and he and another Kings Cross identity, Russell Townsend, had been charged with murder. Russell was a big man, a powerful weightlifter, but not at all the type of person you would suspect of murder.

John Ibrahim, on the other hand, had just become the sole owner of the Tunnel Nightclub, which was only 200 metres down the road from Springfield's. It was on fire, queues every night, and he was well on his way to success. John's only real visible problem was controlling his older brother Sam, who was nearly always out of control. Fortunately for me, Sam and I had a cordial relationship going back more than a decade. Sam was Sam and no one was ever going to change him. He was fearless, and feared by just about everyone. I was fortunate that I had his respect.

John, however, was very different from the rest in Kings Cross. He was focused. He wanted to be successful. He kept to himself, and didn't drink or gamble. He saw successful people and adopted their characteristics. There was only one thing stopping him, and that was his lack of worldliness. But that was all about to change. John had got bail, and came to see me about a dilemma.

His dilemma was not being charged with murder. It was that the love of his life, Molly, had left him. She had packed her bags and left Australia, in fact. I felt for John, who was visibly distressed, as he had no idea where in the world she had gone. He came to see me, and asked if I could assist him in tracing her whereabouts. I agreed and without much difficulty, obtained her mother's telephone details, and then saw that there had been a few reverse-charges calls from a pub in Lots Road, Chelsea, in the UK. Girls always ring their mothers.

I sent a mate of mine who lived in London a photograph of her. So he went to the pub and confirmed that she was, in fact, working behind the bar.

I actually knew the pub in question, and so I told John, and he asked me to take him there, talk to her and convince her to come back to Australia. That all seemed fine but there was one problem. John had just been charged with

Me (far left) and my siblings at my grandfather's house in Ireland the week before we migrated to Australia.

First family photo in our new house in Sydney's western suburbs. Me (back, far right), my eldest sister Ann (back left), Rosy on my mother's lap, Gerry, Dermot and Kieron (front, left to right).

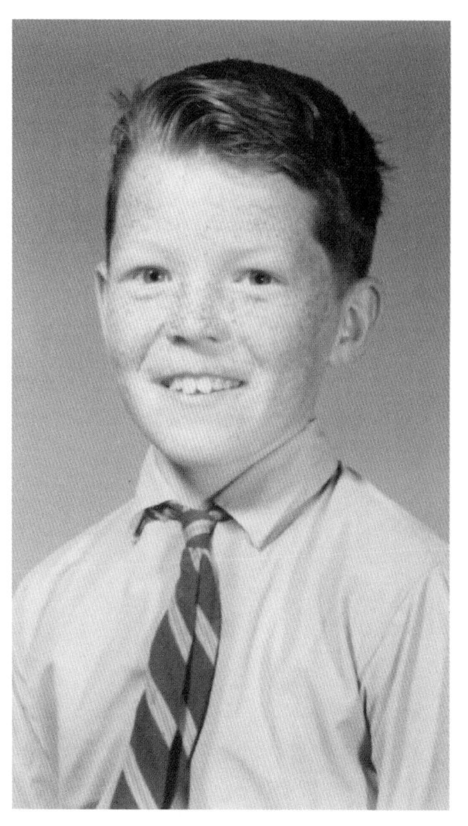

Me at nine years old at primary school in Fairfield.

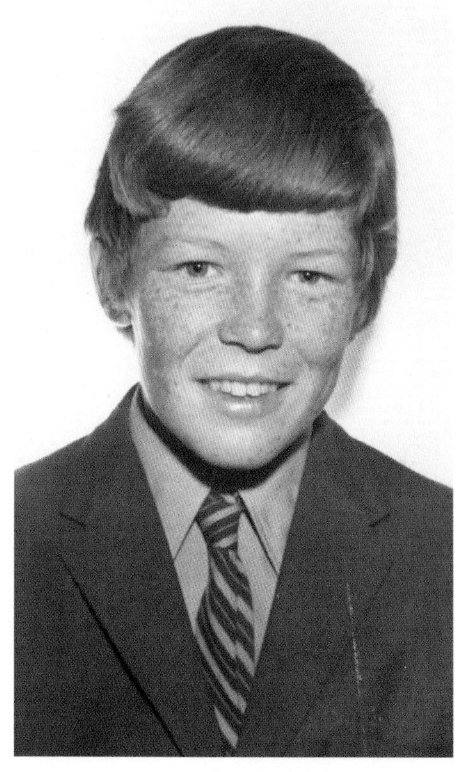

Me aged 12 at Patrician Brothers Fairfield.

A very happy F Troop passing out photo, 1978. Charlie: middle row, second from the left.

A team of good blokes, Parramatta, 1984. Charlie: front row, second from the left.

First picture with my son Danial at Bernie's farm.

Just after the Bathurst Riots in 1985.

A very proud grandfather, Gerald Staunton, with me, 1986.

Kim Staunton and Timothy, my youngest son. She chose motherhood over modelling.

Danial and Timothy, my young sons, at Timothy's first boxing lesson.

Bernie, my father-in-law (left, third from the front), and his daughters and I (front right) at The Cyren Restaurant, Broadway, shortly before his arrest.

RECORD OF INTERVIEW [redacted]
CONSTABLE 1ST CLASS CHARLES JOSEPH STAUNTON AT POLICE INTERNAL AFFAIRS BRANCH ON 27 MARCH, 1987.

PRESENT : [redacted]
[redacted]
Constable 1st Class C J Staunton.

TIME COMMENCED : 1-15am.

Q1. As I have already informed you [redacted] and my assistant is [redacted] we are from the Internal Police Security Unit. I am going to ask you some questions about a carton containing twelve bottles of Black Douglas whisky, 750mil size, together with two grey blankets contained in two plastic bags, which I took possession of from a dark blue Commodore sedan, [redacted], in a garage at your premises at [redacted]s at about 11-20pm last night. I want you to understand that you need not say anything unless you wish, but whatever you do say will be taken down on the typewriter and may later be used in evidence. Do you understand that?

A. I don't wish to say anything about it.

Q2. Do you agree that prior to this interview I told you that I intended to have [redacted] type down the questions that I ask together with any answers you may give?

A.

Q3. Do I take it from your silence to my last question that you do not intend to answer any questions at all that I may ask of you?

A.

Q4. In view of your attitude I intend to terminate the interview.

TIME CONCLUDED 1-23am.

[redacted]
[redacted]

Record of interview where I would not speak or sign, 1987.

CHARLES STAUNTON
Criminal Investigations

21/29 Orwell Street Potts Point NSW Australia 2011
Mobile: (015) 213 851 - Pager: (02) 963 3683
Fax: (02) 360 3289

The old fox's business card.

Richard Clapton with one of the best blokes to grace this planet, Steve Hands.

My friend Marty Clapp (front right) and I celebrating our birthdays at Springfield's, a Virgo party.

Marty Clapp, front and centre, at Springfield's with staff and friends shortly after the opening.

Bill Bayeh shortly before his 16-year sentence.

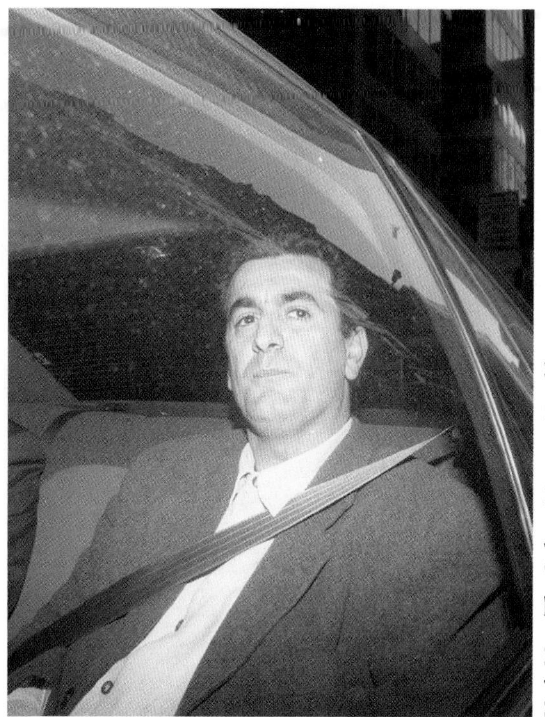

Nick Moir/*The Sydney Morning Herald*

Carol Grey, Miranda Ingrams and I backstage at Wembley at a Madonna concert, taken by Elouise.

A great day at Royal Ascot with Carol Grey and the girls, where fortunes were won.

Danial and Timothy on a visit at Windsor Prison.

Another good bloke, Peter Moore (playing his crutch), and I with another friend in Bali the week before I became a criminal.

Relaxing on a beach in Bali after my release from prison at the Royal Commission.

Me practising at a shooting range in China.

Dubravka and I cruising down the Li River in China.

Divide this bundle by 20 and it's still a million and fits easily into a small bag.

Felix Lyle, the then president of the Bandidos.

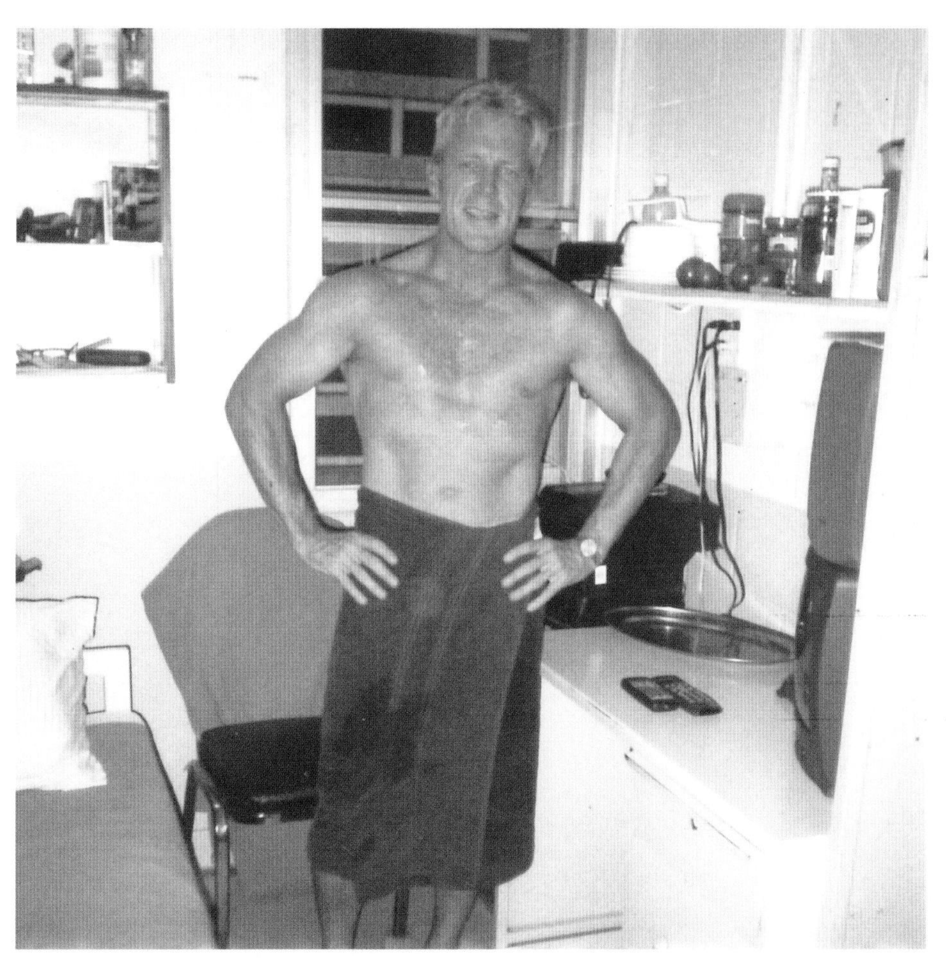

Me in my cell at Cowansville, Quebec.

Citizenship and Immigration Canada / Citoyenneté et Immigration Canada

PROTECTED WHEN COMPLETED - B
PROTÉGÉ UNE FOIS REMPLI

CONFIRMATION / CERTIFICATE OF DEPARTURE
CONFIRMATION / ATTESTATION DE DÉPART

V 071 542 623

Headquarters' use only - Réservé à l'administration centrale

5 6

Case serial no. - N° de cas initial: N903596514

Client ID. - ID du client: 3410 5427

Office file no. - N° de référence du bureau: 2948-97781

NOTE: To be completed for each person directed to leave Canada under removal order.
See back of copies 1, 2 and 4 for privacy statement.
Doit être rempli pour chaque personne enjointe de quitter le Canada en vertu d'une mesure de renvoi.
Voir au verso des copies 1, 2 et 4 l'énoncé sur la protection des renseignements personnels.

A PARTICULARS OF PERSON CONCERNED - RENSEIGNEMENTS SUR LA PERSONNE CONCERNÉE

Surname - Nom de famille: STAUNTON

Given name(s) - Prénom(s): CHARLES

Date of birth - Date de naissance (D-J M Y-A): 16 04 58

Type of travel document - Genre de document de voyage: 2 Number - Numéro: T102227

Place, country, date of issue - Lieu, pays et date de délivrance: Ireland. 12 02 1998

B OTHER INFORMATION - AUTRES RENSEIGNEMENTS

Cause for removal - Motif du renvoi

Detained for removal - Détenu pour renvoi: N

Liability - Responsabilité: 1

Type of order - Genre de mesure: 1 Deportation order / Mesure d'expulsion; 2 Exclusion order / Mesure d'exclusion; [3 Do not use / Ne pas utiliser]; 4 Departure order / Mesure d'interdiction de séjour; 5 Deemed deportation / Réputé avoir été expulsé — 1

Removal under escort - Renvoi sous escorte: 1 Yes / Oui; 2 No / Non — 2

Criminality - Criminalité: 1 Yes / Oui; 2 No / Non — 1

Danger opinion issued - Avis de danger: 1 Yes / Oui; 2 No / Non — 2

APPLICABLE TO DEPARTURE ORDERS:
1) This certificate, when signed by an immigration officer at the port of exit from Canada, is issued in accordance with Section 32.01 of the *Immigration Act*, following issuance of a departure order against you.
2) Section 32.02 of the Act states that if this certificate is not issued within the time specified in Regulations (30 days), **"the departure order is deemed to be a deportation order made against the person".**
3) Section 54(1) of the Act states that **"the order shall be deemed not to have been executed if the person is not granted lawful permission to be in any other country".**

APPLICABLE DANS LE CAS D'UNE MESURE D'INTERDICTION DE SÉJOUR :
1) La présente attestation, lorsqu'elle est signée par un agent d'immigration à un point de sortie du Canada, est délivrée en application de l'article 32.01 de la *Loi sur l'immigration* par suite de la mesure d'interdiction de séjour prise contre vous.
2) Le paragraphe 32.02 de la même Loi dispose que si l'attestation de départ n'est pas délivrée dans la période réglementaire applicable (30 jours), **« la mesure d'interdiction de séjour dont est frappé l'intéressé devient une mesure d'expulsion ».**
3) Le paragraphe 54(1) de la même Loi dispose que **« la mesure de renvoi est réputée n'avoir jamais été exécutée si la personne qui en fait l'objet n'a pas pu obtenir la permission de séjourner dans aucun autre pays ».**

Date signed - Signé le (D-J M Y-A): 01 06 2000

Signature of person concerned - Signature de la personne concernée

REMARKS: INCLUDE NAMES OF FAMILY MEMBERS ACCOMPANYING UNDER A 33(1)
OBSERVATIONS : INCLURE LE NOM DES MEMBRES DE LA FAMILLE QUI L'ACCOMPAGNENT EN VERTU DE L 33(1)

Date signed - Signé le: 26 04 2000

Originating CIC - CIC initial: 2948

Signature

C VERIFICATION OF DEPARTURE (Complete for all persons directed to leave Canada) - VÉRIFICATION DU DÉPART (Doit être rempli pour toutes les personnes enjointes de quitter le Canada)

Port of exit - Point de sortie: Dorval 2476

To final destination country - Au lieu de destination final (pays): Ireland

Carrier - Transporteur: KL

Time - Heure: 19:40

Signature of immigration officer - Signature de l'agent d'immigration

Date of departure - Date du départ (D-J M Y-A): 01 06 2000

CIC involved - CIC impliqué: 2476

D RECEIPT FOR DELIVERY - REÇU DE LIVRAISON

Date (D-J M Y-A)

Receiver's signature - Signature

Official title - Titre officiel

Errors / Erreurs

Utilities / Libres

IMM 0056 (07-1998) B

THIS FORM HAS BEEN ESTABLISHED BY THE MINISTER OF CITIZENSHIP AND IMMIGRATION
FORMULAIRE ÉTABLI PAR LE MINISTRE DE LA CITOYENNETÉ ET DE L'IMMIGRATION

Canada

PERSON CONCERNED
PERSONNE CONCERNÉE 1

My deportation order from Canada to Ireland.

A wonderful gift from the girls at Thomas More on leaving Montreal.

Some of London's best blokes celebrating a great night out. Front: centre, Charlie; far right, Freddie Foreman. Back: second left, George Foreman (Freddie's brother); centre, 'Big Albert' from Birmingham.

Freddie Foreman, England's Godfather, and I celebrating at Guy Ritchie's pub in Mayfair.

Mr Nice, the legendary Howard Marks, and I sharing a pint and discussing the legalisation of marijuana.

Two of the best, Cheech Marin and Tommy Chong, *Up in Smoke*.

Gillian and I
in the Cotswalds
two months after
my release.

Tabitha Ritchie
and I still
loving over a
decade later.

My little sister
Rosaleen and
I sailing the
English Channel.

La dolce vita. Loving my first two grandchildren, Kobi and Kiara.

murder. He was on bail, and a condition of his bail was that he had to report daily to the police.

So, we grabbed the handiest available QC, and raced up to Darlinghurst District Court where his bail conditions were amended so that he only had to report every two weeks.

I booked two tickets, and we were off. We landed in London two days later, and as with most flights to the UK from Australia, we landed at 6.30am. I had rung Elouise, telling her that I was coming back to town, so she booked John and I a very nice suite in South Kensington where she and I had stayed previously. It was 9.30am by the time we checked in and unpacked. John was standing there showered and said, 'Let's go.'

I could feel his ardour. He was a man on a mission. I kept on at him to relax and gain some composure. All the Ibrahims had a sense of urgency. To them patience was not a virtue but a foolish trait used by people who missed opportunities. He wanted to go, right there and then.

I had to sit him down and calm his emotions. He was impulsive, and when you are on bail for murder and 17,000 kilometres away, impulsiveness could have serious ramifications. Suffice it to say, that little talk didn't have any effect at all, and we were in a cab and en route within a minute, arriving at 10.30am. The taxi had not even stopped before John was out the door racing toward the pub.

Through the window he could see Molly setting up the bar. The side door was open, and he disappeared out of my line of sight. I quickly paid the cabbie, and raced toward the door. John had confronted Molly and to say she looked scared was an understatement.

John escorted her outside the pub, but was quickly followed by a large, fit-looking bloke in his mid-thirties. He went to grab John by the arm, so I grabbed him.

Molly was visibly upset. I managed to calm John, who was about to square up to the bloke, who happened to be Molly's boss and the manager of the pub. The manager listened to me. I told Molly that John was just here to make his case with her, and that I would ensure he left if that was what she wanted. The manager backed down, and I had a chat with him while John and Molly walked 100 metres down the road and sat on the grass beside Chelsea Harbour.

They sat and talked for half an hour, then calmly walked back to the pub. The manager was relaxed, and Molly and John smiled at each other. They had arranged to meet that night for dinner, so we both shook the manager's hand politely, and left and went back to our hotel.

When we arrived back at the hotel, I found Elouise had left a message for me to meet her at the Anglesea Arms, a pub in South Kensington, where she and a few of her university girlfriends would be having drinks at about 4pm. I tried to give John some quick tips in etiquette prior to attending. So much for the effort.

Within 10 minutes of arriving, he had the girls in the palm of his hand, his shirt up showing them his scarred torso, and then he had one of the girls organised to take him to the other side of London to score some weed. Within the hour, he had ascertained the social calendar for the following week, which included the Henley regatta and Wimbledon, two dinner dates, and a bag of weed.

I tried to tell him that if we wanted to attend Wimbledon, it was not simply a matter of just turning up and walking in.

For one thing, there was always a queue about four miles long, and it took several hours to get to the front of it. The next morning, we hailed a black cab and within 20 minutes, we were dropped off outside the front gates. The queue, just as I had warned John, stretched for miles.

He tried a few scalpers, and I warned him that it was an offence to purchase tickets from scalpers and that it was not a good idea. With that, he jumped the railing, 10 metres from the gate, grabbed me and pulled me over as well. There were many gesticulations and words from the immediate queue now behind us, and John, as cool as a cucumber, says, 'Don't worry! I'll pay for the lot of you.'

He walked up to the cashier, and said, 'All of them, please.'

The cashier looked out of his booth and acknowledged the next 16 people, all with their hands up. John reached into his money belt and pulled out a large wad of cash, and duly paid for what was now a very grateful lot behind us.

We had a great day together, and got to see some wonderful matches. We even did the strawberries and cream thing, and later in the early evening, returned to the hotel. John had arranged dinner with Molly and I had arranged dinner with Elouise. By the end of the night, John had repaired his relationship with Molly and she was packing to return to Australia.

Where it came from, I have no idea, but John said, 'Do you fancy a trip to Lebanon?'

'Sure,' I said. 'That sounds great.' So John booked two Austrian Airline tickets to Beirut, via Vienna. I was keen to see both cities, and John had been reading an article on Vienna's artistic and intellectual legacy shaped by former residents, including Beethoven and Mozart.

He had been told of the wonderful Viennese cuisine, and it suited him to, as he put it, 'learn something fancy'.

We flew the following day, and caught a taxi to the heart of the city from the airport, directly to the Ritz-Carlton Hotel, situated on the famous Ringstrasse. From there, Vienna opened like a book.

With 27 castles and 150 palaces, as well as cathedrals and museums, it was going to be a cultural experience beyond compare, and there was no time for rest. Two days later, totally exhausted, we were on the plane to Lebanon.

Peering out the window of the aeroplane, we circled over the half-ruined city of Beirut. It was clear that there had been a war, and that the recovery process was not going to be a quick one.

After we landed, we walked across the tarmac and into the third world. The walls of the buildings were riddled with bullet holes, the airport looking like a broken-down shanty town, and as we prepared for passport control, I noticed two burly, unshaven men staring straight at me.

'Charlie, Charlie!' they shouted over the assembling queue. John looked noticeably concerned.

'Do you know anyone here?'

'Not a bloody soul,' I replied.

And as they came through passport control, and marched me to the passport officer, they cried, 'Where is John? Where is John?' They were both smiling and seemed overjoyed to see me. I was getting concerned, as I frankly had no idea who they were, or what was going on, and then they spotted John and grabbed him, hugging, and speaking Lebanese.

It turned out that they were his cousins, whom he had not seen for more than 20 years. I was the only blond person on a flight of 200 passengers with dark hair and olive complexions so I was more than conspicuous, and they had been made aware that he was travelling with me.

We were both manhandled past the queueing crowd and had our passports handed over by his cousin at the passport control point where they were duly stamped, and we were led through to more relatives. Astonishingly, one of John's cousins produced two semi-automatic pistols in the foyer of the airport, in full view of everyone, from under his shirt and attempted to hand them to John and me.

Shocked, we both took a step backwards, shaking our heads. John's cousins assured us that it was perfectly legal. He had a licence, and the new law stated that if you were a licensed person, you could have up to three guns, and you could give them to two others.

We declined the very generous offer and were then taken to the awaiting Mercedes, and at an amazing speed, drove the 80 kilometres down to Tripoli. John's sister had recently become engaged to marry a young man from Tripoli, and we were heading there to meet his family.

Tripoli is Lebanon's second largest city, famous for having the largest fortress in Lebanon. John's sister's future in-laws had the penthouse in a skyscraper next to the international fairgrounds, overlooking the unfinished site, which hadn't been completed after the civil war. I was fascinated, taking in the amazing views over the Mediterranean ocean, and the war-torn panorama, filled with so much sadness and history.

I was looking forward to a very exciting week. Treated like royalty, and with a driver at our beck and call, we started our adventure visiting John's relatives in the mountains.

Heavily armed with pistols and a machine gun loaned to us by the local chief of police, we drove to the Beqaa Valley, situated east of Beirut. Between Mount Lebanon to the west, and the Anti-Lebanon Mountains to the east, Beqaa Valley is just over 120 kilometres long, and about 15 kilometres wide.

Known as the place where the finest hashish in the world is produced, it could be dangerous, but we had a fine tour guide, and were armed to the teeth. From there, we visited Byblos, where we enjoyed the amazing cuisine, including an astonishing variety of wholegrains, more chicken than red meat and fish in abundance. The meze, including tabbouleh, hummus and baba ghanoush were unlike anything served in other countries.

Bill Bayeh's brother Joe, who John and I knew very well, was living in Byblos at the time, and acted as our guide in a city that is considered to be the oldest city on earth, dating back to 7,000 BCE. Byblos had a nightlife comparable to New York, Paris and London, with a dash of the Wild West. Everyone carried a firearm and was prepared to produce it to sort out the slightest dispute.

There were strict rules regarding entry to a nightclub. Single men were not allowed; you had to bring your own girl. In the past, there had been far too many blokes turning up, and leaving with someone else's date, and trouble ensued as everyone was armed.

It was decided that you had to be escorted by a woman in order to gain entry. There was a bar on the outskirts of town frequented by hundreds of very attractive Eastern European women of all ages, so it was never hard to find an escort.

We went to several cabarets that had the full Las Vegas-type shows, and after sitting at a table in the well-known

Cobra Bar, and witnessing a real Mexican standoff where three men all stood up, pointed their semi-automatics at each other, and called each other names after a disagreement, we decided to retire for the evening.

Sadly, we didn't have enough time there. It was time to bail, as it were. John had to be back to report to police. On the flight back to Sydney, he thanked me, telling me I had changed his life forever.

There are many differences between John and I, but we were both immigrants from large families and brought up in the western suburbs of Sydney. We both ended up in Kings Cross and had fallen victim to the New South Wales Police Force.

John has always paid attention, and after our time together he realised there was a lot more to life than the Golden Mile. But he also knew that the Golden Mile could pave the way for him to reach his worldly goals. I guess that is something else we had in common: we knew that the only real police in Kings Cross were the club owners and the doormen who ensured everyone's safety. But the powers that be didn't see it that way and a storm was coming to the Cross.

14

A RIGHT ROYAL COCK-UP

Over the next few months back in Sydney, and particularly in Kings Cross, things became alarmingly tense. The word was out about the Royal Commission into corruption within the New South Wales Police Force, and there were worried people around.

I, however, had met a beautiful young lady named Dubravka Sabljak. I had actually met her years before when I was working at Baron's. She worked across the road at a place called Around Midnight. She had suggested back then that if I was ever single, I should look her up. I reminded her of that, and we started dating immediately. I needed to ease the yearnings my heart was feeling for Elouise.

We decided to get out of town and we travelled to the Gold Coast where I had booked a suite at Jupiter's Casino, which was Australia's largest at the time. I picked her up from her sister's house in Sydney's eastern suburbs, where

I met her father Ivan, who spoke poor English but seemed to give me the nod of approval.

We flew in the early afternoon. As we were walking into the casino to check in, Bruce 'Snapper' Cornwell, who had not long been released from prison after serving a lengthy term for smuggling, approached me.

We had met on a few social occasions in the preceding months. Snapper was a good bloke, and I quite liked him. He asked if I could assist him and a few lads in the collection of a $600,000 debt that was owed by an accountant to some people he knew.

I explained that I was there on a date weekend, and that I didn't really have the time. Still, we had a beer and he explained further. He alleged that a dodgy accountant had fleeced a person known to him of around $600,000 and he was now in hiding on the Gold Coast. They had tracked him down to an address some five kilometres north of the casino, on the waterways that thread through the area.

He had a few of the Sydney heavies with him, but did not want any dramas and since I had a private investigator's licence, I might be prepared to assist them in having the debt settled.

He came back the next morning. Dubravka was at the casino spa and likely to be there for hours, so I was free for a short time. Bruce was in possession of a writ from the district court in Sydney for $19,000. He also came with a giant of a man who he said would be my assistant. I did not want him with me at all. He was big and looked mean, and I wasn't interested, but the boys from Sydney had a plan. I had a better idea.

The giant and I caught a cab to the address. Snapper and the boys were on the other side of the waterway, some

500 metres away and looking into the rear of the property with a pair of binoculars.

The giant and I jumped the front gate, and knocked on the door. From inside came the sound of one very distressed accountant, screaming at us, saying that the police would be there in seconds. He wasn't lying.

The sound of sirens was already getting louder and louder, so I told the giant to leave, and that I would handle the matter. He was reluctant to go, and I had to assure him that he would be arrested but I could talk my way out of the matter. He wanted to stay, and I had to yell at him to go, although his sense of chivalry not to leave me alone for the police was somewhat charming. He really did have to go, though, or we could both be arrested.

Two marked police vehicles arrived within seconds, and at gunpoint, I was instructed to lie flat on the ground. I obliged and questioned the police as to what was wrong. They stated that the accountant had direct alarm access to the local station, as he was living in fear for his life.

I told them that I was a private investigator, and that I had tracked him down to the address with a view of collecting $19,000 as per the writ. I told them that I had been 'in the job' in New South Wales, and that I had just started my own PI firm. They duly checked the paperwork, asked where the giant was and who he was.

I denied any knowledge of such a person. They then spoke to the accountant and he slammed the door in their faces. I asked the police if they could possibly give me a lift back to the casino. I told them a few stories about the accountant that were more than likely not true, but they well knew that he had stolen a lot of money from a lot of people and thought he was an arrogant prick.

So, they drove me back to Jupiter's just as Snapper and the boys were arriving. They thought that I had been arrested, as they were watching across the canal with their binoculars. They were all impressed with the manner in which I had conducted the task, and from there, a very long night ensued.

Dubravka and I had a brilliant weekend, catching up with friends on the Gold Coast. The tables at the casino were more than generous to us, and we returned to Sydney.

A few days later, she rang me and seemed upset. Sometime before, her father Ivan had been arrested for pulling a shotgun on his next-door neighbour. Ivan grew marijuana in his backyard, and had caught the neighbour jumping his fence trying to steal his plants. So he pulled the shotgun on him, and the police were called. Since it was the third time he had been in possession of an unlicensed firearm, he could have been looking at a custodial sentence.

His court case was on the following day and Ivan and the whole family had been convinced that he would be going to prison. I, however, could see a way out.

I rang George Ikners, a barrister I had worked with on numerous occasions, and George had a soft spot for anyone who found themselves in trouble that was alcohol-related – and pretty much all of Ivan's problems were alcohol-related.

The case was heard at Bankstown Local Court and George, Dubravka and I drove there together. George gave a master-class performance, which resulted in Ivan being fined $500 and given a good-behaviour bond, and he walked out the door.

Forever after, I was Ivan's new best friend and I could do no wrong. I was now firmly established in the Sabljak family. They all lived and worked in Sydney's eastern suburbs.

Zdenka, Dubravka's elder sister, was, and still is, the backbone of the family, a tireless worker and one of life's real givers.

Dubravka was at my apartment the following week after her father's reprieve, and I asked her what she would like for dinner, and she said Chinese. So instead of going to the Chinese takeaway I went to the travel agent and bought two tickets to China. It was impulsive, and despite there being lots of work on, there wasn't a court date for a month.

We travelled to Hong Kong the following weekend, and shopped like there was no tomorrow along Nathan Road, the main thoroughfare in Kowloon, starting from Victoria Harbour for about three kilometres heading north. It is lined with shops, restaurants and travelled daily by throngs of tourists.

We stayed two nights, and caught up with Kevin Jolly, a good mate of Snapper's. We went to Sha Tin Races and stayed at the Emperor Byron Hotel, where you can look out of your window and watch the races at the Happy Valley racecourse. There must be a hundred thousand apartments that look directly over the course. It was a great city: lit up like a Christmas tree 24/7. There was street food and fine restaurants standing cheek by jowl. It was constantly busy and full of characters. And there was nothing happening in Hong Kong that Jolly couldn't sort for us.

We then travelled to mainland China. Margaret Shen, the late owner of Noble House, one of the best Chinese restaurants in Sydney, and partner to my mate Barry Forrester, had told me that Guangzhou was a beautiful part of China, and that the only problem with China was flying internally.

Every Sunday for years prior, a crew of blokes had met at 7pm at Noble House for dinner, a chat and then a game of cards, usually Manila. The group consisted of myself; Barry

Forrester; Ross Seymour (a friend of Marty and mine) who would often arrive with Phil 'Gus' Gould, then the coach of the Eastern Suburbs Roosters; as well as two of Sydney's leading rails bookmakers; and two punters.

Barry would start the game after dinner, and Margaret would invariably join in. It was a brilliant way to end a week and Margaret, quite clearly the intellectual of the group, was also the most entertaining. She told me that I was quite possibly the worst card player she had ever seen. I am eternally grateful for that advice.

As Dubravka and I boarded the plane, I could see that there were a few bits and pieces on the aircraft that were held together with tape, and that struck a nervous chord with Dubravka and brought a tear to my eye. Only a month prior Margaret had been killed in a plane crash en route to Guangzhou. She had been travelling as part of a trade delegation on behalf of the New South Wales Government. I had been at her funeral only weeks before. It was one of the saddest days of my life.

Dubravka asked if we should catch another flight, and I said, 'What would the odds be that you would know two people killed in separate plane crashes in your life? You know what? I reckon that Margaret is looking after us.'

On that turbulent flight, I thought fondly of some wonderful Sunday evenings past.

We spent weeks travelling around China. We cruised the rivers, and rather than taking in the tourist traps, we spent most of our time with locals, and we had a truly authentic cultural experience.

We flew back to Hong Kong and then on to Thailand, where I had a few meetings with witnesses regarding pending cases.

On returning to Sydney, Steve Hands got in contact, and reminded me that Joe Cocker was in town and that we should meet up, as he was playing at the State Theatre.

His new music was as good, if not better, than his past. Steve arranged 10 tickets for me, and the usual AAA passes. I attended the offices at Watsons, and invited anyone that wanted to go.

Then I received a call from Nicolai Ion. Nick was a Romanian immigrant in his mid-forties, of very small stature, dark complexion and a big smile. He was so slight he could have easily been a jockey. He lived in Dundas in the western suburbs of Sydney with his wife and daughter. I had met Nick in the early nineties in a restaurant with a friend of his, whom Greg Goold had successfully defended in a criminal matter.

Nick was not an educated man, but he was street smart and had a good knowledge of the newly settled migrant Romanian community. In the 1980s, many Romanians moved to Sydney and Melbourne, and for all the wonderful migrants that arrived, there were some who decided that crime paid in Australia. Alas, for them, they were not all that clever, and Nick knew them all.

A friend of his had just been arrested and Nick wanted advice as to who his friend should seek to represent him in the matter. I heard what his friend had been charged with and realised immediately that he had almost certainly been verballed by the police.

I suggested that he should go to Watsons with his friend, and I was sure that the matter could be resolved to everyone's satisfaction. When cases like this turned up, and they always did, it was a great advertisement for a criminal law firm.

Even more so to ethnic minorities like the Italians, the Lebanese and the Romanians.

Where they came from, no one was ever found 'not guilty'. Sure, you could pay your way out of pretty much anything, but no one was ever found 'not guilty' without a bribe. Their dilemma here was they didn't know who to pay. I had convinced them that a good researcher-cum-private investigator (that would be me) and the law firm that I suggested (Watsons) was who they should pay.

Just as the team at Watsons were all heading to see Joe Cocker at the State Theatre, I got a call from Nick. 'Charlie, I need your help, mate! I am in big trouble!'

'Sorry, Nick, we are all off to see Joe Cocker. I have the whole office going.'

'No, no, no. You must come now. It's very serious. I am in Windsor. Please come now.'

The time was just after 4.30pm and the office staff were already contemplating where we were going to have dinner before the show. I told Paul Hardin what Nick had said. Windsor was some 40 kilometres west of Sydney. I decided I could race out there and be back in time for the gig.

I arranged for Paul to pick up our AAA passes and said I would be back, and off I went over the Harbour Bridge and through the north-western suburbs of Sydney.

At about 6pm, I pulled up on this remote road in the middle of nowhere and stopped next to Nick's beaten-up old car. I approached the car, opened the door and called out, 'Nick, Nick, where are you?'

Next thing out from the bushes comes a familiar voice. 'Don't move, Charlie. Just stay there.'

Out of the bush came half a dozen plain-clothes police, brandishing revolvers. 'What are you doing here, Charlie? Where's Nick?'

Right away, I recognised a few of the police, who were from the Homicide Squad.

'Who are you are talking about?' I retorted.

Detective Warren McDonald, who I used to go to school with and had known for over 30 years, said, 'Come on, Charlie, where the fuck is he? He is armed and dangerous, and has just shot dead two blokes down the road.'

I gave them some time to fill me in, and according to them, Nick had gone to see two fellow Romanians who had sold him a very low-grade kilogram of heroin for a not-so-low-grade price. Nick had gone to their premises a mile down the road to complain about the rip-off.

They had consumed a large amount of alcohol and had taken several grams of cocaine. A gun was produced, and the two other Romanians were now dead. Nick had bolted from the scene altogether, his car had run off the road where it now stood, and he was in the bush somewhere and waiting for me to pick him up.

'Well, there you go,' I said. 'I am on my way to see Joe Cocker. I shall do you a deal. If Nick rings me, I'll bring him in with his legal representatives. If you catch him, then don't question him until we arrive. Is that a deal?'

'Fair enough,' McDonald said.

With that, I sped all the way back to the theatre, making several more phone calls on the way, to Nick's wife, a few of his mates and a few lawyers. I arrived just in the nick (no pun intended) of time for the gig.

Well, the next two days passed, and nobody heard a word from Nick, or the police.

Everyone was out looking for him, from both sides. They all drew blanks everywhere. Then three days later, after a report of a man acting suspiciously at a caravan park a few miles from where his car was abandoned, the police swooped. They nicked Nick looking for food in a caravan.

Do you think they rang me or his legal representative? Did they fuck!

Nick had not slept nor eaten for three days, had taken copious amounts of drugs and alcohol, and guess what? He made a full confession *and* gave them the low-grade kilogram of heroin to boot.

On the Saturday that followed, the races were on at Randwick, or 'Headquarters' as the track was known in the racing fraternity. A month earlier I had set up an account with Jeff Pendlebury, who was one of Sydney's leading rails bookmakers and a mate that sometimes had a Sunday meal with us at Noble House.

I had also set up an account for Bill Bayeh. It was a much better deal for Bill, as at least he would be getting the best price available, and as the betting laws had changed, it was possible to ring Jeff at the track.

I had been following a horse called Aunty Mary, and though she would be an outsider, I was convinced that she would win on this day. I was prepared to have $5,000 on her at whatever price. But, 45 minutes before the race, I received a phone call from Barry Forrester, who was also at the track and calling me from the toilet block. (You were not allowed mobile phones at the track.)

Barry said that a young trainer by the name of Stirling Smith had a horse in the next race, and it would certainly win. I thanked Barry and had a bet of $4,000 each way on the horse. Predictably, it finished fourth, and I lost $8,000. I was so annoyed, and thought that I didn't want to lose any more, so I rang Jeff, and had $1,500 on Aunty Mary at 40-to-one odds. I explained that Barry had just steered me wrong, and that my intention was to have had $5,000.

He laughed and took the bet. Wouldn't you believe it? Aunty Mary got up in the last stride, and I cheerfully picked up $60,000. I backed the next two winners and won close to $100,000 that day.

I paid off Bill's outstanding $23,000 debt with Jeff, which pleased them both immensely, and I told Jeff I would meet him at the Wentworth Park dogs that night. Several bookmakers in Sydney had licences to work both the horses and the dogs. So, I drove to Wentworth Park, just fifteen minutes' drive away, in Glebe, and collected $5,000 in cash from Jeff.

He said we could catch up during the week. He was very happy for me, as he had laid the bet off with another bookmaker. I drove a couple of kilometres down the road to O'Malley's Irish restaurant on Cleveland Street, Chippendale, where my mother and father and several of their Irish friends were having dinner. Just a few hundred metres away, and around 10 years earlier, I had found some Scotch in the back of the BMW. Cheap enough Scotch that had eventually cost me my entire career as a copper.

I stopped and bought six bottles of Dom Perignon for my parents, and was berated by my mother for being a show-off. One bottle of white wine would have been very nice, she said. With that, I left and went to the Sebel Town House. It was the one hotel in Sydney that had the ability to keep secrets, the place where all the big acts that came to Sydney stayed, and was literally in the middle of Kings Cross, just metres from the cop shop.

It had a bar downstairs that Eric the barman took care of, and he took care of everyone who went there. I rang half a dozen mates and turned up with my cheque book and wrote out cheques for $50,000 for them as they were battling at the time. We had a night of it, and like most things that happened at the infamous Sebel Town House, the details shall remain there.

Bill was over the moon that I had paid his debt to Jeff and I told him Jeff was as well. I caught up with Jeff during the week, and he asked me straight where Bill got his money. I explained that he had a coffee shop, a snooker room and two other businesses along the strip, and that they were all cash businesses, and he believed me.

It was then that he offered me a five per cent rebate on both Bill's and my turnovers. Bill and I turned over millions each year, and that seemed like it could be a nice little nest egg for a rainy day. That afternoon, I flew up to Byron Bay, 900 kilometres north of Sydney and the most eastern point of Australia.

My younger sister lived there, and after telling her about my fortunate weekend, she told me of a property that was for sale in Bangalow, in the hills above Byron. It was magnificent. Eighty acres, 30 of which was dense rainforest, with a creek that was inhabited by platypus and was surrounded by macadamia plantations.

The only downside was that it was landlocked, but after speaking to my father, I was convinced that I could put a road through it, once the bypass had been put through by the Department of Main Roads.

The property was only $150,000, due to the issues regarding its landlocked status, so I rang my father, who had just about retired from Neeta Homes. He knew a lot of people in councils that had worked with new developments, and was able to assure me that I could build my own road at a cost of around $250,000. So I paid the deposit. At that moment, Bill Bayeh rang me and asked me to come back to Sydney, as he had some concerns.

I flew back to Sydney the following morning, and caught up with Bill at his coffee shop in Darlinghurst Road. He said that he had to give a detective by the name of Trevor Haken some money.

I quizzed him as to what it was for, and he said that he liked Haken, that he was a good man and he could be handy when it came to dealing with the other police stationed at the Cross. I tried to stop him, but he was having none of it. I suggested that I would hand it over to Haken, as he would doubtless be reluctant to ask for future payments if he thought that I was aware of the situation.

Bill agreed and handed me $3,000.

He had arranged to meet Haken at the Marble Bar, downstairs in the basement of the Hilton Hotel in the city. Impressive was the only way to describe the Marble Bar, with its pillars of multi-coloured marble holding up the arches. It was a Victorian-era bar designed along a Renaissance theme, and could be mistaken for a gallery or museum. I drove there and sure enough, Haken was waiting at the end of the bar. Personally, I had never liked Haken. He always seemed to be a bit dodgy to me. He was not a good bloke. Wimpy in appearance, I certainly never trusted him.

I approached him, looked him in the eye and said that he was very lucky, and that the horse he picked had, in fact, won, and that Bill had collected his winnings and asked me to drop them off to him. He smiled and said thanks. My logic was that if he was wired, I had a defence for any possible skulduggery that Bill and Trevor had been up to.

I was right to be leery of the man. The Royal Commission had started. Kings Cross was its target, a conspicuous and easy one, since it had plenty of form for corrupt activity, all cash and lots of it. The Cross was brimming with informants, and there were no rocket scientists at large. The Royal Commission would get the public salivating, as the media could glamorise the reports, connecting anyone to anything. You couldn't possibly have a better screenplay.

However, the unsuspecting future stars of the screenplay thought that it was just another inquiry that would probably drag on forever. Some well-known identity would be the fall guy, and that would be the end of that.

It didn't take long before that perception changed, and rather quickly at that. The commission had started long before they put their publicity machine in motion. They had seconded all their investigators from other police forces around Australia, and had no New South Wales Police whatsoever.

They had secured powers to tap phones, bug premises and vehicles and had them all in play before anyone knew. They had carefully selected the easiest targets, and unfortunately for me, they had rolled (a term used to describe a person who had decided to inform on his colleagues) none other than Trevor Haken. Unbeknownst to me, he was now an informant.

Witness after witness filed through the commission's doors, willingly jumped into the witness box and lied, and lied again. The publicity was captivating and thrilling for not only a Sydney audience, but for Australia and the world.

I was attending the commission every other day with clients from Watsons, and other law firms. There were spies sent to report back to interested parties on matters that referred to their activities and others.

There were allegations of bribes and standovers, which were more than likely true. For most, these allegations and revelations were embarrassing, but not a reason to panic, since the witnesses giving the evidence were hardly reputable. Should charges follow, it seemed unlikely they would be able to prove any of it.

What was also obvious was that apart from the police, both the Bayehs and the Ibrahims were of real interest to the commission. Bill was becoming more and more agitated. Some of his staff had been approached by the commission to give evidence behind closed doors. They all came to see me as to what they should do. I simply referred them to different lawyers, as there was a potential conflict of interest on the horizon.

Bill had asked me to see Trevor Haken again, and gave me $2,000 to give to him. He also gave me an electronic device that he said he'd bought from George Maamary, a commercial private inquiry agent whom I had met previously. He had a very successful business dealing with matters of industrial espionage.

I laughed at Bill, as I had never seen such a device; not much bigger than a pager, it looked just like one. He had been assured by George that if you were within 10 feet of a listening device, the pager would vibrate and alert you to the fact that you were being eavesdropped on. Still not entirely convinced, I went to the designated meeting to see Haken at Birkenhead Point, a very fashionable, recently built development on the inner western harbour shores of Sydney.

As I approached Haken in the bar, the bloody device went off, and started vibrating. Shocked and confused, and now somewhat concerned, I grabbed two beers and sat down with him.

I handed over the $2,000 and said, your mate said to give you this. He nodded, then started on the Royal Commission. The questions that he was asking seemed in contrast to any previous conversation that I'd ever had with him, and being as aloof as possible, I finished my beer and left.

I went directly to see Bill and told him what had happened. He in turn went directly to see George Maamary, and asked to buy two more devices. I was now convinced that Haken had rolled, and would be repeating our conversation to the police. I feared that there would be ramifications for me, though I was not entirely sure what they would be.

I was not concerned about the payments that I had made to him on Bill's behalf, as in the broad picture they were insignificant, and if a prosecution was pending, I felt sure I could defend whatever allegation might be brought by the Crown.

Jeff Pendlebury rang me, and during the conversation he mentioned that Bill was losing and losing lots, and his debt was now well into the hundreds of thousands. I told him not to panic, as Bill would be good for it and that if he didn't pay, Jeff could always take his house.

Jeff said he didn't want to do that, and was more than happy to receive a few thousand each week, as he had long stopped worrying about Bill ever backing a winner and had decided to just hold the bets himself.

I had a lengthy conversation with him, saying it was almost certain that the New South Wales Crime Commission would take Bill's house from him, and that he should at least take a lien on the property. (A lien is a legal right granted by a homeowner that serves to guarantee the repayment of a loan. If Bill couldn't pay, Jeff would be entitled to seize Bill's house. When a lien is placed on a home, it means the owner can't sell it or transfer ownership.) He was concerned, and in spite of all my assurances that he should not be, he was not prepared to do it.

It didn't take long to find out what was going on. Haken was wired at our meeting and the Royal Commission was collecting information with the assistance of other listening devices and informants in play by them and their investigators. They knew their super informant had been exposed, albeit in a small circle, but nonetheless he was no longer the asset he had been the day before.

Within days, I was handed a subpoena to attend and give evidence at the Royal Commission hearings. I was annoyed but there was a side of me that was relieved. For a long time, I had wanted to break my ties with Kings Cross. The Cross had changed, and not one bit for the better. Being subpoenaed to appear before the commission was like a crossroads and I knew which way I was going.

I knew that I was likely heading to prison. I knew what sort of questions I would be asked and I wasn't prepared to give an inch. The police and the commission were coming after me and my mates, and my choices were either to be a rat and give everyone up, or go to prison. I didn't have to think twice. Someone had to stand up to them and that person was going to be me.

I knew I would miss my kids, of course. Kim was now living in Nelson Bay where her parents Bernie and Rhonda had bought a café after selling their rose farm. I would travel up there every other weekend to spend time with my boys. It still saddened me that Kim and I had split. Although we spoke regularly and I was only a few hours away, I did miss the family that we had together. However, Kim was doing a wonderful job as a single parent – a much better job than I had ever done. I knew she would continue to give the boys a loving and stable environment while I was in prison, for however long that would be.

I wanted to be represented by the best legal team at the Royal Commission, and phoned Elizabeth Fullerton to ask her if she was available. To my mind, she was the smartest QC in Australia and I had figured that the commission would come out, guns blazing. I could not be represented by Watsons, as there were numerous conflicts of interest.

Elizabeth recommended I contact Gary Stewart, a lawyer that she had often been instructed by, to instruct her in my matter.

The night before my appearance in front of the Royal Commission, I summoned all my mates and arranged a last supper, as we called it, at a bar on Bondi Beach. A dozen people turned up and partied hard till closing, and then Dubravka and I went home and prepared for the morning.

I thought I knew what it would bring, and I was ready.

15

THE CHANGING GUARD

The scene was set, and the following morning, with legal team in tow, I fronted the Royal Commission. It was very brief and cursory.

I refused to answer their questions, and within minutes, Justice Woods, the royal commissioner, sent me out a back door, and down the stairs, where I was bundled into a car and taken across the road to the Supreme Court. There I was charged with contempt. From there, I was taken to Long Bay Gaol, where I was to remain until I answered the questions and purged my contempt.

On the way, as we drove down Anzac Parade, a main road leading out of the city, a road that I had travelled thousands of times in previous years. I had my fingers crossed that this whole matter might somehow blow over in the very near future.

We arrived at the Remand Centre at Long Bay, a place where I had been many, many times before, except in a very different capacity. This time I would be staying. There was the usual booking in at reception, the strip search and receiving the prison uniform, all greens.

There were familiar faces on both sides of the fence, and general acknowledgements. I was taken through to a cell complex and directed to a cell on the first floor. I had been there before more than a decade earlier during a prison guard strike, back in the early eighties, and I had been assigned to that very block.

Not much had changed in 15 years, certainly not the décor, and on entering the cell it appeared neither had the bed linen. The cell door closed behind me and as I sat it re-opened and a young, fit prison guard appeared.

'Staunton, you had better come closer to the post. You have just been on every television channel and the other inmates are taking an interest.'

He explained that there was a cell next to the guard's post, and that it would be safer for me to be there. I assured him that I had nothing to fear and that I knew several inmates and that they would certainly look after me if necessary. He shook his head at me, as if to say I was a fool, and moved me anyway.

I had missed dinner that evening, and the cell door was locked behind me. I lay on the bed contemplating life, as you do, when the guard opened the door and asked me if there was anyone I wanted to ring. I said if I could ring my sons, that would be appreciated. He took me out of the cell and to his post where he made a reverse-charge call to Kim, who was still legally my wife even though we had been separated for some time.

Tim, my youngest, answered the phone and was very excited for a seven-year-old. 'Dad, I just saw you on the television!'

'I know, son. Timmy, I want to explain to you and Danial what it's all about.'

'I know, I know, Dad. Dobbers wear nappies.'

A tear leaked out of my eye. A few years before I had come home from work to find some minor infraction had been committed by one of the boys. I asked them who had done it.

Timothy had looked at Danial and pointed. 'It was Danial, Dad.'

'*Never* tell on your brother,' I said sternly. Timothy looked upset, and started to cry. I said, 'Where's your nappy?' I wanted him to remember this important lesson. 'Only babies dob. Dobbers wear nappies.' I had instilled in the minds of both my boys that you never give someone up. That if you got caught doing something wrong or illegal, then you copped it sweet. Loyalty and integrity, especially to family, were core values I wanted my boys to learn. And here we were years later, and this seven-year-old son of mine remembered, understanding that you never 'dob', and that made me feel very proud.

I went back to my new cell with a further sense of vindication regarding the day's actions. The Royal Commission had played a card. I was the first person to test their resolve, and by refusing to answer they got all the publicity they needed. I was neither a policeman nor a criminal and yet I was now in gaol, indefinitely. It clarified for everyone who had not been paying attention: if you were not prepared for an indefinite prison term, there were three choices. Talk, lie or roll.

At 11am the following day, the cell door was still closed. Not a word spoken, and I was wondering what the routine at the prison was. Then the cell door opened electronically and standing in the doorway was Peter O'Brian, my old mate from Maroubra who had lived with Mum and Dad for months when he broke his leg. He was now Detective Sergeant Peter O'Brian, and he did not look happy. I was totally shocked as he said, 'G'day mate. You had better come with me.'

Somewhat disoriented, I walked out of the cell and followed him down the landing immediately followed by two prison guards. He walked me to the cell that I had been placed in upon arrival the evening before. The cell was streaked with blood, and everything in it smashed and strewn over the floor.

I assured him that it had nothing to do with me, and with a stern rebuke, he stated that it had everything to do with me, and pointed to a card placed on the front door of the cell indicating the name of the prisoner in that cell. It read 'Staunton'. When I had been moved by the very astute young prison guard the previous evening, he had overlooked the name on the door.

Peter advised me that everyone in the prison had access to television and newspapers, and that after the media circus when I had refused to answer, everyone believed what had been reported – that an ex-policeman had been sentenced to an indefinite term in prison for refusing to answer questions at the commission. As he rightly pointed out, there is no such thing as an ex-policeman when it comes to prison.

Another inmate had been placed in the cell, and he had been brutally attacked by three other inmates, all the time screaming that he was not a policeman, and that sadly, he was in a critical condition. With that realisation hitting home, the warden came to the landing and told the two guards that I was to be taken to solitary confinement immediately. As they stated, they had a duty of care to protect me.

Peter escorted us down, and there were screams as we walked the gangway as the inmates realised that there was a policeman in the house. Peter spoke with me briefly, and asked if there was anything I needed or anyone that I needed to inform. He asked about my resolve on the actions I had taken, and I assured him I would remain firm, and with that, we shook hands and he left.

Then there was a further little drama. 'Who do you bloody think you are? Who is Antonio, and what is Tre Scaleni's, and who is this Ms S?' the warden yelled at me.

I stated that he knew very well who I was, and that Antonio was the owner of a very fine Italian restaurant in Liverpool Street in the city, and that it was called Tre Scaleni's, and anything regarding 'Ms S' was none of his business.

Apparently Antonio had been told by a number of lawyer customers that as contempt of the Royal Commission was a civil matter, not a criminal one, I was entitled to have my food delivered to the prison. I was also allowed to have daily visits, as opposed to a sentenced prisoner's single weekly visit.

I was also permitted to wear my own clothing. Antonio being the adorable Italian restaurateur that he is, had cooked my favourite meal, placed it in a hot box and had it chauffeured to the front gate of the remand centre, with a note reading, 'For my good friend Charlie Staunton. Please let me know if you need any more'. He had attached a copy of the restaurant's menu.

Ms S, a special friend of mine, had sent a hand-delivered envelope, addressed to the warden personally, containing $500 in cash. The envelope also had a note with specific instructions that the funds were to be immediately placed in my prison account. She had not given a return address, and the courier wasn't taking it back.

There was also a personal note for me, which he allowed me to read, but as there was no name or address on it he would not allow me to keep it.

It read:

My darling, saddened to hear of your situation, I do know that the first week can be difficult, and that this small gift will get you your necessary requirements instantly. I am here for you. You know how to contact me. Love, Ms S

What a good girl! The warden, however, wanted none of me. He had a prison to run, with 600 inmates that would be less than happy if it seemed that I was getting privileges that they were not. I more than understood his predicament.

But what about the law? I didn't make the law, and the law stated that a person held in contempt of court was entitled to things that other inmates were not. I had made my decision according to the law, and I was prepared to accept the consequences. But it seemed that no one wanted to uphold the law when it was too difficult.

To be fair, I was not all that perturbed. I had apprised myself of the law both inside and out; this was never going to be a quick process, and I had decided to take on the establishment. No prison wants an inmate that knows his rights. Most certainly, this warden did not.

I was taken to solitary confinement and given a spam sandwich and a carton of warm milk. Immediately, I thought my diet would be the first bone of contention.

Gary Stewart visited me the following day after conferring with Elizabeth Fullerton. I had not known Gary before the commission, but he came with a good name, and there could be no better recommendation than one from Elizabeth Fullerton. I asked him to bring me a copy of the Prisons Act of 1952.

It was the book that contained the rules and regulations for both sides, on the inside. I wanted the rules in front of me and wanted to quote them verbatim to anyone who felt that, for reasons that suited themselves, they would not adhere to them. Not that it would have any bearing on the warden at the remand centre as he had just signed my papers and was having me escorted immediately to a protection prison out Bathurst way. He stated that he had a duty of care and that he could not protect me in Long Bay and *blah blah blah*.

I argued that I would release him from his duty of care, and that I could sort things out in the general population myself, if it would allow me access to the entire population. No chance, was his response.

I was going to be difficult. It was a profile case and he wanted none of it or me and the next morning I was in a prison van heading for Bathurst. Kirkconnell was the name of the prison, located in the whimsically named Sunny Corner, a small village, population 92, situated 30 kilometres east of Bathurst. It housed 270 prisoners who, for whatever reason, were deemed to need protection from other inmates. That usually meant they were informants, paedophiles, rapists or police.

So, from my perspective, I would much rather have stayed where I was. On arrival, I was introduced to the warden, a very large Maori man who had obviously spoken with the warden at Long Bay. He did, however, have a different attitude, and was far more amenable when it came to my rights as a civil inmate.

He asked if I could assist him in allowing my rights to be honoured, and that seemed to be a way forward to me. I was taken to the cell complex, which was much more relaxed than Long Bay, and I was assigned a cell with a very intimidating Samoan gentleman by the name of Telofu Kurapa, who stood about six foot two tall and was 17 stone.

He seemed on first impressions to be quite amiable, and we introduced ourselves and he gave me the top bunk. The next few days passed. I was busy filling out reports to receive daily visits. I informed the warden that I was in fact a veget-arian, even though I was not. I had been made aware that the quality of food served in prisons was going to be a shock to my system, and thought I could get a better deal as a vegetarian.

There were three former policemen doing their time at Kirkconnell. One for murdering his wife, who kept pretty much to himself, and two ex-detectives from the old Motor Squad who each had only a year left on their sentences.

That left 266 inmates that I had no idea about; who they were or what they were in for. Telofu kept telling me that he was in for fraud. That's what they all said, and if that were true, they were very unlikely to be serving time in a protection gaol. It did not bother me, as I was able to keep pretty much to myself. The warden did his best to accommodate most of my requests.

The Royal Commission could no longer keep under wraps the fact that Haken had rolled, and sensationally released the secret footage of him paying colleagues bribe money via the hidden camera in his motor vehicle. That certainly opened Pandora's Box.

It also confirmed to me what I was already thinking. George Maamary was almost certainly going to be a wealthy man.

Weeks passed rather quickly inside. Dubravka would drive up at every opportunity, and we managed our intimacy with discretion, as there was no security ever rostered during my visits. She could bring food, and we could sit in the visiting area undisturbed for hours at a time. Ivan and her mother Anna would visit at every available opportunity as well.

I was now part of the Sabljak family, and Ivan especially wanted me to be his son-in-law.

While I was able to make phone calls both legal and personal, keeping my mother happy was another question. I had embarrassed her, and she thought it a disgrace that one of her children had ended up in prison, no matter the reason. She would not accept a call from me for the entire stay. Dad, however, was at least able to talk to me.

I rang one night, and out of the blue he asked if I knew the whereabouts of Trevor Haken. Taken aback, I asked why and how he knew who that was. He said that he had kept abreast of the media reports regarding the Royal Commission, and that he was aware that Haken was in a witness-protection program of sorts. Well, you could have floored me there and then, but I assured him that I hadn't a clue as to his whereabouts, nor did I particularly care.

Then Dad blurted out that Haken was in Far North Queensland, and even gave me the location. He explained that a work colleague of his, whom I also knew, had been on holidays, and had bumped into him.

I questioned him regarding how his colleague would have known Haken. He assured me that all his friends had opinions about the commission's activities, as did most of Sydney, what with the daily revelations on the national news. I told him to keep that information to himself, and to advise his work colleague to do likewise.

We said our goodbyes and I returned to my cell. When I arrived there, Telofu was in the process of making a bong. He had a Granny Smith apple in one hand and a broken biro case in the other. He stuck the biro tubing in the apple core at different angles, made a cone out of aluminium foil that he had pinched from the kitchen, and then mulled up some weed and away he went. Clever lad, I thought. He offered me a toke. I had previously only had a handful of joints in my entire life, and thought: *Fuck it. Why not? What are they going to do? Send me to gaol?*

We sat back and told each other some war stories about Kings Cross and life in Sydney, and then shortly before midnight I turned and screamed at him. Telofu had his not fully erect, but not flaccid either, cock in his hand and wanted me to look at it. Instantly attentive, I could see that it looked deformed. In his other hand, he had a black pearl.

He told me he had used a razorblade to insert the five black pearls under his foreskin, and wanted to know whether I could assist him with the sixth and final one. He seemed to be somewhat annoyed when I refused, and I can assure you that that was the last time that I shared a joint with a giant Samoan with a pearl-studded penis.

The following morning after no sleep and much deliberation (more so over the phone call with my father and less so about Telofu's enormous deformed cock) I contacted the Royal Commission. It wasn't so much that I gave a shit about Haken, but his wife and children were more than likely with him and if my dad could find him, then anyone could, and I thought they should know.

I also thought that would be the end of the matter. Not so. I was picked up within days, and driven back to Sydney to front a closed-door session of the commission. It was all very brief: I told them of the conversation, but they did not acknowledge either way as to the likely truth of what I had told them. I assured them that I had not disseminated the information, and before long was straight back to Long Bay before I was to be transferred back to Kirkconnell.

On the way back to Long Bay, as always, I was segregated from other inmates, but similarly separated on the other side of the van was Ivan Milat, who was also returning from court after a day's hearing for the backpacker murders in Belanglo State Forest. I had worked with the blokes that arrested him. That must have been a task, as you would walk past him in the street and never suspect a thing.

I wondered how it was possible that Ivan Milat and I were on any sort of scale whereby our profiles were deemed to be similar enough that it was required for us to be placed together. This bloke was charged with and later convicted of murdering seven backpackers, all between 19 and 22 years old. He had buried their bodies in a forest south of Sydney. He looked ordinary to say the least. I stared directly at him for the half-hour ride back to Long Bay Gaol, puzzled as to how such an insignificant wimp could have terrorised and brutally murdered so many innocent young people.

I had had the chance to speak with Elizabeth Fullerton and Gary Stewart before being transferred back, and it was agreed that I should seek a transfer back to the Sydney Metropolitan area.

I had a cordial relationship with the warden at Kirkconnell, and on my return, had a meeting with him. He advised me on the course of action I should take in order to be successfully transferred. He was right, and I was returned to Long Bay a few weeks later, this time to a different section.

I was still segregated from other inmates, but had made applications to have internal visits from inmates that I knew. One of them sadly was Bruce 'Snapper' Cornwell. He had just been pinched again, and was refused bail. He had inadvertently spoken to an undercover policeman, and, well, let's just say his problems were far worse than mine. But he was, as always, enjoyable company and we spent many a day discussing his case, and the daily revelations of the Royal Commission.

The new warden did not want me at Long Bay either. He wanted me transferred to Windsor, just down the road from where Nick had murdered the two Romanians, and where Bernie, my father-in-law, had lived. It was a new prison that had been built only a few years earlier. That did not seem a bad idea to me.

It would also mean that I would see Marty, who had in my absence pleaded guilty to a pathetic made-up charge by the Department of Public Prosecutions, relating to his problems of nearly six years before. He wanted to free himself of his whole past. That I could understand, and I felt for him, but to allow those lying bastards any sense of righteousness infuriated me, and he knew it.

That said, if you must do time, you may as well do it with your best mate. It was late afternoon when I arrived at the John Curtin Correctional Centre at Windsor and as things go, it was a very modern prison – only one inmate to a cell, and each cell had its own toilet and shower. Marty had heard on the grapevine that I would be on the afternoon prison van and met me at reception. He knew that he was in for an earful and duly got it.

But it had not been the full abuse that he deserved. That would come later. It was good to see him, and I was welcomed – well, that was until we got inside the prison blocks. I had been assigned a block and cell, and Marty led me in.

On the way, we stopped at each block and Marty, in a loud voice, summoned all the inmates of the block to the foyer and called upon any inmate in the block who may have a problem with me for being a former policeman, or for any other reason, should come forward there and then and deal with me, and if any two inmates had a problem, they could deal with both of us.

He recited the same speech across every block. There were no takers for Marty's offer. He then escorted me to my cell in the same block as his.

Over the next few days he tried to justify why he had pleaded guilty to a ridiculous made-up charge by the Department of Public Prosecutions. He explained that his house and that of a very good friend of ours were being used as surety for his bail from the rubbish charges from years earlier and that he wanted the matter finalised once and for all. Even understanding that, I could not understand why he would ever let the Australian Federal Police have any sort of victory.

As prisons go, Windsor was great. Marty had arrived a month before me, and being the proper bloke he was, had the respect of virtually everyone. As the prison was in the west, and just before the Blue Mountains, there were people he knew from both Sydney and Bathurst, and we had the run of the place.

Marty organised a family day, and with the help of Steve Hands, he organised a concert involving Sydney's best musicians who happened to be a crew of great blokes. We also had several wonderful young ladies who were more than happy to purport to being 'backing vocalists'. The corrections staff had no idea at all, not a clue, and the frustrations of many a long-serving inmate were relieved.

The commission again called me back, and offered me an opportunity to purge my contempt, and again, I refused. But it was coming up a year and I had had enough. You can read the Prisons Act in an hour. The screws were so lacking in moral rectitude that they could arbitrarily turn a key and deprive me of my liberty, let alone my rights under the Prisons Act, without even knowing the facts of my case.

No! It was time for me to get out of there. By all accounts, the commission was busy. I had my sources of information. Elizabeth, whom I trusted implicitly, had told me that even if I purged my contempt, that may not secure my release immediately. The Supreme Court would have the final decision and could impose a sentence more than the time served already.

That meant my plan had to be, at best, just a plan. I weighed my options, and decided, based on the law and parity in sentencing, that at most I would receive a further two months after purging my contempt. I had ascertained the anticipated schedule for witnesses to be called at the commission. There was, logistically speaking, no availability for a person of interest such as me to be scheduled for at least two months. I only had to turn up and answer the few questions that I had initially refused to answer – and I knew that these were only superficial.

Then I would have purged my contempt, and they would be forced to send me across the road to the Supreme Court, where I would once more be sentenced. Then they would re-subpoena me at a future date to answer further questions, and see what they could get from my evidence. My plan was to be out of prison and out of the country before they'd had a chance to re-subpoena me.

I had been assured by a staff member of the Royal Commission that it would be nearly three months before the commission would re-subpoena me, and that they were keen to let me back in the community, having their surveillance teams and listening devices in place, as well as informants who knew me. They believed that if I went to see people who had rolled and were giving them information, they would have a real chance of hearing the conversation.

I was ready, and the date was set. I contacted the commission and told them that I was prepared to purge my contempt and was called two days later to do so. The gallery was full of reporters and concerned others. Much to their disappointment, it was all quite boring and within minutes, I had purged my contempt and had to be taken to the Supreme Court to be sentenced for the contempt.

Despite a brilliant oratory from Elizabeth, the Supreme Court decided that I should serve another month. That was disappointing, but fine for me. The correction bigwigs decided that I should serve that at Long Bay, and that suited me as well. My logic was that I would have a month, maybe two on the outside, before I would be re-subpoenaed.

There were things to do, and people I had to see. The Prisons Act states that an inmate can be released at midnight on the final day of his sentence with the permission of the warden. I made an application and was granted permission. I feared that the Royal Commission could be waiting at the front gates of the prison at 8am (the usual release time), with a subpoena in hand. It is not common knowledge that inmates are entitled to be released at midnight. Had they subpoenaed me in the morning, then my plans would have been scuppered.

I also knew that if I was out of the jurisdiction, then I could not be served and would never have to appear. That was the plan. Dubravka picked me up at midnight. I just wanted a beer and as it was nearly 1am we drove to the Cross and stopped at Dancers Nightclub. It had only just opened and was owned by Bruce Hardin, Paul Hardin's father.

Bruce was old school, a proper grafter, and he had an almost paternal interest in me. I had done a job for him a few years earlier, and he was impressed with my work and was always concerned about my welfare. When I walked into the club, he was more than pleased. At first he thought that I had escaped, and that would not have bothered him had it been true. Like I said, Bruce was old school and hugged me like a long-lost friend. He demanded service from the staff immediately. We sat and drank, and I told him about the past year, and his only concern was that I was okay.

He had sunk most of his money into his new business ventures, and as he said, he was cash-strapped at the time, but that did not stop him going to the safe and handing over the contents to me. He owed me nothing, and gave me his last. Like I said, proper old school, and a very good bloke!

Dubravka and I then headed back to Bondi. Over the past year, she had cleared out my apartment in the Cross and put things in storage. My little sister had given her the use of her apartment in Bondi, as she had been living in Bali for some time with her partner. It was a nice apartment and only 300 metres from the beach.

The decision to stay in town temporarily had been made a week prior to my release. I had two choices: get the midnight release, and be on the plane to Bali at 7am, or hang around and try to save Bill and a few others, and take the punt that the Royal Commission would rather follow me than re-subpoena in the hope they could gather more information. I chose the latter.

The following day I drove to Bill's house, and from there, we drove to a café in Rose Bay, a very wealthy part of Sydney's eastern suburbs. There were Bill and I sitting at one table, and I am quite sure that seated at every table that surrounded us were police, working for the Royal Commission. It was somewhat comical. There is an air about people who sit in restaurants and cafés in Rose Bay, and these blokes stuck out like sore thumbs.

I did feel sorry for a very nice couple, Wally 'Diamond Wally' Adominska and his girlfriend Janey, whom Bill and I both knew, who just happened to come by our table. They sat for the briefest of moments while congratulating me on being released. They left, and went to the car park where they were detained by several plain-clothes police, searched and had their details recorded.

It became obvious then that the Royal Commission were still investigating, and what was more obvious to me was that they were no longer investigating the police but that they were investigating Bill. I pleaded with Bill to leave town, and move to Queensland. I told him who the informants were.

He was having none of it. He was not going to relinquish control of his business interests. I tried to explain to him that every person he knew was either bugged, or worse, was colluding with the Royal Commission. I spoke to other people who were involved in commission matters and to several police.

I spread the word that I was going to Bali for a week and made a busy schedule of appointments for when I returned. All were fictitious, of course. I drove to Nelson Bay to spend a few days with my sons, and tried to explain to them what was going on. They seemed to understand every word. Their mother and grandfather Bernie had taken good care of them.

On the night before I left for Bali, I went to see Bill. I was sure it was my last chance to talk some sense into him. He had moved out of his house and was renting a very large apartment near the Police Academy.

When I arrived, I sat with Bill and his wife Tanya, and pleaded with them to get out of Sydney, let the commission run its course and see where the cards fell. Bill asked me not to leave the country, and then asked me to be the godfather to his newborn daughter. I felt honoured, but I wouldn't be attending the christening. My mind was made up. I was leaving. Then the doorbell rang, and it was a guy who had done odd jobs for Bill now and then, but had also somehow been involved in Bill's arrest years earlier.

Years before, I had tried to speak to him as a potential witness in that matter. I had also taken a statement from another one of Bill's hangers-on. The Royal Commission seemed to think that I had coerced statement from both of them.

It was obvious to me that this guy was wired. He was asking questions designed to elicit answers that would amount to an admission of guilt on my part. I was sure that the commission had an agenda and I wanted no part of it. I told Bill that I was leaving, and went to the door. Bill escorted me out, and handed me an envelope with $5,000 cash.

We shook hands and I told him that the guy in his kitchen was almost certainly wired, and had to be working with the commission. I pleaded with him once more to head to Queensland, and come back in a few years when everything had died down.

I left and, in the morning, Dubravka and I flew to Denpasar, Bali. On the flight to Bali, I went to the toilet, then as I was going back to my seat, I saw a smiling face and was greeted with a 'Hello, mate.'

It was another very good bloke whom I had not seen for well over a year, Peter Moore. Peter was a good man; he was the licensee of the Windsor Castle, a trendy pub in the very fashionable suburb of Paddington, between Kings Cross and Bondi Beach. His family also owned the business.

He asked me if I had escaped. I had known Pete for years, though not well, but when he would finish work at the pub, he and his staff and any remaining customers would invariably end up in the Cross, as far back as the Baron's days. He was always well behaved, and being an old surfie, always had a good team in tow.

He told me that he had just started a business in Bali, and was moving there permanently. We agreed that I should come past, and we could catch up. I put it on the list of things to do. We landed, and my sister Rosy picked us up from the airport, and drove us to her house, which was in Jimbaran, a suburb south of the airport. It was great to catch up. We had not seen each other for two years, and she had a daughter, and their business was moving forward. She was in the rag trade making jeans.

I brought her and Gary, her partner, up to speed, and for the next week, we toured the sites and finally, after the year I'd had, I could relax. I had no intention of returning to Australia as everyone expected, until the Royal Commission had played its final hand. My only real concern was a financial one.

There were many offers of assistance from far and wide. But I needed my independence, and daily thought of what new career could come my way.

I tracked down Peter Moore, who along with a mate, had built a villa complex in Seminyak, the suburb immediately north of Kuta Beach. Seminyak back then was full of artists and very trendy people, intermingled with the multicultural tourist trade. It was a hub of activity. The villas themselves were exceptional. They oozed class. I thought immediately that as an investment, they were better than gold.

From the moment I walked into the first villa, I said to Pete that I would be more than interested in being part of a venture such as the villas. Over the next few weeks, Dubravka and I stayed at the villas a lot. Pete generously gave us exceptional mates' rates. Rosy was impressed that I had been accepted into the trendy set, and enjoyed the company of another group on the island.

She came over one afternoon and asked who Monty was. Taken aback I asked where she had heard that name and she told me that at 4am the previous night, their phone at home had rung and that there was a man with an American accent called Monty who'd asked for me. She had, not surprisingly, berated him for waking up her daughter, and told him that I was at the villas.

He assured her that he was a friend, then asked her if I could be available on her number at a reasonable time the following day, and she told him that she would try to make it happen.

Monty was a client and friend of mine from back when I was dating Elouise. I'd always liked him and he owed me money. He had been released from prison while I was in Lebanon with John Ibrahim, and had been deported to the United States. I had assumed from there he would have made his way back to Lima, and would by now be living back along the Amazon River somewhere with his family.

How could Monty have found me? I thought. No one knew where I was in Bali. I had thought it possible, but not likely, that I would never hear from him again.

So I went to Rosy's at the designated time, and sure enough, he rang. He was all apologetic about not contacting me in the year that had passed while I was in prison, and that he had huge personal problems after being released. He said he knew he owed me, and wanted to assist in any way possible. He told me he was in Amsterdam and invited me and Dubravka to join him at his expense so we could catch up.

He owed me plenty, and if he could pay, even by instalments, I could return to Bali and, with Pete's knowledge, could start up my own villa complex. That was as good a temporary plan as any, and after watching the Australian news and seeing that Bill had just been arrested by the Royal Commission's extended arm, there was no reason for me to return to Australia any time soon.

Monty was as good as his word, and wired me $10,000 within an hour of the call. I booked two tickets to Amsterdam.

I saw Pete again before leaving. I said that I would be back soon hopefully with some money and we could build our own villa complex.

He wished me luck, and Dubravka and I were off.

16

AMSTERDAM: THE HASH CAPITAL OF THE WORLD

Schiphol, Amsterdam, is the third busiest airport in Europe, and in my experience, the easiest airport in the world to navigate. You can walk through customs, down an escalator and a train will have you at Amsterdam Central in 15 minutes.

Upon arrival, Dubravka and I did exactly that. We had booked one of the many small boutique hotels near the Vondelspark, 47 hectares of urban parkland in the centre of the city. I had arranged to catch up with Monty the following day, and so Dubravka and I went sightseeing. Our first port of call was a 'coffee shop', which is not to be confused with a café that sells actual coffee.

I had heard about the coffee shops and did not believe that it could possibly be legal. There was something of a paradox regarding legality, however. It was legal to go to a coffee shop, purchase marijuana and to smoke it in the coffee shop. It was also legal to be in possession of marijuana outside, and just as legal to be in possession of half a kilo in your own home.

But, it was not legal to smoke in public, and even though you would never be arrested, you could be cautioned by the police and even be given a small fine.

Every coffee shop had a menu, either on the tables or behind the bar. Selections were typically divided into weed, hash, pre-rolled joints, and sometimes 'cookies', which were biscuits or brownies baked with marijuana. Prices varied by quantity and quality. Coffee shop employees were extremely friendly (and why wouldn't they be?), knowledgeable, and well accustomed to clueless tourists.

For the first 33 years of my life, I could never understand why people needed, or wanted, to take drugs. I had only ever had half a dozen joints, and it did little for me other than put me to sleep. My first dabble with cocaine was when Kings Cross went mad for it again in the mid-nineties. It was easy to obtain, and distributed on a scale not dissimilar to the coffee shops in Amsterdam.

I had stayed clear of it at places like Springfield's, where the music industry treated it like supper after a hard day's work. By way of my introduction, I was seduced by a beautiful young lady with promises of heightened erotic pleasure. I thought, *Well, it won't kill me* and the offer was fairly exceptional, so I tried cocaine for the first time.

Being well intoxicated at the time, I found myself feeling instantly sober after just one line. I finally understood why so many people took it, and I must confess it became a staple part of my diet for well over a year after that.

My views on drugs were not complicated. People took drugs because they wanted to take drugs – just like smokers smoke and drinkers drink and fat people eat. All of which will ruin your old age – and possibly your youth – if you consume too much. I have often thought that moderation in every aspect of life should be the way forward. Balance; if you do the crime, do the time, and don't whinge about it later.

Amsterdam was different from Sydney. Their version of the Cross was the red-light district where pot smokers could be seen meandering aimlessly along a warren of alleyways and canals. Prostitutes rented small rooms and stood naked in their windows, bathed in the glow of red lamps before potential customers and sightseers. Policemen pedalled easily alongside visitors keeping an eye on the scene.

And if you need a joint just to soak up the ambience, there were more than 200 registered coffee shops that would satisfy your every taste.

Dubravka and I sauntered along the canals of Amsterdam that night, in awe of its diversity. In the morning, we rose early and again passed the morning negotiating the canals and the cycleways that encircle the city.

After lunch, Dubravka went shopping and I met up with Monty. It was good to see him. We sat and caught up. We didn't waste time discussing prison, as former inmates often do. We talked more about what the future held for both of us.

Amsterdam had been Monty's choice of places to meet. He had been there before; Australia and the US were out of the question, and he was not all that keen on the British. I was just glad to be there. I told him about Bali, that I had a friend who could be helpful if he was inclined to come there and build a villa complex. Monty was a timber merchant and looking to revitalise his business. We even thought of shipping his timber from the Amazon to Indonesia.

He explained his financial situation, and said that it would be some time before he would be able to pay me all of what was owed, but assured me that he would make regular payments, and I believed him. There would not be a consistent flow, but it would eventually all be paid. I was more than happy with that, he gave me another $10,000 cash there that day, and we then caught up with Dubravka and decided to head out for dinner.

Dubravka had a friend from Australia named Jacqueline who was born in the Netherlands, and was now living and working in Amsterdam. She was a very good sort.

The four of us hit the town that night. It was late, and we all decided to stay at Jacqueline's apartment, which was much closer than both our hotels. I crashed immediately. Dubravka was in the shower and as I lay in bed, in walked Jacqueline butt-naked. As pleasant a sight as that was to me, when Dubravka came out from the shower she went ballistic, and not at Jacqueline either.

In her mind it was my fault that her girlfriend was coming on to me. Earlier that night, we had decided we would stay at Jacqueline's place for a week or two and see the Netherlands, while Monty worked on trying to gain contracts for his timber.

Instead, Monty and I quickly dressed and departed for our hotels. Dubravka arrived at the hotel mid-morning and rather than being apologetic, continued with her tirade. She had decided that while waiting for news from Monty, we should stay with her aunt and uncle who lived in Germany in a small town called Dinslaken in the Wesel district and just north of Duisburg.

I knew of Dinslaken as it had a well-known harness racing track. (No surprises there.) Rather than continue with what would surely have been a loud and endless domestic, I agreed. By doing so, it quietened her and logistically, the idea was sensible. Duisburg was only an hour and a half from Amsterdam Central by train, and I had liked every other member of her family I had previously met. They seemed to me to be good stock, and within an hour, we were boarding the train to Germany.

I had rung Monty at his hotel, and given him the phone number of Dubravka's aunt, and he said he would keep in touch.

Stephan and Boya, Dubravka's aunt and uncle, were wonderful. They had not seen her for years and were more than receptive to us both staying with them for as long as we wanted.

I found plenty of work to do in their garden and their son's friends were all about the same age as Dubravka and I, and so we were constantly invited to local events. A few weeks passed and there was no word from Monty. Then, one night the phone rang, and he asked me to meet him back in Amsterdam.

I went on my own the following morning, and we met at an Irish-themed pub that we had been to before. He told me that things were not looking promising on the timber front, and that he would have to travel back to Peru and help his family.

He said that in the time I had been in Germany he had met with some marijuana distributers, and that they knew people in Australia. He had mentioned my name and they responded with, 'We have heard of the Prince.'

When he questioned them further over a few beers, it appeared that people in the international underworld were following the events of the Royal Commission back in New South Wales, and that I had been designated the Prince (referring to 'Royal Commission', and 'Charles', thus Prince Charles, and then abbreviated to the Prince). He, as I, found it mildly amusing, and he said that they wanted to meet me.

I asked if I knew them, and he said it was unlikely, but then he could not say for sure, as I knew quite a few people in many countries. I asked him if he knew their names, and he did not. He thought that they seemed like good blokes, and said that he would take me to the bar where they regularly drank. I had nothing better to do for the next few days, and off we went.

It was a pleasant summer evening, and we walked for some way down the sides of the canals past the boats full of tulips in all their splendour, vibrant in colour, past the red-light district to a much quieter part of Amsterdam and a bar with no name.

It had a few tables and chairs outside, and sitting there were two very well-dressed men, enjoying the glorious sunshine with a refreshing lager. As we approached, one of the men stood and said, 'Look. It's the Prince.' I smiled and walked over to him and shook his hand. He looked me in the eye and said: 'Manfred.'

He indicated his associate, who stood and shook my hand; 'Bram. Nice to meet you, Prince.'

We sat down. The atmosphere was convivial, to say the least. They said that they had been following the Royal Commission and that it was the talk of the town.

At that time, placing a camera in a car for surveillance purposes, as Haken had done, was a new form of technology and if you were a criminal, I guess it was something that you should at least be aware of. They both said that they knew people in Australia, and that they had me checked out, as they put it, and the word had come back positive; in other words, I was a good bloke and could be trusted.

I thanked them, and we sat, and had more than a few beers, and smoked a very nice piece of Moroccan hash. We then went to dinner, and enjoyed a wonderful Thai meal and a few more beers, and the night burned down to the early hours of the morning.

Monty and I left, and I stayed the night at his hotel. At breakfast the next morning, he said that Manfred had asked him whether I would be interested in coming to work for them. I asked what it would entail, and he said he was not sure but that it would almost definitely be in the marijuana business. I said, it would depend on what part of the business and asked him to set up a meeting.

I believed that marijuana and hashish were far less evil than alcohol; that the detrimental ramifications on society were far fewer. And also that the people involved in the industry on a whole were far more socially conscious. Those I knew were non-violent people. Just because Big Brother had deemed these drugs illegal did not make them immoral in my mind.

The following day I met up with Bram. Manfred had a previous engagement. Bram was well into his sixties, tall and dapper. He was an articulate Dutchman or possibly German. I never really could discern between the two accents, so he could have been either.

He told me that he had been married three times and had three children, one to each woman, and that he was single now and intent on staying that way as the women he had been married to had cost him a fortune. He told me that he was in the coffee-shop business, in a manner of speaking, but on a much larger scale, and boasted that he had never been arrested, and neither had any of his associates.

The afternoon continued over several beers and a joint, and I felt relaxed in his company. It appeared obvious to me that he knew a hell of a lot more about me than I knew of him. He mentioned that he spent a lot of time in Pakistan, Thailand and Cambodia, and that most of their business was based overseas. He gave me the history of his business, from the beginning of his involvement in his early twenties, and he said had never been busier than right at that moment.

So, it came to crunch time. 'What is it that you would like me to do for you?'

'First, I must ask you if you have any problems dealing with marijuana or hash?'

'No, but that would depend on exactly what the job description is.'

'We shall start with the financial side. I would like you to make payments for me to suppliers and staff. You would have to transport large quantities of cash to different locations in the world and hand it over to the people that I tell you to.'

'What does large mean?'

'Millions of dollars, and you will be very well reimbursed for your trouble. Let's say you are with the company for a year, you will certainly be able to start your villa complex in Bali, and within a few years you can own Bali.' He smiled at me, and said, 'Go away and think about it, but I would be happy for you to start work on Friday.'

It was Monday. I went back to see Monty, and told him what Bram had told me at the meeting. He said it sounded promising, and he had asked around and the guys seemed genuine. He said he knew nothing at all about that line of work and that any decision I made had to be made by me alone. We went for dinner again that night and did not mention either

Bram or his company. Instead, Monty asked me for Kim and my children's numbers, and said that if anything went wrong, he would look after them. He was heading back to South America the next day and I had some serious decisions to make.

We shook hands and, sadly, it was to be the last time that I ever saw him. I caught the train back to Dinslaken, and thought long and hard about the proposition from Bram. I questioned the illegality of it and had issues with that, however, I had no problem with the morality of it. I knew people who smoked hash. They were without exception very nice people and had very normal moral compasses. Not like the people who smoked skunk. In Australia, as with America, the crackdown on the sale of hash and marijuana had forced suppliers to go indoors and cultivate hydroponic weed better known as skunk. Skunk is much stronger than any hash or weed, and I believe the cause of many mental-health issues. Yet another example of do-gooders making the rules without the knowledge necessary to grasp what really happens in life.

There was another matter: geography. You would be a fool to get involved in the hash business if it involved Bali or Indonesia. If you got caught in either of those countries you were looking at the death penalty. In Australia, the introduction of the 1989 Sentencing Act and 'truth in sentencing', which aimed to crack down on parole periods, meant that the time you were sentenced to was the time you served. So for million-dollar hash deals, at that time it was best to steer clear of Australia, as well as the United States. But for Europe and especially the Netherlands, well, it was a totally different ball game.

Back in Dinslaken I was reunited with Dubravka and I told her that I had met some blokes and that I was considering doing some work for them. I explained that the work was a bit dodgy, and would require some international travel, and that perhaps we should, for now, be based in Amsterdam. The thought of living in Amsterdam outweighed her concerns over dodgy activities.

I told her to stay put at her aunt's until I returned in a week's time. The following morning, I returned to Amsterdam and headed straight to the University of Amsterdam. I found out where the law faculty was and asked if it would be possible to do some research.

I told the curator that I was an Australian law graduate and my dissertation was going to be on the lack of parity regarding sentences of crimes relating to drugs across the world. He thought that sounded interesting and had two faculty members assist me in my research. That could have been difficult, but I had dealt with lawyers and members of the legal profession for years and had the answers to any questions that they could come up with. Based on the day's research, if one were to get involved with trafficking hashish or marijuana the two best places would be Canada or the Netherlands.

I thanked them and as I left, I jokingly said, 'Well boys, I'm off to Canada!' and they both laughed and wished me luck. I went for dinner alone that night to a quiet little Italian place tucked away in a side street. As I sat reading the various sentencing likelihoods of each country and setting out a graph, I was astonished by the contrast in parity that different countries applied to sentencing.

I rolled a joint and sauntered along the canals and back streets of Amsterdam as tourists and locals passed me by with the occasional nod and smile. I was relaxed as I was confident I had just secured a dream job.

There were perks with the job: international travel, fine hotels, all expenses paid. The thrill and the danger. I had been a policeman and as far as international criminals go, Manfred and Bram were not what I had expected. I now had the opportunity to make lots of money and I would soon be able to save the world in a different way. I knew so many people who were struggling back in Australia, and money could solve most of their problems. To me this new adventure was a no-brainer. I would not be hurting anyone, and would have the opportunity to help so many people while having a right bloody adventure. And as for the legality, who really gives a shit about marijuana?

The following day I met with Bram at the Van Gogh Museum in Amsterdam South. He took me on a fast-track tour of the famous Impressionist's works and interjecting at times to tell me of the job that he wanted me to do. He needed a million guilder taken to Bangkok the following day and said that he would pay me 10,000 Swiss francs to deliver it, and that he would cover all the expenses, meals, accommodation and any other costs incurred by me including entertainment.

I asked what the payment was for, and he said it was not necessary for me to know. I assured him that it was as his business, as he had stated, was illegal and that if I were to take part in assisting him then I could be regarded as a co-conspirator.

He paused and then whispered that his company had taken a delivery of a large shipment of hashish from Pakistan, and that it had been long sold in Canada, and that the funds were dribbling in and that people along the way had to be paid.

'And my job is to be the paymaster. I'm in,' I said without hesitation. I felt this way because my job would be at the back end of the proceedings – the drugs had already been delivered. So if I were caught with the money, I'd lose it, but I'd only get a very minor prison sentence. In my book, it was well worth the risk.

With a very broad smile, he shook my hand, looked me square in the eyes and said, 'Welcome aboard, Your Royal Highness. You will be known as the Prince.'

I smiled and we completed the tour of the museum, his knowledge of the Dutch master far superior to that of the tour guide. We left and went to an apartment in a part of Amsterdam that did not seem as affluent as the parts that I had been over the past few weeks. He pulled a bag from under the bed and produced 1,000,000 guilder, which was just over US$600,000. It was only a thousand notes, as the guilder were in denominations of a thousand, so it sat not much more than eight inches in height.

He handed me six money belts and gave me another: five thousand guilder for expenses. The instructions were to get a flight from Schiphol the next day to Bangkok, take a taxi from the airport to a hotel near Patpong Road, and then to call him on this number, and he would direct me from there.

He handed me the money and the bags, placed inside a small leather bag. 'You can keep this if you like,' motioning to the leather bag.

He shook my hand. 'Good luck. We will see you in a week.'

We exited the room and walked out the front door. He went one way and I went the other. As I made my way back to the hotel, I stopped at a travel agent and booked a return trip to Bangkok, Thailand, and requested that I have a suite at the hotel that Bram had mentioned near Patpong Rd.

I paid for the ticket and went back to the hotel. I had never had so much cash at one time, and found it amazing that so much wealth could be housed in spaces smaller than a shopping bag. I loaded the money into the six money belts in equal portions, and strapped them on.

I put my shirt and trousers on and looked in the mirror. It was noticeable, all right. Too much so for my liking, so I strapped two of the belts around my lower thighs, and looked in the mirror again. I didn't notice a lump but the belts moved around a bit. I applied some gaffer tape to the belts and there was no more movement.

I supposed I was ready.

I woke to another glorious summer day. I made sure that I had no metal on my body or clothing including buttons and zippers, no belt other than the money belts, which only had plastic zippers. Then I checked out of the hotel and walked up to Amsterdam Central and caught the train to Schiphol.

I checked in my luggage and proceeded to the departure gates. Nothing special; I wasn't nervous. While it's not always possible, I always try to keep calm when I need to; my father used to say, 'If you worry, you die, and if you don't worry, you die, so why worry?' and it has always stuck with me. Directly in front of me in the queue was an elderly lady well into her seventies, walking at a snail's pace. As she walked through security the alarms went off and she kept walking. I had my focus directly on the security man standing in front of her. He seemed to be alert and attentive but had not moved.

She continued, and he didn't stop her, or even attempt to do so. I caught his eye and was given the nod to proceed, so I did. No bells went off, and I smiled at the security guard and continued past him. He then said, 'Excuse me, sir. Can you come this way?' and pointed to a cubicle to the left of the metal detector. I looked at him with a sense of bemusement, and asked what the problem was, gesticulating with my hands that I had not set the bells off.

He replied that it was just random and that could I follow him to the cubicle and that he wanted to pat me down. Let me tell you here and now, if you have ever felt your pulse racing either through fear or excitement, multiply that feeling a hundredfold, and that's what went through my body, there and then. I kept telling myself to relax, it could actually be just a random search, so I shouldn't panic. It was a civilised country, there were laws, so whatever happened would not finish there and then in the following thirty seconds.

He is about to pat me down. I have six money belts on my person that contain 20 years' salary for this bloke. Keep calm, were my only immediate rational thoughts.

I entered the cubicle, looking for an escape route. The wall was just a sheet. *I could burst through the back. I might have to belt him, but then where to run? There is security everywhere, it's a bloody airport.*

Relax, relax.

He asked me to raise my hands and I did so. As he got to my waist, he raised his head and looked at me. I said, 'I have my money belt.'

He looked up and I lifted my shirt, so he could only see the first two belts. I dropped my elbows to my side, and unzipped the tops, revealing the upper edges of a large number of notes. He looked me in the eye, and I said without hesitation, 'Baht.'

He looked at me and gave me a thumbs up, and said thank you, and waved me on. You can have a thousand baht and it may look like a fortune but it was only enough to buy a burger. Lucky for me, the guard knew the value of baht! It was my only chance to get out of there unscathed and it worked.

Can you imagine? My first job and I haven't got fifty metres and I nearly lost the boys a million?

I went straight to a bar and ordered a pint. The flight was delayed nearly an hour, which was not a problem, as I wasn't expected for another day. I had a good night's sleep on the plane, albeit with some discomfort as the tape on my legs was beginning to rip the hairs off every time I moved. I landed in Bangkok not long after lunch and was extremely alert, almost paranoid. I had only to get through customs and I was as good as home.

There are rules for the airport among the criminal class, at least: don't look around, never make eye contact, grab a pamphlet and appear to be interested. Then, feign a sudden awakening when asked to produce your documentation. Don't make small talk. Listen to what the official says, and be compliant. I followed the rules and I walked straight through, grabbed my bag and an hour later, I was sitting in a bar on Patpong Road watching a ping pong ball being ejected from between the legs of a very attractive Thai lady.

I had the million locked away in the room safe and was now walking around, drifting in and out of different bars, catching the sexual exploits that appeared everywhere. I had a nice meal and went home to bed, awaiting my instructions.

As soon as I woke in the morning I rang Bram, and he told me to go to Soi Jaruwan, sometimes referred to as Patpong 3, which has long catered for gay men.

Not my scene, but then police being police, it was probably not an area where they would be either. He gave me the name of a hotel, and said that the person I was to give the money to would be sitting in the bar of the hotel, reading a motor mechanic magazine. He would have a Thai bank note with a serial number on it that would match the one Bram now read out to me. Most importantly, that was my receipt for the million.

I headed off to the gay capital of Bangkok, and walked into the hotel. There, right in front of the bar sat a well-dressed man in his late fifties, not looking as tanned as someone from Bangkok should be. He met my gaze and smiled, but then, so had every other bloke in the street, and said, 'Mister Prince?'

Embarrassed, I acknowledged it was indeed me, and he handed me a 100-baht note with the same serial number that Bram had given me. I handed him the bag, and he stood, shook my hand and walked out the door. That was it.

For those few brief moments of fear, I had gained an all-expenses-paid trip to Thailand for a week, and was earning 10,000 Swiss francs. I arrived back in Amsterdam after a very enjoyable week in Thailand. I rang Dubravka in Germany and asked her to meet me in Amsterdam and she agreed. Little did she know, I had a surprise for her.

While all neighbourhoods in Amsterdam are effortlessly cool, some parts of the city go the extra mile. Nieuwmarkt en Lastage, which trails south from Central Station toward the river Amstel, has several diverse areas, and was developing into one of the most architecturally innovative parts of the city.

It was a hip part of town, and I had met a cool bloke in a bar by the name of Marcus Van Dijk, a musician who played guitar poorly, and his singing was worse. But at forty, he had a zest for life like no other. He had fallen head over heels in love with a Brazilian girl called Kiania, who had not long turned 20, and was a good sort.

He had met her at a gig where he was performing, and she appeared to be tone deaf, as she thought he was a rock god and asked him to come back to Sao Paulo in Brazil, and live with her.

He jumped at the opportunity, and so he needed someone to rent his apartment long-term. He had taken me to view the apartment and it was amazing, as most artists' places tend to be. I paid him upfront for the first six months, and he was over the moon.

Dubravka arrived in Amsterdam, and I avoided telling her what had transpired in Thailand. Instead I focused her attention on the opportunity to live in Amsterdam and took her to view the apartment. She was delighted, and instantly started making plans to refurnish it.

I scheduled a meeting with Bram. We met at the same apartment where he had given me the cash to take to Thailand, and he said that he was pleased, and laughed at my story of terror at Schiphol airport prior to leaving. He informed me that there was a much bigger job that needed tending to in Montreal, Canada. That it would last for possibly two to three months, and asked me if I was up for it.

He said that it would be worth a couple of hundred thousand to me personally, and was, as he put it, a relatively easy gig.

'Abso-fucking-lutely.'

We chatted for a while, and I told him of the apartment that was available and the area. He thought it a very good deal, both price and location-wise, and ran me through the local rules and regulations, insisting that I not take the lease in either mine or Dubravka's name and that he would assist in that regard.

I had to see Marcus the musician and fix him up with more cash for the apartment as he was about to leave with the love of his life. I also had to tell Dubravka that she could stay in Amsterdam and sort out the apartment, or head back to Australia, or go back to Bali. It was neither here nor there to me, as I was going to be busy for the next few months.

Dubravka decided to stay with her aunt and uncle in Dinslaken, and over the next month or two travel to Amsterdam, and with the help of her cousin and his friends, put her personal touches on the apartment.

Bram gave me a list of instructions for when I landed in Montreal, not specific but general, and more general tips than absolute 'musts'.

So I was on my way to Montreal, come hell, high water or thigh-deep snow.

17

MONTREAL WELCOMES PRINCE CHARLES

I had just spent the last few months in the warmer climes of Bali and Thailand, and some exceptionally warm weather in Europe, while waiting for the Royal Commission to finish. Well, on landing at Mirabel airport in Montreal, to say it was cold would be a gross understatement.

I cleared passport control, grabbed my luggage and sailed through customs. I jumped into the first cab I saw and told the driver take me straight to a department store.

I was freezing. The temperature was -2 degrees, and I was wearing a t-shirt and a pair of jeans.

He drove me to the centre of Montreal on Rue Sainte-Catherine and stopped outside the Westmount Square shopping centre, and waited. I raced inside, and bought two of the heaviest winter jackets available.

From the airport to the city centre the entire landscape was covered with snow. The roads were clear and layered with salt, but as we approached the CBD I thought it could have been the gateway to any ski resort. The cabbie dropped me off at a small boutique hotel in Old Montreal, and I was excited about embarking on a new career.

After my experiences with the faculty members at the University of Amsterdam, I had made a decision. My occupation was now and forever going to be 'student' and I intended to begin by studying liberal arts. Plus, what better cover for my current occupation? I was a graduate doing my masters and if the business continued, as I believed it would, then a doctorate would be in my future. There could be no better place on earth than Montreal to assume the identity of a student. The city has always been ranked in the top five QS World University Rankings, and depending on your degree, you were spoilt for choice.

The city itself is the largest in the province of Quebec. It sits on an island in the Saint Lawrence River and named after Mount Royal, the triple-peaked hill at its heart.

French is the city's official language, and although Canada is supposed to be bilingual, Quebec is not. Having said that, Montreal is not dissimilar to France in that every second person can speak English, they just don't. Still, the city must be one of the most diverse on the planet.

The city itself has a distinct four-season climate with very hot, humid summers and very cold snowy winters. It has an underground city colloquially referred to as Downtown Montreal. It houses a brilliant underground rail network that connects the entire city, so that you could, should you so desire, leave your hotel in the morning and walk underground for the entire day without having to come up to street level. Montreal is a city full of history and culture, but it also has an ice hockey team (the Habs) that the entire city supports.

I was a very happy man. I could blend in without drawing attention. I spent the next few days travelling around the subterranean city, occasionally surfacing to get my bearings.

I found an apartment downtown with a secure underground car park with a lift, which I would need for the job. I rented a mobile phone and sent the number back to Bram in Amsterdam. Then almost a week later came the call I was eagerly awaiting. Bram rang and said that I was to meet a person at the Sheraton Hotel on Rene-Levesque Boulevarde, which was less than a mile from where I had rented the apartment. The meeting was set for 1pm the following day.

He then asked me to pull a note out of my pocket and read him the serial number. I did; it was a $20 Canadian bill and I read him the number. He said I was to sit in the bar adjacent to the check-in desk and to be in possession of, if not reading, a copy of *Horse and Hound* magazine, the oldest equestrian magazine in the United Kingdom, but freely available in any bookstore, of which Montreal had plenty.

Apprehensive, yet excited, I arrived and sat in the bar, ordered a coffee and opened the latest edition of *Horse and Hound*. Within minutes two very tall men arrived, both in their mid-forties. The more vocal of the pair was a redhead and the other greying, both were smartly dressed and neither looked out of place in the bar of a five-star hotel.

They approached me and said in unison, 'Prince?'

I nodded and asked them to be seated. They both ordered a beer, and as the waiter left to get their order, they asked if I had any paperwork. I produced the $20 note and handed it over and they checked the serial number with a piece of paper from the redhead's pocket. They nodded to each other and handed me the set of keys to a motor vehicle, and a receipt for the car park.

The redhead told me to go to the car park, take the vehicle to wherever I was going to store the contents, and that they would have a few beers and wait for me to return. I was trying to act as though I had done this a thousand times before, and desperately trying to seem professional. The truth was that I did not even know what was in the car that I now had the keys for. I was assuming that it would be money. The keys had a tag attached with the registration number of the vehicle, so I assumed it was a rented vehicle, and duly set off for the car park.

I quickly found the vehicle, which to my surprise was a small van, not a car, and it had no windows in the back. I jumped in, drove up the driveway and around the block, and was in my underground car park in less than 10 minutes. I got out and opened the back of the van. At the rear was a small trolley and behind it were several cardboard boxes with lids that reminded me of file boxes like I had seen in legal firms.

I popped the lid of the closest box, and it was crammed full of cash, all Canadian notes. I popped the lid of two more and they were identical. All full of cash, and numbers started flying through my mind. There were twenty-three boxes, and if, as I imagined, they were all full, there was a bloody lot of money there.

I could fit four boxes on the trolley, so I loaded it and caught the lift from the car park to the second floor. When I got to the room, I popped the lids on all four boxes, and they were all full of cash in different denominations. A quick glance at the first box, and I had figured that there was roughly $400,000 in the box, and that particular box had predominantly $20 notes in it. It took me the better part of an hour to empty the van and secure the money. Well, 'secure' doesn't seem quite the right term, as I just stacked the boxes in the wardrobe. One of the boxes had a money-counting machine inside and no cash.

I locked the door to the apartment and drove the van back to the Sheraton and parked it in the same spot that I had left an hour and a half earlier. I walked back to the bar where the boys were waiting. They were all smiles and asked if all was good, and I nodded and said sure.

The waiter passed the table and the redhead said, 'Three beers.'

I sat and as cool as could be, mentioned the ice hockey, as it had appeared on a television at the end of the bar as I walked in. It started a conversation about how the Habs were about to move to a new stadium just around the corner, and that their season was reasonable, but not much to get excited over and by then the men were ordering another beer. I said that unfortunately I had work to do, and made my excuses. I stood and we shook hands, and I handed them back the keys to the van, and parted ways with the two men.

I walked down the street, then dived into subterranean Montreal and caught a few different trains to nowhere in case there was anyone on my tail, and then appeared in a different part of the city and walked back to the apartment. I called Bram.

'Okay. I've received the boxes.'

'Good. Very good. You should have a counting machine there, so start counting, and I will call you at midnight your time.'

He hung up. Eager to get started, I stopped at the famous Schwartz's Deli, a cultural institution in Montreal on Saint-Laurant Boulevarde, and grabbed a couple of smoked salt beef sandwiches and a six-pack of Labatt blue beers. It was about five in the afternoon when I arrived back at the apartment.

I took all 23 boxes and placed them on the bed, stacked on top of each other. I set the counting machine on the desk and grabbed the first bundle from the first box, and started flicking away with pen and paper in hand. Hours later, and I mean *hours later*, the tally was at $23,719,000.

I sat back, turned the television on, and thought and thought and then thought again. *Who the fuck gives a bloke that they have never met and don't know 20 million fucking dollars?*

I knocked off the rest of the beers, all the time shaking my head. Bram rang at midnight on the dot.

'So, what's the tally? It should be $23,500,000.'

'No, it's . . .' Before I could say, 'it's more', he ranted.

'Those sons of bitches! Those bastards! They robbed us last time.'

I had to interject. 'Hang on, hang on – its $23,719,000.'

There was a pause. 'Great! If you see the delivery guys again, tell them it was the correct weight.'

'Sure, I thought that was a test.'

'Charlie, you have $20 million of my money. *That's* the test. Count it again, and make sure, and I will call you in the morning.'

I started the laborious task of the recount, boiled the kettle and made a coffee. Just then, a thought entered my head. *I don't know these blokes. I have well over $23,000,000 in cash. I can just . . . disappear. I know people all over the world.*

I could ring my mate Reggie Bourke back in Australia. He would be well up for a heist and he, or any one of a dozen blokes on the planet, would be in Montreal in the morning and we could start up anywhere in the world.

I shook my head and promptly lost that evil thought, but I do confess it definitely crossed my mind.

As the night slowly evaporated, I noticed there was some dust in the bottom of the counting machine, I swiped my finger over it and after looking at it, it occurred to me that it wasn't dust but cocaine. I scooped it up, racked it and had a line.

Gazing out the window, watching the first flakes of snow fall over the streets of the city, I thought it wouldn't take nearly as long now to do the recount. The sun was up by the time I finished. The total amount had not changed by one cent. $23,719,000. And a bit of trivia: if you ever put that many notes through a cash-counting machine, the vibrations of the flickering notes will leave you with roughly a gram and half of cocaine.

Bram rang not long after, and sounded pleased that the count was over and told me to get some sleep and that he would ring me the next day. By now, sleep was no longer high on my agenda, so I packed the boxes away, and headed up the hill to 1313 De Maisonneuve Boulevarde to arguably the perfect breakfast location in the city. The place was called Eggspectations, where you can have any egg breakfast you can think of cooked to perfection.

After breakfast I walked around the city, amazed at the efficiency of the snow-removal teams. Downtown, in the subterranean city, you might never know it was snowing but pop your head above ground and it was a different story altogether.

As I walked through the snow-lined streets, the bitter air chilled my bones. I just couldn't shake the mental picture of $23,000,000 in cash sitting at the end of my bed and smiling, I shook my head.

Bram called just after midday and suggested I go to a luggage store, and purchase a number of suitcases of varying sizes to work out what size fitted $1,000,000.

Coincidentally, I was just 50 metres away from a luggage shop, and scurried in out of the falling snow. I bought two suitcases somewhere between the size of carry-on, and an average checked luggage size. Back at the apartment, I counted out a million, and closed the bag. It fit easily, and so I tried to put in another million, but the bag would no longer close.

So, I went back to the luggage store and exchanged both the bags, adjusting the sizes to fit a million or two million, whatever may be required. Of course, if you wanted a couple of million in $10 notes then it would take up more space, but once you have seen a million in $20 notes you can adjust accordingly dependant on the denomination.

Bram called.

'Hello again, Prince. I need you to take $300,000, and go to the Sheraton Hotel again. There will be a guy there, and he will be sitting in the bar, reading the *Financial Times*. His name is Jim. He's been in the business for years. He will have some bags for me. Be there at around 4pm.'

He read me out a number and said that it would be the serial number on a bank note, and that would be the receipt for the $300,000. I went back to the luggage store and bought a hold-all bag that would carry $300,000 easily. From there I returned to the apartment and filled it with the cash, then made my way back to the Sheraton Hotel.

I could see two men sitting on a sofa, and one of them held a *Financial Times*. I was annoyed that there were two men. It doesn't take two men to take a bag like that. As I approached, the shorter and somewhat more portly of the two stood and with a smile said, 'Prince.'

I nodded and sat. He introduced himself as Jim and introduced his companion as Ken.

I shook both their hands and immediately felt uneasy when Jim looked away as he shook my hand. My hackles went straight up. You are always going to be on the back foot with me if you can't look me in the eye when you shake my hand. That said, after 30 seconds of chat, Jim handed me a note with the correct serial number and I handed him the hold-all.

We sat and ordered beers. Ken asked if I would accompany them to his room where he would give me three bags. I asked if he could go and get them himself and he replied that he wanted to show me how they worked, and that it was not appropriate in the foyer of the hotel. I agreed and went with both of them to a room on the fourth floor.

Once inside, Jim opened the bag and emptied the contents on the bed. He went to the wardrobe and produced three sports bags, black in colour with a compartment for a squash racket. He undid the zipper and placed his hand inside, indicating what appeared to be the bottom of the bag. He tugged a very strong Velcro strip, and the fake base of the bag came free revealing a secret compartment.

I thanked him and Ken, and though they tried to get me to hang around and chat, I made my excuses and left. With the three sports bags over my shoulder, I left the hotel and quickly disappeared into the depths of Montreal, resurfacing in another part of town and took a cab to the vicinity of my apartment.

Back at the apartment, I rang Bram and told him that the job was done.

'What do you think of the bags? How many notes will they hold?'

'I think they should hold easily a thousand notes without being noticeable from above in the main compartment.'

He seemed pleased. 'The next few days are going to be very busy for you. I need you to hire a car.'

He told me to take the rest of the day off, and that he would call me in the morning. I needed no further I encouragement. I showered and headed out for dinner.

I was spoiled for choice in Montreal, but when I'm on my own, I prefer somewhere with a bar and good wait staff, and as my French was non-existent, I preferred the Irish bars in and around Rue Cathcart, downtown.

The Old Dublin was Montreal's oldest Irish pub, and the staff's first language was English, which made life easier for me. As I was sitting at the bar, I noticed on the television that there were two pundits talking about the Montreal Canadiens (Habs) the local ice-hockey team. Their talk was about how they were leaving the Montreal Forum, the arena that had been home for 70 years, and were moving to the new Molson centre just around the corner from the Old Dublin. The opening game was in two days' time.

I commented to the barman that I had never seen a game of ice hockey live, and that I may go to the first game at the new centre. The three staff behind the bar roared with laughter. 'You have no chance of getting a ticket to a game like that! They've been sold out for weeks!'

I wondered whether, if they'd known about the $23,000,000 I had at home in the wardrobe, they would have thought the same thing? I left and went back to the apartment, and all the news on the television was about the big game at the new Molson Centre. I had made up my mind: I was going to the game.

Bram rang early in the morning, instructing me to go to a different hotel at the end of town and drop $3,000,000 off to a Pakistani man. I was to again be at the bar with a *Horse and Hound* magazine, and he would have a note bearing a serial number that Bram recited to me.

I went to the hotel and within minutes, two extra-large men with beards, who looked to be from that part of the world, approached me while I glanced through *Horse and Hound*. This time, the pair said quite softly, 'Mister Prince,' with an expectant look.

'Yes,' I said. They both sat and ordered a tea, and handed me the receipt and a set of car keys, telling me that the car was parked in bay 72 on the first floor. I left and headed down to the car park.

They had said that the car was white, and had a large boot. What they had not mentioned was that it was a fucking 1994 Rolls Royce Corniche. There was no way that I was driving a Rolls Royce through the snow in Montreal to an underground car park in a very modest part of town and load $3,000,000 in the boot. So, I exited the car park, walked down the street, hailed a cab and went back to the apartment.

Upstairs in my room, I loaded two suitcases with $3,000,000 and put the bags on the trolley. I caught the lift to the ground level and, hailing a cab, went back to the hotel. I went down to the car park and tossed the bags in the boot and walked back to the hotel with my trolley.

The two men looked somewhat apprehensive when they saw me dragging a trolley. I handed them back the keys to the Corniche, and with a resolute look said, 'Are you fucking mad turning up in a car like that? You may as well put a neon sign on top saying, "Look at me".'

To make matters worse, they gave me a dismissive look as if I was paranoid. They stood and smiled, we shook hands and they both left. I finished a beer and walked back to my apartment, and on the way stopped at a traffic light was the Corniche, the two of them sitting as if they had not a worry in the world. I rang Bram and told him that I had delivered the money, and how amazed I was that they had turned up in a Rolls.

He laughed out loud. 'They've always been eccentric, but those guys have been around since the invention of the wheel. Don't worry.'

He added that I should keep $2,000,000 aside and that I would have to bring that back to him when the job was complete over in Montreal.

'Charlie,' he asked, 'have you ever been to Pakistan or Afghanistan?'

I assured him that I had not. He suggested I should work on my tan, as I would have to go to that region within the next two months. My fair skin would stand out like dog's balls, and may even get me shot.

'You're fucking kidding,' I said, amused. 'There's snow everywhere here in Montreal. How am I going to do that?'

'Ask any woman.' He laughed and hung up.

Great, I thought. *That just leaves me with another $18,000,000 to get through. More deals with strangers. More awkward chat ups than a first date. More hotel foyers. More fucking Prince this, Mister Prince, that.*

Sod this. I'm going to the ice hockey.

18

THE HABS AND THE HAVE-NOTS

There was no word from Bram for days.

I was becoming *au fait* with Montreal and its cosmopolitan nuances.

It was the night of the opening of the Molson centre. I grabbed $10,000 out of a box in the wardrobe and at 6pm walked down Avenue des Canadiens-de-Montreal where the Habs were to play the Ottawa Senators in the first game at the new arena.

Outside there were crowds gathering, the new arena being the largest indoor sporting venue of its kind in the northern hemisphere. It held 26,000 spectators and there was a buzz in the air in anticipation of the game beginning. Down on the street, there were a number of scalpers trying to flog tickets at well above face value. I had anticipated that it may cost in the region of $1,000 to score a ticket. I approached the first scalper.

'What sort of tickets do you want?'

'Good ones, please.'

He said I could have a pair of red circle seats for $500, the 'red circle' being the first six rows around the rink, directly behind the Perspex screen that protects the spectators from being struck by the puck.

Pleased, I took the two tickets and handed him $500. I walked directly to the Old Dublin bar and asked Lina, a very attractive waitress who had just finished work, if she would accompany me to the game.

The two barmen, Jacques and Phillip, who only nights before were adamant that it was an impossible task to buy tickets were clearly impressed, and even more so that I was now being accompanied by Lina. I escorted her home, where she showered and dressed, and we walked back to the Molson Centre, and sat in the third row next to the Montreal dugouts.

The game exploded from the outset. A brawl erupted between the teams, and ended with two players standing toe to toe, exchanging blows. What amazed me was no one interfered with the two remaining combatants.

When the last man standing turned to the crowd and raised his hands with a victorious salute, the referee walked over to him and the other combatant who had regained his feet, indicated that the two of them had to depart the rink. They had two minutes on the bench and that's it. I can tell you, it was easy to see why it was the most popular sport in Canada.

Certainly, it was no place for the faint of heart, and you needed to be a tough bloke to play a sport like that. Mark Recchi, the goal-scoring machine, was playing his first season with the Habs. He scored the opening goal, and the locals went ballistic. The game ended at 3–3, and I had just experienced one of the best sporting events of my life. Lina asked me to stay with her that evening, and as alluring an offer as that was, I respectfully declined and went back to the apartment.

At 5am, the phone rang and it was Bram.

'Good morning, Prince Charles! Can you go back and see the two eccentric Pakistanis at the same place, and give them another $2,000,000? And can you split up the bags this time? They said that the two you dropped off before were too heavy.'

Can you believe that? I dropped off $3,000,000 in cash to some bloke I didn't even know, and his only comment was that it weighed too much? But then who was I to argue?

I met them in the late afternoon, and this time I brought five small carry-on luggage bags, placed them on my trolley and marched down through the snow-lined streets of Montreal, and straight into the hotel foyer. As I approached the two Pakistani men, they had a look of bewilderment on their faces at seeing the trolley stacked with new suitcases.

I asked where the car was, and they gave me the key. I marched off to the car park and placed the bags in the boot and returned to the foyer and we sat and had a beer. They handed me a receipt and explained that at their end of the journey home, they had a number of stairs to climb as the lift in their building was not working, and it was extremely difficult to carry the bags up five flights of stairs.

I accepted their explanation and then they asked me why I had come marching down the street with the trolley and suitcases?

'Well, the weather is shit, there is snow everywhere and the Rolls Royce stands out in the area where I'm living. No one pays any attention to a tourist dragging a load of suitcases along the street.'

They seemed satisfied with the explanation. We had a few more beers, and then we parted company. Back in the hotel, I rang Bram, telling him that it was all done.

He said that it would be weeks before anything else would happen and that I could leave Montreal if I wanted, and store the money somewhere secure, or I could stay. Whatever I preferred.

I just wanted to know if I would be done by Christmas, as I wanted to travel to Bali and fly my sons and their mother in Australia up for Christmas, since it had been some time since I had seen or spoken to them. He said that for sure it would be complete and that could even help him as he had to pay someone, and they would be in Bali at Christmas as well.

After hearing this, I rang Dubravka at her aunt's home in Dinslaken, and told her to go to Amsterdam and get a flight to Montreal. Then I rang Kim in Australia, and asked if she and the boys fancied a trip to Bali at Christmas. I even offered to pay for her boyfriend to come as well, if she would leave the boys with Dubravka and I. She accepted the offer, and I booked them a hotel, and rang Peter Moore and booked his best villa for two weeks.

I rented another apartment a few hundred metres down the road. By now, I only had 15 boxes left, and the denominations were all larger: $50 dollar notes, $100 dollar notes, and half a box containing a mixture of the old grey and new pink $1,000 notes. It seemed hard to believe that the old grey notes were actual currency, but there was easily $10,000,000 in both of the Canadian $1000 notes.

(High-denomination bank notes were popular in organised crime as they made moving money so much easier. So not surprisingly, they were withdrawn from circulation by the bank of Canada on 12 May 2000, at the request of the Royal Canadian Mounted Police as part of a program to reduce organised crime. At the time, there were 2,827,702 in circulation. By 2011, fewer than a million were in circulation, and the RCMP said that most were held by organised crime. That was a scare tactic if ever I heard one. Nonetheless, I still have 10 of them.)

I settled into the new apartment, which had a full-time concierge named Pierre. Three days later, Dubravka arrived. I still had the other apartment where the boxes were in the wardrobe. She questioned me like a seasoned detective as to what on earth I had been doing. I had to plead the fifth amendment, as the Americans say, refusing to answer. She was not remotely happy, but at least she didn't lock me up. She just refused to sleep with me for a week.

But a week of fine dining in an epicurean city like Montreal did the trick, particularly after I took her to see Harry Connick Jr. at the St Denis theatre in the Latin Quarter. It is an intimate theatre, albeit one seating more than 2,000 people, but when Harry came off stage and ambled through the crowd and serenaded her from the adjacent seat, all was forgiven.

Bram rang earlier than expected, saying that plans had changed, and that the remaining funds had to be disbursed. Over the next few weeks, I was quite busy. I had six meetings in the following week but Dubravka contented herself with excursions around the exquisite characterful neighbourhoods of Old Montreal and the Latin Quarter.

The snowfall in the city was extraordinary, and driving was hazardous, in spite of the best efforts of the snow-removal crews. My next delivery was $2,000,000 to the Delta Hotel, a four-star hotel and less than a mile from the apartment.

Much to my surprise, I met a very elegant French-Canadian lady in her forties, immaculately attired with a voice that spoke in such a beautiful French accent, I could have listened to her for hours.

When she greeted me with 'le Prince', rather than embarrassed, I felt somewhat regal as I nodded and looked her in the eyes.

'*Oui, madame*,' just rolled off my tongue.

She looked delighted and said, '*Parlez-vous français?*'

Suddenly not feeling so regal, I responded with, '*Non, très petit*.'

She smiled. 'English is fine.'

I had a small suitcase that I had just carried down the street. We sat and had coffee, chatting about the snow, and the wonders of Montreal for nearly half an hour. Then, looking at her watch, she stood and approached me and kissed both cheeks.

'*Au revoir, mon ami*,' she said, as she walked out the door of the hotel carrying the suitcase. I felt a surge of emotion. I hoped that we would meet again, as I admired the very chic lady walking out the doors.

But enough of that!

I had a driver waiting to take me to New York. It's a seven-hour drive if things go your way, and I had tickets to game six. The Yankees baseball team were playing the Atlanta Braves, and if the Yankees won, they would have the series. They had lost the first two games, but had come roaring back in the next three.

I was sure there would be no game seven, and I had told Bobby Noble, a good mate of mine back in Australia, that I would get him a Yankees shirt. It was impulsive, but David the barman at the Old Dublin had agreed to drive there and back in exchange for me getting him a ticket.

We were off. I had a Canadian driver's licence, so we passed the border without incident and arrived with a few hours to spare. David had arranged the tickets. The Yankees won 3–2, and 56,000 fans went absolutely mental.

We stayed the night in New York, and drove back to Montreal the next morning. I had Bobby's shirt and had experienced a sporting event of mammoth proportions. David dropped me off at the Old Dublin.

I decided to traverse the snowy footpaths back to the apartment instead of going underground, as rays of sunshine pierced the clouds. My thoughts wandered back to New York. The rays disappeared slowly behind the grey above, and I came back to the real world as the temperature dropped. I hustled my way underground and went back to the apartment.

Later that evening, I went to buy some cigarettes and as I was walking along St Catherine, I came to a set of traffic lights. I stopped with other pedestrians at the intersection and noted a marked police car in my peripheral vision. The lights changed, and the police car moved forward and stopped on the other side of the intersection.

Two officers leapt from the vehicle and approached me. 'Stop, stop, you. You were jaywalking.'

That was bullshit from the start, and as I glanced toward the police car, I saw a shadow in the rear of the vehicle. They asked me for ID, and where I was staying in Montreal. I handed over my Australian driver's licence, and lied about my address in Montreal.

One of them took down my particulars, and as I tried to manoeuvre my body to see if there was someone in the back of their vehicle, one of them purposefully blocked my view. The address on my licence was actually that of Detective Sergeant Gary Spencer, who was still in Sydney. I imagined him being harassed by the Royal Commission about me and our relationship. Spencer had just married Sergeant Donna Murphy, the new licencing sergeant at Kings Cross. I imagined their house being raided and her giving Gary an earful!

'That fucking Charlie! This is all your fault!' She would berate him for the next decade.

It's quite hard to keep a humorous thought in your mind when you have two lying policemen trying to screw you over. They gave me some bullshit about a caution this time, then scurried back to their vehicle and sped off down the street.

I had been compromised. I was certain of it. I threw the mobile phone in the next garbage bin and quickly disappeared into the underground and made my way to another part of the city where I rang Bram on a different number.

I explained to him the ruse used to stop me and that I was sure that there had been someone else hiding in the car. He didn't seem to have the same concerns I had; he had recently read that there was a blitz on jaywalkers in Montreal. It was as a result of Rudy Giuliani, the mayor of New York, having had such a success with his zero tolerance approach to crime.

My reaction was that there could only be a 10 per cent probability of that being the case. Bram said he could have someone else turn up in a few days, and continue with my work. Although I suspected I had been made, I had already set the times and dates for the meetings to distribute the rest of the money. It would be as difficult, if not more difficult, to alter those arrangements, and I was confident that those plans had not been compromised. So, I declined his offer.

I went back to the other apartment, and told Dubravka that she would have to leave immediately. She again pestered me about what was going on, and I again declined to elaborate, which pissed her off no end, and she was more than happy to go. I went and saw Pierre the concierge at the apartment building and checked us out but paid the total amount, which was a further three weeks' rent.

He said that wasn't necessary, and I told him I'd just backed a winner and that he had been so kind in taking care of both Dubravka and me. He was a good bloke, and I liked him.

Three days later I had completed the task. All the money, bar $2,000,000, was gone. I was bringing that cash back to Amsterdam with me. I still had two of the smuggling bags, and the money left would easily be concealed in them.

I sorted the other apartment, and took a room at the Ritz Carlton, located in the luxurious Golden Square Mile on Sherbrooke Street west. I walked the streets, farewelling some very nice people that I had met in the previous months, and rang Lina from the Old Dublin. She joined me that evening for a cultural delight at the Place-Des-Arts, the home of the Les Grand Ballet Canadiens, and then a magnificent supper in the hotel restaurant.

The next morning, I had the concierge at the hotel arrange a driver to take me to Pierson airport in Toronto, a six-hour drive away. If I had been compromised, there was a better chance of leaving undetected from Toronto rather than Montreal. I had one sports bag in my checked luggage with just over $1,000,000, the other $1,000,000 in my carry-on luggage. I placed the bag on the track for the x-ray scanner, and it went straight through.

I arrived at Schiphol late in the afternoon, and caught the train to Amsterdam Central where a very pleased Bram met me at the station. We walked through the laneways to the apartment that I had been to with him on a number of occasions, and I opened the concealments and removed the cash. I handed him the bank note 'receipts' for over $20,000,000, which themselves had a face value of nearly $500.

Without even blinking, he waved me off and said, 'Buy a beer.'

I told him again about my concerns regarding being stopped by the police, and he was convinced it was Rudy Giuliani's fault and not to worry so much. I left him that afternoon, and we were to meet the following day at the unnamed bar where I had first met him months before.

With that, I rang Dubravka, and met her back at our new apartment. The weather had turned in Amsterdam, and the sunshine that I had left months before was long gone. As I strolled back to the apartment, I tried to convince myself that I had not been compromised in Montreal, but the niggling doubt remained.

I should have gone with that gut instinct. I could have made some calls and found out more information. Instead I shrugged it off, and that was a big mistake.

I had been given $100,000 by Bram as payment, and a promise of more over the next few weeks, and I was more than happy. Walking back and passing the smiling faces of so many people in the coffee shops, I felt a sense of achievement as if I had been part of a community service, and in no way felt any sense of wrongdoing. Why was marijuana illegal?

It made no sense, and even less as I saw a bucks' night of 10 English hooligans drunk and falling over each other, screaming obscenities at passers-by.

Without exception, in the previous months in Montreal I had not had dealings with any person that a fair-dinkum society would have any objection to. The law may have its objections, but then as Mr Bumble said in *Oliver Twist*, 'The law is an ass'.

Dubravka and I planned our trip to Bali, and I contacted Kim and made arrangements for her and the boys' flights to Bali in three weeks' time. Just when I thought that I could see a bit more of the northern hemisphere, Bram called and asked if I could fly to Hong Kong in two days' time. I said, why not?

I met him the next morning, and he gave me back one of the smuggling bags which had $500,000 in it and asked me to deliver it to a man who would be sitting next to the piano at the Holiday Inn hotel on Nathan Road in Hong Kong.

An easy job for me, I had been to Hong Kong many times before. I could catch up with Snapper Cornwell's mate Jolly, and have 'breakfast with the stars' (a morning gallop for the horses competing in the group one races on the weekend, and a chance to speak to the trainers and jockeys). That was on at Sha Tin in a few days, and Jolly could surely get us an invitation.

Dubravka was interested in a course some spiritual guru was holding in New York, and asked if she could go. I told her to crack on, and she could meet me in Bali in a few weeks.

I left for Hong Kong the following day. Jolly had booked me into the Emperor Lord Byron, which overlooks Happy Valley Race Course. He had scored us tickets to 'breakfast with the stars' and had arranged an appointment with a diamond dealer.

I had made the decision to ask Dubravka to marry me, and the last time I was passing through Hong Kong, Jolly had told me that he had a mate who could get very good deals on diamonds. I sailed through customs with around $600,000, and Jolly met me at the Emperor Lord Byron. We went straight to the diamond dealer in Kowloon, near Victoria Harbour.

Over the past year, I had listened to the girls talk about diamonds and remembered that Dubravka liked an emerald cut, so I walked in, handed Jolly's mate $10,000 cash and asked him to have the diamond that I selected set in a white-gold ring. I told him I would be back in about 10 days to pick it up. The same ring at the jewellers down the road was $30,000, so that made me happy and would please Dubravka as well.

Jolly and I went to the Jockey Club that night for dinner, where he was always being befriended by wealthy Chinese men as his badge number was 88. The number 8 has long been regarded as the luckiest number in Chinese culture, and 88 symbolises fortune and good luck. Jolly regarded it as his pension.

The following day, I took the bag with the $500,000 to the Holiday Inn. I had been there at least half a dozen times and it was a very busy hotel. I knew where the piano was, as on occasions, usually intoxicated, I had tinkled those very ivories. I arrived at the hotel, walked straight up to the bar and in full view of the piano, a man in his mid-thirties, well-dressed and tanned caught my eye and smiled.

I smiled back, and he approached the bar, asking if I would like a drink.

'Please, I'll have a vodka and tonic, tall glass and lots of ice.'

He ordered the drink and came and sat next to me.

'Thanks, have you got something else for me?' I asked.

With that, he looked me in the eye, and his face beamed, as he put his hand on the inside of my thigh and said, 'Oh yes, I surely do!'

Taken aback, and not knowing what to do, I looked past his beaming face and could see directly behind the reception desk, a Pakistani man sitting rather nervously right next to another piano.

I apologised to him and stood, putting $100 Hong Kong dollars on the bar next to his glass and walked away from his no-longer beaming face.

I walked over to the Pakistani man, and asked if he was waiting for someone. He said the magic words, 'Mr Prince', and we left the bar and walked down Nathan Road, where he handed me my receipt. I gave him the bag and we parted company.

I rang Jolly and he said he would pick me up the following morning at 7am, and we would cab it to Sha Tin for 'breakfast with the stars'. When we arrived, a well-known Sydney trainer had a horse running on the Saturday, and on seeing me there, came over and thanked me for assisting his son who had found himself in a lot of bother some two years prior. He told me that I should back his horse, as it was very likely to win.

I thanked him and left $20,000 with Jolly to place the bet for me, as I was heading to Geneva, Switzerland that evening. I said my goodbyes to Jolly and told him that I would be back in a week to pick up the engagement ring, and, hopefully, the winnings from the horse.

That evening I flew to Geneva, arriving mid-afternoon. Geneva is not unlike Montreal in that its main language is French, and it's a hive of activity. Nearly every ex-pat person you meet is involved in banking or finance of some description.

As smart as they all look, and as convincing as they may sound, their moral compass could well do with a shake-up. I truly believed that the people that I had found myself with over the past months held themselves to a far higher ethical standard than the bankers of Geneva.

I was only there for 48 hours, and had booked a hotel on Lake Geneva, which had a panoramic view of Mont Blanc as the backdrop. I was only there to pick up a bag of passports for Bram, and was to drop them off to him in Amsterdam before returning to Bali. I set the alarm to coincide with the running of the race at Sha Tin.

I rang Jolly, who was at home listening to the race on the radio in his apartment in Hong Kong. He turned up the volume so I could hear the race through the telephone. Sure enough, that horse romped in, and started at 4/1, so I had a very nice $100,000 to pick up on the way to Bali.

After a very hearty breakfast, followed by a massage and spa, I met with Bram's associate, and took possession of the bag containing the passports. I flew back to Amsterdam that afternoon. I went directly to our apartment and organised with the neighbour to take care of things, and said that Dubravka and I would be returning in about three weeks.

I then caught up with Bram and gave him the passports and he asked me how many I wanted. I told him that I did not want one, and he laughed and handed me one. There was a passport in the bag with a different name, but it had my picture in it. I laughed as well, as I had not given him a photo of me and yet he had a new passport in a different name with my picture.

I took it from him, and we parted on the agreement that I was to be back in Amsterdam no later than 15 January.

19

THE PRINCE GOES TO AFGHANISTAN

As I was walking out of the apartment the following morning, the phone rang.

It was Bram and he asked me to meet him for coffee. He mentioned a café, not a coffee shop but a breakfast café that I knew, and I met him there 20 minutes later. When I turned up, he asked if I could make a quick dash to Islamabad, Pakistan.

There was an urgent need to drop off $1,000,000. He assured me that getting through customs was a very simple task, but I had to be alert and security-minded as I would have to drive to Jalalabad, very close to the Afghan border, and that as Kabul had just fallen to the Taliban, it would likely be very dangerous. Then he handed me a bottle of spray tan and said that I would need it.

'What's the spray tan for?' I asked.

He said that as an Anglo-Saxon male with blond hair, I would stand out so much that I would be stopped by every soldier or policeman that passed my way. And should I be seen in Afghanistan by the Taliban, I would surely be taken captive. He gave me a pamphlet for a wig store in Amsterdam, and suggested that I dye my hair or purchase a dark wig before leaving. I chose to get the wig as the last time I had some colour put in my hair it burned my scalp.

I said that I had already booked my flights to Bali, and that I was going via Hong Kong to pick up the engagement ring for Dubravka.

'Forget the engagement ring!'

He then proceeded to offer me fatherly advice on the perils of marriage, adding that I could buy five engagement rings if I did the job. I sat holding the bottle of spray tan, and thinking of how exciting it would be, and agreed to do it. He smiled, and handed me the itinerary.

'Get a flight to Istanbul tomorrow morning. I will have a man meet you at your hotel. He already has one of the smuggling bags, and it will have the money stashed inside. You can spend the day in the markets, as he won't arrive until late in the evening. The following morning, get a flight from Ataturk airport to Islamabad. Turkish Airlines flies there daily, and it's a six-hour flight.

'You will sail through customs in Islamabad. Get a real taxi from the airport in Islamabad. Do not under any circumstances take a lift from someone who tells you he will give you a lift to the hotel. You will likely never be seen again. Stay at the Marriott Hotel. It's in a great location, and the security is good. Give me a call when you arrive, and I will tell you what the plan is from there. Oh! And start with the fake tan.'

I left Bram and went to the wig shop, and the man serving told me that I looked better as a blond, but the wig that I had selected was okay. I assured him that it was for a fancy dress party, not that he really cared.

I went from there to the travel agent and booked a flight to Istanbul, then went back to the apartment, packed a bag, and went for a massage. That evening, I relaxed at home with a very nice piece of hash and a few beers.

I rang my sons back in Australia, and they were as excited about the impending holiday as I was. I was even pleased that Kim was bringing her boyfriend. I was glad she was dating someone else and wished her all the best. I was looking forward to having the family together again.

I slept like a baby and rose early to the rain pouring down, and I jumped on a tram to Amsterdam Central, and caught the train to Schiphol, where I boarded the flight to Istanbul.

My first shock was how cold it was there. It was early afternoon, and the temperature was just eight degrees. Amsterdam had been warmer. I'd had the travel agent book me a hotel not far from Hagia Sophia. If you don't have long in Istanbul, there is only one thing to see and that surely is the Hagia Sophia, now a museum. This domed monument was built originally as a cathedral, around about 530 A.D.

I checked into the hotel, and was back out the door like a flash to book a tour of the magnificent building that took me till 8pm. I wandered the street markets, the aromas of the rich spices triggering an irresistible craving in me to taste some exotic street food, and then I returned to the hotel where I was met by a very short man in his mid-fifties, his hair ruffled like straw and eyes that pierced like a laser beam. He saw me entering the hotel and approached me.

He introduced himself as Ayaz, and asked me if I would like a coffee. I nodded, and we left the hotel and walked

100 metres down the road through a bustling marketplace to a small coffee shop with a number of men outside all smoking a *nargile*, a large multi-stemmed pipe. In Australia, we would just call it a fancy bong, but then I wasn't in Australia, and it is certainly part of the culture in Turkey, and all over that part of the world.

Ayaz acknowledged a number of the men outside, busy chatting away and smoking the nargile, and we entered the coffee shop. Ayaz nodded to a staff member, a young man barely out of his teens, who then disappeared to another room and emerged with a smuggling bag. He handed the bag to Ayaz, and pointed to a red door and said to me to go and check the contents.

I left the table, and went into what was a very small toilet, and separated the Velcro, revealing what appeared to be, without counting, $1,000,000 or pretty close to it. I came back in less than a minute, and handed Ayaz a note with the serial number that he required as a receipt, and he pointed to two of the men smoking a nargile at the front of the café and nodded to them.

'Thank you, Mr Prince. They will escort you back to your hotel.'

I parted with a nod, saying, 'Be lucky.'

He nodded and said, '*Inshallah*.'

I was escorted back to the hotel by the two blokes, neither of whom looked all that smart, but I figured their size alone would deter any would-be assailant. We did not speak a word on the short trip back. They knew exactly where we were going, and nodded at me at the door of the hotel. I thanked them, and they left. I went straight to bed, as I had an early flight to Islamabad the following morning.

I woke to a sunny, cold morning. I had a coffee in the hotel, and caught a taxi to the airport. I checked in my bag, and carried the smuggling bag on as hand luggage. The flight was delayed by over an hour, and Ataturk airport is hardly the sort of place where you want to be stuck. Eventually we boarded, and the flight departed, and six hours later, I landed in Islamabad.

I once again sailed through customs, and just as Bram had advised me, dozens of very dodgy characters asked if I needed a taxi. I declined, and walked out of the terminal and caught a regular yellow cab.

The traffic was bad from the airport, and it was nearly 10pm by the time I got to the Marriott. I rang Bram and told him that I had arrived at the hotel and that all was well. He said that I would be picked up in the morning at 10am by a man called Baddar, which means 'he is always on time'.

He said to wear the wig, and to put extra spray tan on my face and hands, and that we would be driving through the country roads to Jalalabad, across the border and into Afghanistan. Be alert again, he told me, reminding me that Kabul had just been taken by the Taliban, and it was a very dangerous part of the world with the Taliban now in charge.

He assured me that Baddar was a good bloke, and that I should let him do all the talking, and to keep the bag with me. I was up very early, and seriously looked like I had just dived head first into a mud bath. With the wig in place, I could hardly recognise myself in the mirror. I didn't look Pakistani or Afghan – I looked like a very dirty Englishman.

With the wig and a scarf, I didn't stand out unless you were standing in front of me. Bag in tow, I headed down to the reception area of the hotel and suddenly felt paranoid, like everyone was staring at me. I had breakfast and waited, and just as Bram had said the night before, at 10 on the dot, Baddar walked into the foyer of the hotel. He walked up to me and smiled as he said, 'Ah, Mr Prince, I see you have been catching some sun.'

I laughed, and he said we should go. He had a new Suzuki Margalla, and seemed quite chuffed with it. He lifted the back seat and suggested that I place the bag under it.

We set off and travelled through the city to the northern countryside of Pakistan, and there were a number of army vehicles on the roads. Baddar explained that with the problems in Afghanistan, there was heightened security across the border regions between the two countries. The journey was only 250 kilometres, but was going to take at least five hours, as we were not taking the conventional route.

Even though we would be crossing at the Torkham crossing at the end of the N-5 National highway, we had an appointment of sorts with Afghan Border Police and the Pakistan Frontier Corps. The Durand Line, arguably the 'border' between Pakistan and Afghanistan (depending on what tribe or nationality you were associated with) has been in dispute for centuries.

Around 3pm, we approached the border, and Baddar prepared me for the crossing. He parked the car about 500 metres away, and told me to wait. As I sat in the car, many a local passed, carrying their goods and chattels as they approached the security stations in front of them. Baddar was gone for nearly half an hour. Eventually, I could see him walking back to the car with a smile on his face. He jumped into the car, and said: 'We are good.'

We drove toward the crossing, with a few cars standing stationary in front of us, the occupants handing over their passports and identity documents.

I was becoming a tad nervous as the heavily armed border crossing staff carried on. Baddar drove to the security person on his side of the car and handed his passport to him through the window of the car. The very solemn-looking, sweaty soldier with his rifle hanging over his shoulder looked in all directions as he pretended to be scrutinising the passport. He held it for a few seconds without even opening it, handed it back to Baddar and we drove straight through the Pakistani side, and then straight on through the Afghan side.

I asked Baddar what had happened, and he said that he had told both sides of the border that my Afghan wife had returned to her family and taken our daughter with her, and that I was there to see if I could negotiate a deal and talk her into coming back to England. He had paid $200 to each side, saying that I did not want it known that I was in Afghanistan.

Amazingly, they didn't even want my passport or to speak to me. We headed off to Jalalabad, 144 kilometres away, although he was now driving off the main highway. Baddar was singing along as we drove through a number of small villages. You could easily see that the region was plagued with problems and I was saddened seeing the expressions on the faces of the locals. The children, however, like kids the world over, seemed to be oblivious as they kicked a soccer ball through the barren fields.

As the sun was setting, we stopped at an intersection and drove down a dirt road to a farmhouse, surrounded by trees laden with tangerines, ripe for the picking.

Baddar parked the car. 'You better bring the bag with you.' I trusted Baddar as Bram seemed a good judge of character and swore by him. But I was alone in the middle of a war zone with a million dollars in cash, and what's more I was the only boy in town without a gun. I had placed my trust in the crew but it was still a bit nerve-racking.

I lifted the seat and took the bag out, and followed him to the door of the farmhouse, where we were greeted by a man wearing a *kufi* on his head and a *shalwar kameez* (the traditional male dress consisting of a loose pair of trousers and a long shirt). He welcomed us, and asked us to join him for some food. A tall imposing figure, he looked fit, and even though he had a few grey hairs, he did not appear to be yet in his forties.

Baddar introduced us. 'Asad, here is the Prince. His name is Charlie!'

Our host was introduced to me as 'Asad the lion'. As I was about to set foot inside the house, Baddar pointed to my feet, indicating that I should remove my shoes. We entered the house and I was impressed with its cleanliness and the feng shui organisation of its layout. In a nanosecond, three women – all stunningly beautiful – walked into the room, smiling. I was pleasantly surprised, but Asad angrily told them to leave. I was dismayed. It's always safer when there are women present. But this was the last place on earth where you would want to be a woman. It was very clear they were there to have children and do as they were told, and sadly I doubt that will change in my lifetime.

I handed him the bag, explaining to him how to pull apart the Velcro. He slowly pulled out the notes from the bag, and placed the money on the table, flicking through the wads and stacking them in front of us. Without any calculation, he placed the lot back in the bag, and took it away to another room. When he came back, he handed me a note with a serial number, and shouted at the women to return. He spoke in Dari, the most common language in Afghanistan.

They hurried back to the room. Asad shouted at them again, and they left once more, but quickly returned with tea and sweets. Asad asked if we'd had any problems at the border, and Baddar said no. He told Asad that we had to be back at the border before 10pm as that was when there was a change of shift.

He nodded in agreement, and the women then reappeared with plates of food that they placed on the table in front of us and left immediately. We ate, and I only spoke a few words, while Asad and Baddar chatted together. After the meal, Baddar stood and said that we had to leave as the roads were quite treacherous later in the evening when there were more trucks, and we left.

And then came a surprise announcement from Asad: 'I will see you soon, Prince Charles. Very soon.'

'Oh. Oh! That would be good.'

Baddar and I left. I asked him as soon as we were out of earshot. 'When will I see him again?'

'I don't know. Probably in Amsterdam once the job is done.'

As Baddar had predicted, the traffic was a nightmare. We took the highway back, and the combination of poor lighting and plenty of trucks kept Baddar on his toes. There seemed to be an extra military presence on the roads and though I may have been paranoid, they all seemed to look at me when they passed. We stopped again just before the border, and again, Baddar got out of the car and went to the control point. Just as we had earlier in the day, we sailed through both sides. I gave a huge sigh of relief, but that was short lived as the trip back to Islamabad was treacherous as well, the roads bad and the traffic, both military and civilian, heavy. It was 4am before Baddar dropped me at the Marriott. By this time, I had tossed the wig and couldn't wait to get back to get the spray tan off my face and hands. I bade him farewell, and went into the hotel, and was that tired I just fell asleep.

When I woke up it was midday. The spray tan had come off all over the pillowcase and the sheets, and I felt embarrassed by it. But frankly, the only real thought in my mind was to get out to the airport. I checked out, caught a cab back to the airport, and rang Bram. He was reassured as I told him that all had gone well, and that I would be back in Amsterdam at midnight as I had a direct flight back.

He said that he would see me the next afternoon, and we could catch up for dinner. I bought two lemons at a stand on the way to the airport, and a pack of wet flannels and started scrubbing my face and hands and did not stop scrubbing until I arrived in Amsterdam. I caught up with Bram that evening, and tried to grill him on where I had been, and who the players were. He was evasive enough for me to catch the drift that it was strictly on a need-to-know basis, and so we left it that.

He wished me a Merry Christmas and handed me another $100,000, reminding me to be back before 15 January. Dubravka was still in New York, and would not be arriving in Bali for another week, which would allow me to spend a few nights with Jolly on the way through.

I landed in Hong Kong and again checked in at the Emperor Lord Byron, where Jolly turned up that night with my $100,000 winnings.

We partied long and hard into the night, and the next afternoon, I went and picked up Dubravka's engagement ring. Then I was on the plane to Bali.

20

THE TRANS-CANADA BLUES

Pete Moore picked me up from the airport, and by dinnertime, we were on the beach with a Bintang (Bali's local lager) in hand.

Kim and the boys arrived the following day, and I picked them up at the airport and we drove back to the villas, where I told her a more than believable story about what was happening in my life. I still had to come up with a larger explanation that justified how within a few months I was now flush with cash. Trying to spin it as being the proceeds from a winning bet was never going to cut it, but I had some time as Kim and her boyfriend were going to be staying at a different hotel while Dubravka and I spent time alone with the boys. I was looking forward to the family time, as I had not had much of that in the previous few years.

Dubravka arrived from New York the following day, and I proposed. She accepted.

Dubravka and I travelled the island with Danial and Timothy, and had a brilliant time. It had been a long time since I had been able to have any quality time with the boys and I really appreciated it. Sadly, the time flew by and, as much as I wanted it to continue, I had to be back in Amsterdam. Dubravka kept on at me about what I was doing but I figured the less she knew the better. I'm sure she thought that it may have been dodgy, but for the sake of peace, she let it go.

I was making so much money at this time that I was beginning to think I would not have to return to Australia; that I could support Kim and the boys and help out a few mates that were battling.

Kim and the boys flew back the day after Boxing Day, and I flew to Amsterdam on 12 January. Dubravka stayed in Bali and was heading back to Australia to pack all our belongings with a view to moving to Amsterdam on a permanent basis. I landed at Schiphol, and after seeing Bram a few days later, was on a plane back to Montreal.

Strangely, I was pulled aside by customs and had my luggage searched. Not that unusual, perhaps, but it did seem odd at the time. I was allowed to proceed and went outside the terminal and rang Pierre at the serviced apartment block downtown.

He greeted me warmly, before informing me that a policeman had been there asking questions about me, just days after I had left. He told me that he had told them nothing, and that the policeman had said if I were to come back that Pierre should contact him on the number that he had left. Pierre then gave me his name and the number, and suggested that I not come back to the apartments but wished me all the best and said he would not contact the policeman. 'If you need anything, just call me and I will help you.'

I thanked him profusely, and hung up.

I walked straight into a newsagent, bought a card and a stamp, and posted $1,000 to Pierre, who had proven himself a very good bloke. I rang the number, and the phone was answered by a man speaking in French. I asked what number I had rung, and he answered in English that it was head office of the Royal Canadian Mounted Police. I hung up, and rang Bram and told him what had happened. He said that if I felt compromised, I could get on the next plane, leave immediately and he would send someone else.

I said that I would find a hotel in a different part of town, and would speak to him in the morning. I then caught a cab to St Denis and took a room in a small, unassuming hotel on the fringes of the Latin Quarter. That night I could think only of the jaywalking incident and if I was right, who could possibly have been the person in the back of the car? It was throwing me off like a bronco. The car was a Surete du Quebec police vehicle, which was the state police. How could that car be connected to the RCMP?

I stayed awake until the early hours of the morning, then I rang Bram. I asked him if he had heard anything from anyone else that might throw some light on the situation. He couldn't help.

I asked what was going on, and if what I was doing had any connection to America, or Australia, where harsh penalties applied to our activities, and he assured me that it did not. He said that all the monies that I had collected and distributed were in relation to a previous shipment that had been transported and delivered nearly a year before in Canada. At that time, I had been in prison in Australia.

He said that there was a new shipment arriving, which was coming from Pakistan, and was about to land. I was to meet a few people in the next few weeks and pay them monies that were owed. He said the new job would need attention in a few months, but that everything seemed fine with regards to this new venture.

'Listen. Do I have to meet anyone . . . new?' I asked. I was suspicious that anyone new might be connected to the police who had tracked me down at Pierre's hotel.

'Oh, yes. Only one person, but he's not connected to anyone, and knows nothing about past or present deals. Your only job with him is to give information about certain things which are not connected to you.'

'Right. I see.'

'Do you feel safe at the hotel?'

'I do. As long as I don't have to meet anyone else I don't know, then I'll stay here.'

He said that I should meet with the new man that day, and not to tell him anything about the information I had received from Pierre. Just get the guy's number, and have a meeting place organised, and then all that was left was possibly to see Jim the bag man, then I could come back to Amsterdam. I said I would stay.

The next morning, Bram rang and asked me to go and meet the man at a bar downtown, and get his details. We had nothing to discuss; I just had to get his contact number, and have a pre-arranged meeting place. I met with the man, who was tall and very well dressed. Possibly German, he had a very curt manner about him, although he was pleasant enough. I didn't know it then, but this was Vagn Larsen, and we were to see each other again sooner than either of us expected. We exchanged contact details, and arranged a meeting place for a later date, should it be required.

The following afternoon I spoke to Bram, who instructed me to go to the Intercontinental Hotel downtown, and see Jim and Ken, the two men whom I had given $300,000 and who in return had given me the sports bags used to smuggle money. I met with Ken in the foyer of the hotel, and he suggested that we go to his room. I tried to back away from that, since he had another bloke with him.

Something was off as far as I was concerned. I could sense it. The other bloke just didn't look right. He seemed a bit dopey almost. Far too friendly.

Apropos of nothing, he said, 'It's been a long month. I still have my sea legs.'

I stared blankly at him as his words meant nothing to me, and we eventually caught a lift to the twelfth floor, and then came out of the lift and walked up the stairwell to the next floor. I questioned him about why we were taking a long route, and he replied, 'With you, I can never be too careful.'

Scratching my head as to what he was talking about, we entered a room on the thirteenth floor, and to my surprise, there were three other blokes in the room. All of them had beers in their hands, and seemed to be having quite a party. Ken started the conversation, saying that the shipment had arrived, and I told him that I had no idea what he was talking about. He alluded to the fact that he had skippered a boat across the Pacific, and that when they were unloading the hash, the seas were huge and that they all nearly fell overboard.

I questioned him as to why he had not rung me back months previously. We had said that we would catch up for a drink and he said that he'd tried, but that there had been a Chinese lady on the other end of the phone. That to me seemed more than a bit odd. In fact, it was all more than a bit odd.

Suddenly, I had an epiphany: *Fuck! All these blokes are coppers.* Their behaviour, their mannerisms, the fact that none of them had a tan or a decent haircut was a dead giveaway. There was no way these blokes could have spent a month at sea and yet look as pale as they did. My mind started racing at the speed of light. I had to get out of there, and quick smart.

I kept up with the pretence that I was only the messenger, and knew nothing of what they were on about. In this surreal scene, the beers kept flowing, and my mind seemed blocked. I could not work out what was going to happen. Eventually, I sort of relaxed a little. I decided on a plan. I needed a reason to leave, so I proposed that they had to be paid and that I had $2,000,000 back at my hotel and that I could go and get it for them and bring it back in the morning. Of course, they immediately said that we could go and get it now.

I explained that for reasons that they did not need to know such a thing was impossible, but I could be there early in the morning and pay them. No policeman on planet earth would ever let $2,000,000 in cash go begging. Their reactions, their facial expressions, all made it very clear that they were in fact police, but they agreed that my plan would be acceptable.

Ken asked me again for my number, and I gave him the same number as before and he wrote it down. With that, I left the room and hit the subterranean city in an instant, making certain I was not followed. By this time, I was seething.

I rang the number I had just given Ken, and as he said, it was answered by a lady with an Asian accent. Bram had set up a code to be used when exchanging phone numbers. Ken hadn't known how to flip the digits to get the right number. Everyone else in the organisation knew how to decipher it, except Ken.

I went to a telephone box and placed a call to Australia, where I briefly spoke to a person I knew who would know if I had been mentioned in police dispatches. He asked if I was involved in any way with hash importations, and I said no. He said if I was, to stay away as there was a big job on, and that Australians were involved; that it was huge and was far from finished.

I rang Bram and told him, and he said that his company had nothing whatsoever to do with Australia, and said that the only policeman there was me, and that I was paranoid. I said that I was done with this job, and he would have to get someone else to deal with Ken. I advised him that in my opinion if he continued dealing with Ken, he would be at risk, as I was 100 per cent sure that his friends were police.

It was the first time I didn't believe what I had been told.

I eventually found my way back to the hotel as the sun slipped below the horizon. Exhausted mentally and physically, I took a shower. Sitting on my bed, I counted out the remaining $10,000 and flicked through my electronic organiser. My mind was whirling. I felt like the police were breathing down my neck.

Little did I know how close they really were.

21

THE LAW COMES KNOCKING

23 January 1997

Knock! Knock!

I stowed the cash and the organiser and then in stormed the troops, including the man I had known as Ken. The traitor. My instincts had been correct. I should've followed my gut. As angry as I was to realise I'd been betrayed, I stayed calm.

You have been in this situation a hundred times before, Charlie. Just pay attention; take notes; look for mistakes. They will surely make some . . . All police do.

They tackled me to the ground and dragged me out the door. As we passed the reception, I said, 'Hang on. Hang on. I have to pay my bill.'

A bemused look crossed the faces of the Royal Canadian Mounted Police. The French-Canadian guy behind the desk watched on, a look of astonishment on his face.

I placed my cuffed hands into my pocket and took out my wallet, removed a credit card and handed it to him. Everyone seemed faintly amazed.

What they didn't know was that the card was not in my name, but one that I had obtained with a false passport that Bram had given me a month earlier. The receptionist placed the card in a machine, and slid the top of the tray, leaving an imprint.

The receptionist handed me a pen and I signed the slip. He gave me my copy, and I winked at him and walked away, leaving the card in the tray.

That was the second obstacle I'd hurdled. Had the police seen that card, they would have known the name I'd been using, and they could have checked with the bank and found a trail of all the places I'd been.

After a cursory search of the room, they hadn't found the $10,000 cash, or the electric organiser with all my encrypted numbers. *So far, so good.*

I had to smile. Michelle, the very cute and hardworking chambermaid, was going to turn up in the morning, make the bed, and find a wonderful surprise. I hoped she'd toss the organiser, and enjoy the cash. She had told me two days prior that her wage was rubbish, and that she needed to find a better paying job. She'd appreciate the hefty bonus.

I was placed in the back seat of an unmarked police car, three bulky policemen, two RCMP and one American DEA agent squeezed in against me. It wasn't a long drive from St Denis to RCMP Headquarters. Barely 10 minutes later, the car thumped down into an underground car park. I was yanked out of the back seat, marched upstairs to an office, and sat at a table.

The head RCMP officer involved in the operation was strutting around the office giving orders – all in French – to different people. He came over and said in broken English in his drawling French accent, 'Charlie, you are in a lot of trouble. We have you. There is no way out for you other than to help us.'

He was bullshitting and I wasn't falling for it.

Ken and the chief DEA agent then came over to the desk, and took a seat opposite me. Ken was the undercover operative who had purported to be the skipper of the boat that was to bring the hashish to Canada.

I thought back to the two other times I'd met him. The first nearly three months prior, when I had handed him a bag containing $300,000 and he had given me 10 sports bags that were specifically made for carrying large amounts of money through customs undetected. And the second meeting just yesterday when he and all his police mates had been having a party at the very fashionable Intercontinental Hotel in Montreal.

He handed me a folder with a dozen or so mugshots and surveillance photos. 'Charlie,' he said almost politely. 'It's not you we want. You can walk away from all of this. We have spoken to a number of police in Australia and we have been asked, if possible, to give you a break. Evidently, you have looked after a number of police back there. So we are prepared to do that, but you must help us sort out this shit. The alternative is . . . You will spend the rest of your life in an American federal prison. I have your extradition papers here.'

I paused, thinking about what he had just said. Did these blokes have nothing better to do? I hadn't hurt anyone; I'd spent my life being there for everyone else. They must have known that I would never talk or give anyone up.

'Thanks very much, fellas. You can take me to my cell now. I'll see you in court in a few days.' I rocked back in my chair.

The RCMP commander suddenly raised his voice and said, 'You stupid idiot! You are fucked!'

'Yes, sure I am. I'm ready. Let's go.'

I was then taken to a cell block. Just a cage really. Not even a front wall. Just bars.

Next to me, in a similar-looking cage sat Vagn Larsen, who I had met only a few days before. Unbeknown to me, Vagn was about to become my co-accused. He didn't even look at me, let alone acknowledge me.

We remained there in silence for more than an hour, and then a number of vehicles were driven into the docking area only a few metres away. Both of us were taken from our cages and re-handcuffed, and placed in separate cars. We were each accompanied by two DEA agents.

We were driven through the snow-lined streets of Montreal to the Regional Reception Centre located at Sainte-Anne-des-Plaines, a maximum security remand centre near Mirabel International Airport.

From my days driving a prison van, I was very familiar with what was about to unfold, so I was not in the least concerned. On arrival, we passed through many towering gates and well-lit grounds all covered in metres of snow. It was a frigid night, five degrees below. I scanned the skyline, observing towers surrounding the outer perimeter, all with heavily armed guards patrolling the catwalks.

Electric gates and shutters opened and closed behind our vehicles. We stopped in a garage-like area, and were removed and taken to a reception desk where we were uncuffed and strip-searched. I was surprised we were allowed to slip back into our own clothes, albeit minus our belts. Then, we were presented before what can only be described as a check-in clerk. It was not in many ways different from checking into a hotel. 'Name, address, have you stayed with us before, any requirements?'

Then, we were asked, 'What religion are you?' And 'Are you affiliated with, or a member of, the Hells Angels or The Rock Machine?'

The biker question related to a deadly war in progress between the Hells Angels and their arch-enemies, the Rock Machine. The prison population of Quebec was split into two categories: Hells Angels or Rock Machine. As I had no known affiliations, I let the check-in clerk decide. By now, the early hours were grinding me down to a numb stump. It was what-the-fuck-o'clock and I just really needed some sleep. We were both taken to a cell complex and given a cell with a bunk bed.

I took the top bunk, which had a dirty window next to it, and as I gazed out at the snow falling, and the armed guard in the tower, exhaustion overwhelmed me and I fell into a deep sleep.

*

I awoke to the sounds of doors clanging and voices from outside the cell door. Vagn was already awake and motioned with his finger to his lips that we should not speak within the confines of the cell. I complied with his wishes. It was not long before the door opened automatically, and a prison guard came past our door and indicated that we should both come with him.

We followed and were marched down a corridor past numerous other prisoners, keen to see who the new inmates were, and if they knew us. We were taken to a stores department and each given a bar of soap, a towel, a toothbrush, trousers and t-shirts.

The guards took us back to the cell complex, which consisted of eight cells – six of which had two inmates, and the other two were single-occupancy cells. There were tables and chairs in the complex, and a single television attached by a bracket to the wall and a water fountain. Everything was painted blue, and there was not a single friendly looking person in the place. Meals turned up at 8am, 1pm and 6pm, all brought down the corridor to each separated complex by an inmate regarded as a trustee.

We were told it would be two days before we would be taken to court in Montreal, where we could make an application for bail and that if we wanted the phone was available to speak to a lawyer or we could make a call to a relative but that it would be at their expense. There was no point in ringing a lawyer, even though I knew plenty, as there would be little anyone could do from Australia. If I did require one, I could probably get the legal aid solicitor that would surely be at our arraignment to make any call I required.

I really wanted to ring Dubravka. I knew that she would be at her sister Zdenka's place, and I wanted her to know about my arrest before she saw it on the news, as it was surely going to be reported. I rang Zdenka, and as always, she was happy to hear from me. I told her that I had been arrested, and in her motherly way, she wanted to know firstly, was I all right, and what did she have to do? A good woman, Zdenka. No matter what you did she only cared about your welfare and how she could help. I assured her that I was as well as could be expected, and asked to speak with Dubravka.

I waited in the dense silence of the long-distance call. Bumps, groans and noises. Static. Dubravka came to the phone. She had been asleep. I told her that I had been arrested, and that I was in Montreal and that it did not look good. There came a piercing shout of 'No!' through the phone, deafening to my ear, and she started crying. I told her roughly what it was all about, and her tears kept coming.

Zdenka took the phone off her sister, and again, she asked me: 'What do you want me to do? Anything, Charlie. Anything you need, we are here for you.'

I told her I appreciated all her efforts, and advised her not to panic.

'It may be a week or so, but I will contact you at the next available opportunity. Can you please, please, make sure that Dubravka stays put, and doesn't venture out of Australia until I contact her?'

The next two days passed without incident, and Vagn seemed to make contact with other inmates far more easily than I was able to. For me it was French television and sleep with the occasional coffee thrown in. Then on the third day, we appeared on a transport list of prisoners that were to attend court in Montreal.

Vagn and I were taken back to reception at 6am and given a Spam sandwich of sorts and a coffee, the international breakfast standard in prisons. We were then strip-searched, cuffed and shackled, and placed in the back of a prison van.

We were transported to Montreal, where we waited in a holding cell to be called for a mention.

A call came from the staff in the holding centre at the court for Vagn and me. Our appointed legal representative was here, and so we were taken to a cubicle, where a somewhat plump, bearded man in his late fifties named Jack Waissman said that he had been retained to look after our interests. 'I'm awaiting disclosure from the RCMP, and the Crown, and that could take weeks. Bail is unfortunately out of the question, and it will likely be at least a month before we hear anything.'

That was to be expected, and he said that he would put money in both our accounts, so we could purchase things from the prison canteen. He asked if we needed any messages conveyed to anyone, and not to be concerned about any fees, as they were taken care of by Bram. All stock-standard to me, and I left him with Vagn, and went back to the holding cell.

We fronted court at the appointed time, and they read the charge: that I had conspired with others to import a commercial quantity of hashish. There was no need to plead at the time, and eventually, at 7pm, we ended up back at the remand prison.

Jack Waissman had given me a set of facts about the case, and I was somewhat confused as to what role the DEA was going to allege I had played. Twenty-five tonnes of hash had left Pakistan in August, and had travelled the high seas and somehow, eight tonnes had ended up in Australia, which pissed me off no end. I had never wanted to be involved with any offences in Australia. It also appeared that some of the $300,000 I had given Ken months before was for warehouse rental to store the hash when it finally arrived in Montreal. Right: $80,000 for warehouse rental? I mean, I could have bought a house for that. I was sure someone in the DEA had scammed that money.

To me, it was just the American DEA doing what the AFP had done with Marty years before. They had themselves an informant, Jim, and, just like the Royal Commission, had rolled him, and as in Marty's case, had broken every international law in order that they would be paid handsomely, and have a year-long holiday at taxpayers' expense. Do I sound pissed off? You fucking bet I was.

I am not a fool, nor am I trying to claim some kind of moral high ground, but what I was sick to bloody death of was smart-arse police and prosecutors who seem to think that they have licence to amend the Crimes Act to suit their own agendas. Clearly they were breaking the law and using threats, promises and inducements on witnesses and defendants to secure their next five-star holiday, and increase their basic wage by tens of thousands of dollars. There wasn't a good bloke among them.

I didn't know Vagn at all, and still didn't know what his involvement, if any, was in the matter that we were facing. He seemed to be quite an accomplished businessman, involved in artwork primarily from different parts of Asia. He was well travelled and had a wife who was more than capable of taking care of things at home without him. In the whole time had been together so far he hadn't talked to me about the case, and as we were still not aware of what our actual roles in regard to any conspiracy were, it seemed right that we did not discuss it.

Meanwhile, Dubravka had decided that she was going to move back to Amsterdam. She had her aunt and uncle in Dinslaken, only two hours away from Amsterdam. She had enough money to get by, and as Canada allowed conjugal visits, it would be easier for her to fly from Amsterdam, as opposed to Sydney.

The American DEA applied to have both Vagn and me extradited, and neither of us wanted that. However, I was well up for the fight, and had there been a Canadian counterpart to Watsons legal team I was sure that we could have ended up having everything dismissed. Sadly, I had instead the services of one Jack Waissman, a man far more interested in how much money he could make than adequately defending his clients.

Alas, Vagn believed in Waissman, and my life was not going to become any easier. I was going to have to sort things out by myself.

It took just over a month to get the limited disclosure (the information the prosecution has relating to the alleged offence). Waissman had it brought to the remand centre by an associate. I then spent days going through it.

Let me state some of the facts for you. About twenty-five tonnes of hash originally from Pakistan was placed on a container ship, but not in Pakistan.

The hash was unloaded in the middle of the Pacific Ocean, from a container ship to another vessel. Eight tonnes were unloaded from that vessel further south in the Pacific Ocean, and loaded onto another boat bound for Australia. Then 17 tonnes of hash was unloaded from the first vessel to a US navy ship north of Vanuatu, and from there taken by helicopter to the US. This was why the American DEA were involved and wanted to extradite me.

The bloke I had met who had called himself Jim was an informant, and had been arrested in the US the previous year on a minor matter that may have earned him a custodial sentence. *May have*. Anyway, he was offered a deal where those charges were dropped.

Jim had previously worked with what was now called the Pacific Mariner Cartel, Bram and Manfred's company. He introduced the DEA to members of the cartel, including me. I had given Jim and the DEA agent Ken $300,000 at the Sheraton Hotel in Montreal.

I had also met Ken, the DEA agent, again at the Intercontinental Hotel in Montreal the day before my arrest.

I had been charged with other named people in relation to the importation of hash into the USA so the DEA had made an application to extradite me. But I could defend that charge either in the US or Canada.

They had nothing – well, nothing that I couldn't defend. That said, they did have an application for extradition, and since you cannot dispute the facts, the hash was imported to the USA (just not by me), there was the looming possibility we could both end up in the US to face the charges.

Even more frightening at the time, remand prisons in the US were crammed full and there was a system in place that had prisoners travelling the countryside on buses, stopping at different prisons for the night. The next day, it was back on board the bus and on to another prison. This could last for months.

The judicial process in the US, like most Western countries, was long-winded and impossibly slow. A trial could take 18 months, or even longer. As for the sentencing for such a large importation, 30 years was a realistic ballpark figure.

These were my options. If I was extradited to the US, pleaded not guilty and defended the charges, it would be a minimum of eighteen months to two years awaiting a trial. I was sure I could win, but the DEA couldn't be trusted *not* to cheat. Lose in the USA, and it was 25 years minimum for sure.

Try, somehow, to beat the extradition? Unlikely, but possible.

If, and it was a big 'if', I were able to beat the extradition, then defend the charge in Canada, it would mean I would spend a minimum of twelve months in the remand prison, where the conditions were very poor. But if I was successful, I would be free in around 18 months.

Plead guilty to the charge of importation of the hash in Canada, being a first-time offender and with no history of violence, I would get 10 years and would be eligible for day parole after serving one-sixth of that sentence. After serving one-third, about three years, I would then be eligible for parole, and would be deported.

The decision?

I told Waissman to talk to the prosecutor, and see if the Crown would accept a guilty plea immediately – conditional on them dropping the extradition to the United States. The alternative was that I would defend the extradition, then appeal and drag it out for as long as possible. Then I would plead not guilty in the US if I was unsuccessful. Then if I were to lose, I would then appeal in the US against a conviction, and drag the matter on for the next five to six years.

The result?

The prosecutor accepted the pleas, and both Vagn and I pleaded guilty in Montreal and were sentenced to nine and half years each.

I was relieved. The stress of not knowing what would happen had passed. I now knew exactly when I would be free.

The definite date would be after serving one-third of the nine-and-a-half years: three years and two months.

Before I'd taken the job with Bram, I'd investigated the possible penalties. I'd weighed my options and taken the risk. The money, the travel and the adventure had all been thrilling. I'd known the stakes and reaped the rewards. I'd come a long way from the humble New South Wales policeman and I knew there was no turning back. There was no point in complaining about my sentence. Do the crime, do the time; I just had to get on with it.

22

LIFE IN PRISON

Within days, Vagn and I were sent to a classification prison, where we were to be assessed. We arrived in the late afternoon, and were given a double cell together, along with the usual Spam sandwich and a cup of tea. We awoke to a cold, sunny day, and were keen to get some fresh air. In the remand prison, you only got an hour a day outside, and for the most of our time there, the temperatures were well below freezing. So, a little sunshine and fresh air were a welcome change.

At 10am, the gates opened to the yard, an area the size of a football field, covered in bitumen. It had recently been cleared of snow. We walked around the perimeter, a mesh fence topped with razor wire and supervised by guards in towers, armed with rifles.

We joked about the possibilities of escape, in the same way that people joke about winning the lottery (it's never going to happen but, you know – what if . . .?). It was good to breathe some fresh air, and we were looking forward to the month-long classification process being completed so we could reach our permanent homes for the next three years.

As we walked the yard in pairs, just like most of the other inmates, contemplating our imaginary escape, I could see a number of inmates gathering ahead. They were looking at a newspaper, and as we got closer, I got the impression they were pointing at us as we neared. As we passed them, I distinctly heard one of them say, 'It's him, it's him.'

The article had to be referring to Vagn and me, as we had just been sentenced. Judging by the looks on their faces, whatever it said was not making them happy. I told Vagn that we should separate, as it must have mentioned that I had been a policeman. He reluctantly walked on, and I did another lap of the yard. Then the siren sounded indicating that it was time to re-enter the block. Vagn had passed the gathering, but they remained, so I slowed down in the hope that the area would be clear as I was returning to the block.

I leaned down and grabbed two stones that fit neatly in the palms of my hands. As I approached the gathering, I had my sights firmly set on what I believed to be the leader of the pack. I was about to take the first step, my eyes focused on the ringleader and ready to let rip, when I was struck in the back of the head and knocked to the ground.

Instantly, boots and fists began to pummel me, all hitting different parts of my body. I assumed the foetal position and covered up as best I could, and then there was the loudest bang I had ever heard. The guards in the towers fired a number of warning shots into the air, and with that the group dispersed and fled back into the block.

Dishevelled and somewhat battered, I picked myself up and wiped myself down. I was escorted by two prison guards back into the block where piercing eyes followed me. On the far side of the block, the instigator was being held by two other guards. Then a senior guard came over to me, and said that I should come with him, that forms needed to be filled out. He also mentioned in passing that the ringleader would be heading to a maximum-security prison.

He had with him a copy of *La Gazette,* the daily newspaper in Montreal, and on page three, there was a picture of Vagn and me, with copy stating that I was a detective from Australia, and that I had just been sentenced for the importation of a large amount of hash into Canada.

He wanted me to sign a complaint of assault against the ringleader. I refused.

'Then you'll have to be placed in segregation,' he said.

I refused that as well, and unlike in an Australian gaol, he walked off, saying, 'I have to get another paper for you to sign, saying that you refuse segregation.'

I nodded, and he left. Most other inmates were already sent to their cells, but as I was walking back to mine, a portly grey-haired gentleman in his late fifties approached me, with some difficulty. 'Good man. You have no more problem here in Canada. I tell everyone, you and your friend are with me.' He smiled, and waddled off to his cell. His legs were obviously paining him.

I went back to my cell, and Vagn, after making sure I was okay, made it abundantly clear he was not happy that he was now associated with a policeman, and rightly so.

It was bad enough doing time in *any* gaol, let alone in a foreign country, only to find out that your co-accused was a copper! Jesus. Just when things were looking up in our relationship as well. Not much was said for the rest of the day or the following morning.

At 10am, we were sent to the laundry where once more, I spied the portly old man. He was seated at a table. A very fit-looking young French-Canadian man in his twenties came over and shook Vagn's hand and then mine. 'How you doing?' he asked. 'I'm Frank Cotroni Junior, and this,' he indicated with his hand, 'is my father, Frank Cotroni Senior.'

Frank Cotroni was head of the Mafia in Montreal. Known as the Big Guy, he was one of Canada's most colourful and flamboyant mobsters, and was the boss of the Cotroni crime family. Frank, Frank Jr and twenty-two others were arrested shortly after Vagn and I, and had just been given seven years each.

Frank Jr said that his father had liked the way I had handled myself, and that he would ensure my safety in prison. He said that he had arranged to go to Cowansville Prison and suggested that if we had the chance, that we should go there too.

The Big Guy called a guard over and told him to put Vagn and me to work in the laundry. The laundry was by far the best position to have at the prison; it kept you out of your cell all day, and in prison terms it was one of the better gigs going. The guard came straight over to Vagn and me and said, 'It looks like you have a job.'

I walked over to Frank, who looked me square in the eyes. We shook hands and smiled, with a nod. A good bloke.

Both the Franks went to Cowansville the next week. The weeks flew by at the classification prison. Vagn and I ended up at Cowansville as well. Once again, we endured the rigmarole of being checked in and Vagn and I were assigned to the same block, in opposite cells.

It was a pleasant change, as for the past three months, we had shared a cell. Now we had our own cells, and could sort out how we wanted to live for the next three years.

Frank Jr and Vagn seemed to get on well, and Vagn was quickly introduced to the prison heavyweights and as much as the Big Guy had my back, I was never going to make friends, not with the heavyweights anyway.

I had already asked Jack Waissman to get me a copy of the Prisons Act, the Corrections Conditional Release Act and a copy of Canada's Charter of Rights and Freedoms. I had to find out what, in fact, the rules were, and not the rules that you were told by the people in charge. It took a week and more until I had grasped the entitlements fully, and the ones that immediately affected Vagn and me, regarding parole and our entitlements both to early release and work release.

The rules also affected visits, especially conjugal ones, as in our case, any likely visitors were not living in Canada. I also investigated our general rights regarding what you were allowed in your cell, and what you were entitled to with regards to diet. Armed with some recently acquired knowledge, I immediately made an application to the warden to have my file amended to show that I was converting to Hinduism. The next day he saw me outside the cell block, and called me over and he asked why I wanted him to know that I was changing my religion.

I informed him that it was important enough for Corrections Canada to ask me what my religion was the day I arrived, and so I wanted my records up-to-date. He shook his head as if I was mad, but assured me he would amend my records and then continued along back to his office.

I waited three days and then while waiting in the queue at the canteen, I called the supervisor over and asked him for a box of food. He told me to fuck off and I went directly to the warden's office and said that I was not given any food. He asked what the fuck I was talking about.

I informed him that I was now a Hindu, and that my food had to be blessed prior to cooking and that it was a tradition of my sect that this be done. It had to be a member of my religion who blessed the food, and as I was the only member of my religion in the prison, only I could bless the food and cook it.

He shook his head, and told me to get lost. I told him I would appeal his decision to Ottawa and the Headquarters of Corrections Canada, and he suggested that I should do just that and not to bother him again with such rubbish. Two weeks later, I received a notification from Ottawa informing me that the warden was not correct in refusing my religious rights and quoted the relevant Sections of The Charter of Rights and Freedoms. The warden was compelled by law to accommodate my rights and I should see him and resolve the matter.

Well, 10 minutes later, I was at the warden's door, file in hand, and he called me into his office. He started with, 'Sit down, Staunton. It appears to me that you are going to be trouble. It seems that you have won this battle. Now tell me how I am supposed to implement this?'

'Listen, warden,' I said. 'I didn't make the laws regarding the legality of importing hash into Canada, nor did I make the laws regarding sentencing, or how a sentence is to be served.

But you can be sure as shit I am going to make my stay with you is as bearable as possible for myself. The sentence I have received is what it is, and there are rules and regulations that govern that sentence, and I can assure you that Corrections Canada will adhere to those rules.'

He narrowed his eyes and pointed a finger at me. 'Listen to me, mister. I have a prison of 600 inmates, and that includes some of society's worst. If they ever learned to read, and had any idea of what their entitlements could be, let alone what they really are, then the system would fall apart. So. I am all ears. How are we going to deal with this particular issue?'

I held up my hands. 'Mate, I don't want to blue with you. How about you supply me with a box of food each week from the kitchen, and I will buy an electric wok and I will just cook for myself and I'll never have to eat that rubbish you serve up in the canteen.'

He nodded. 'Okay, as long as you do not disseminate this information to any other inmates.'

Crossing my fingers behind my back, I said, 'Agreed.' A blatant lie.

Next on the list was what we were entitled to in our cells. The rule was that each inmate was allowed a total value of $1,500 worth of personal property in his cell, including the value of his clothing, and a watch.

Now a bit of creative thinking was required when it came to this subject, as the Cartier watch I had just purchased in Switzerland cost me $2,000. So, I probably should have given them the strap back and walked around naked for the next three years. But that not being an option, I told the property officer that it was a Thai knock-off and was worth about $10.

They presented me with a catalogue from one of Canada's largest department stores, and, of course, there are some barred items but not that many. First on the list, a television, followed by a radio, electric wok, a kettle and a toaster. I convinced the property officer my clothes were also cheap Thai fakes, so their value was minimal.

Then came the linen and bedding. I ordered two goose-down pillows that cost $147 each, a mattress and five 1,000-thread-count Egyptian cotton sheets, two bathrobe towels, a set of four linen napkins, two serving dishes and cooking utensils, a china mug and cutlery for two people. That got me to exactly $1,500.

Then the arguments started. I'm not sure why but the first issue was, who would buy their own linen and pillows or mattress or towels, since they were supplied by Corrections Canada? Well, I pointed out to the property officer that I had the pleasure of his company for three years, of which I would spend a minimum of one of those years sitting or lying on that mattress and resting on the pillows and that there wasn't a chance in hell I was going to do that on someone's hand-me-downs. The pillows were as putrid as the mattresses, and the sheets were soiled and paper-thin. He actually thought about rejecting my list, but soon thought better of it and allowed me the entire list.

So, with the first two issues out of the way, and my cell feeling a bit more comfortable, it was time to work on the visits and a daily routine. Regarding the visits, you had to prove that you had a relationship with the pending visitor prior to being sentenced. The reason that was a condition was because otherwise everyone would just ring the local hooker and get her in for the weekend. Vagn and I were never going to have a worry, as we clearly had a provable history.

The normal entitlement was a weekend every six weeks but if your visitor had to travel from overseas you got five days every three months. There was a block of six apartments inside the prison complex, but segregated from the area frequented by the inmates. Each apartment was self-contained, and the inmate could order his food from a supermarket in the local township at his expense. We were both approved for visits, but it did take over six months to qualify and have the paperwork sorted.

Vagn and I disagreed on the subject of parole. Waissman advised Vagn that he should sue the Canadian Government as foreigners were not entitled to day parole as they did not have a work permit. Under the Charter of Rights and Freedoms, no person should be discriminated against because of their race. Clearly, they were discriminating against both of us. That would mean that for the second sixth of our sentence, we would not be allowed out on day parole, and Vagn was arguing we should be allowed day parole and be allowed to work.

I sued, however, arguing that because we were not allowed to work we should be deported at the time that day parole would apply to a Canadian citizen. In effect, we would be deported at the completion of one-sixth of our sentence. If I won, we would be released within a year. If Vagn won, which he surely would because it was a clear case of discrimination, we would be granted day parole after completing one-sixth, and then have to do work release for a further 18 months. Which case would be decided first?

We had already served 10 months before the litigations commenced. I prayed daily that I would have a result before him.

Vagn spent most evenings with the prison heavyweights, playing cards. He was mathematically inclined, and a very good player and the big boys liked him.

I got on much better with the Rastafarians. They convinced me that time in prison passed much easier if you smoked hash every night before going to bed. They assured me that a smoke of the 'chalice' (the name they bestowed on their bong) was like a sacrament. It brought you closer to God, and apart from that, it made you sleep better.

I was not so sure about the God bit, but it sure made you feel better as you drifted off to sleep. For me even more so, since I had a wok and a food store, so I could cook away at whatever time I wanted, if I got the munchies.

The bloke in the cell next to me, Conrad 'Twitch' Austin, befriended me. He introduced me and vouched for me in the black population of the prison. Twitch was a Rastafarian from Kingston, Jamaica, and conceivably, the only innocent man I ever met in prison, either in Canada or Australia. He was about 30 years of age, with a perfect set of dreadlocks. Twitch was a terrific bloke, and had the ability to score a block of hash with just an hour's notice.

A notice appeared in our block advertising that the Thomas More Institute, an academic institution located in Montreal, was offering a program of university-level studies in the liberal arts. There was an option to earn a Bachelor of Arts degree in affiliation with Bishops University. When I saw that they had graduated 15 Rhodes Scholars, I signed up immediately.

There, I met Fred Dubee. He was a deeply intellectual man. His mind and thought-processes unlike any person I have met in my life. He was also a very good bloke.

Fred took a liking to me at the first meeting in the chapel at the Cowansville Correctional Centre. He offered me a chance at a BA, and assured me that I had the pre-requisites to attain the degree. I found him a bit of a square on the first meeting. Likeable, but wary as to why such an intellectual would be at a prison bothering about what society would deem, at best, the dregs.

Fred would turn up at Cowansville every week, with a group of scholars from Thomas More. They had a weekly lecture in place, and with very few inmates interested, battled on regardless. Further education was their only mission.

I was mightily impressed, both with Fred and his mission, and we bonded. Fred took me under his wing, and we wrote a joint paper on hallowed places. My hallowed places were Wembley Stadium and Uluru. Fred's choices were Highgate Cemetery in north London (the burial place of Karl Marx, among many others), and Hagia Sophia, the domed monument built as a cathedral in Istanbul, Turkey, which I had seen for myself.

After gaining a very good result on the paper with Fred, I went back to the cell block and ordered an ounce of hash from a good bloke whom I won't name as he may one day get parole. It would take a little over a week to come and the price ($1,000) was seriously inflated, but it would be delivered to my cell.

I also had a job as the 'block buffer' which meant that I had to polish the floors of the block each day with a buffing machine. I could finish that within two hours, and then go to the gym and train until lunch.

Then I would find one of the other inmates who had a job as a sweeper or a yard cleaner, and sit in my cell or head to the library and play backgammon until I went back to my block to prepare dinner.

I played a lot of backgammon during the days in Cowansville. I played regularly with two blokes, the first being Maurice Dubois, who was in for a number of robberies.

Poor old Maurice seemed to have more domestic problems than anyone I have ever met. He was constantly on the phone to his wife, and he was sure she was having an affair with someone. He went on and on about it. He was desperate to get out, and counted the days. Unfortunately for him, when I met him he had another seven years to go. Frankly, I didn't give him much chance of her waiting for him.

The other bloke I befriended briefly was an English speaking French-Canadian who seemed to be a bit of a 'Jack the Lad'-type. Cocky, and always looking for a score, Stephen Baxter was 32 years old, a bit scruffy, with long blond hair. He talked extremely quickly, and it was not uncommon to have to ask him to repeat what he had just said.

I was supposed to meet him in my cell one day after he had finished sweeping the block, and when he didn't turn up, I went looking for him. I went to the gym and the canteen and down to the administration block and he was nowhere to be found, so I came back to the block and went to his cell.

The door was ajar, and a towel was covering the peephole used by the warders to check on inmates.

I yelled at the door. 'Hey, yo! Steve! Are you in there?'

I thought maybe he was on the toilet, and when there was no response, I pulled the door aside and there right in front of me was a huge, white, hairy arse pounding away, chock-a-block up the other sweeper from the block. Steve turned, and when I saw his erect penis, my lunch did the 100-metre sprint over my tonsils, and I vomited there in front of his door, and walked away.

I went back to my cell, and 10 minutes later, Steve was standing outside my open door. 'Hey, man. What's up?' he said with a grin.

'What do you mean, what's up? You were just belting one into the young bloke.'

'Ah, don't worry about it. I'm not a poof, he is, but I'm not.'

'I don't give a shit. I'm just surprised that you were just shagging him.'

He tried to explain that he was a 'giver' and not a 'taker', thus negating any possibility of him being gay. He was just horny. Either way, it was a dreadful sight, and one I had no desire to see again.

I tended to stick with Maurice after that, who I tried to get to see the prison doctor, as I was sure that he was suffering from depression and every time he hung up the phone to his missus, I became surer.

I also received word that Bill Bayeh had just been sentenced to 16 years. If ever there was a victim, it was Bill. How on earth anyone can justify punishing Bill still escapes me to this day. I spoke with Bill a number of times during his time in gaol.

We had a system whereby I would ring someone, and he would ring them at the same time and we had a conference call! Can you believe that it's possible for a maximum-security gaol on one side of the planet to make a call to another maximum-security gaol on the other side? Thank Christ we aren't terrorists! The criminal police that assisted him resigned from the force, with a pension. He got 16 years, and did the lot.

Oddly, I was busy every day. Between the normal daily routines, I had a list of clients in the prison. In prison, the answer to every request was 'no'. No matter what the request was, it was denied, and so I quickly became the in-house legal representative for disgruntled inmates. The guards hated me for it, but that didn't bother me at all. I quite enjoyed it at times, thinking of myself as the prison-bound version of Christopher Murphy, the most hated lawyer in Sydney. Well, hated by the police.

I also did a lot of cooking. I would usually start my prep at around 4pm, just before the bulk of the inmates would return from their jobs. I would take food orders from the guys in the cells around me and we would all sit and have dinner around 6.30pm.

None of us were going to the canteen to eat the food supplied by the prison service. The guards hated me for that as well; they would usually be eating sandwiches they brought from home, and had to put up with the aromas of my cooking wafting past their offices. Surely another nail was being bashed into my coffin.

Finally, it was time for Dubravka to come for a visit. She was back in Bali, this time for another guru retreat. This particular one was where you are not supposed to speak for two weeks.

I rang her the day after she finished, and she told me that she was coming, and that she had lost the engagement ring while sitting in the surf on the beach at Seminyak. I was annoyed by this, as well as for other reasons. She did not seem that keen to come to Canada. But she was on her way and I ordered the food for the week.

Monday 11am, and a call came over the PA system that I was to attend the visit. She had arrived, and as much as

I wanted to see her I had my reservations as to how we would interact after a year apart.

The week went fine: it was a break from the tedium of the prison, but the spark between us had about faded. Dubravka was travelling from one country to the next, and everyone that I had spoken to or who had written to me, were not very complimentary about her antics, and I felt sure that she would not last another year, let alone two.

I saw Jack Waissman the following day, regarding the current progress on Vagn's case and mine, as to who would be heard first. He was unsure about it, but still had a dig at me for not heeding his advice. I asked him to bring me $1,000 in cash, on his next visit. The ounce of hash I had ordered was about to arrive and I needed to pay for it. The look he gave me seemed to insinuate that he had to pay out of his own pocket, but we both knew Bram had supplied him with plenty of money to look after Vagn and me and could get more if needed.

I really did not like the bloke at all. He had no choice, though; he was holding money for me and said that he would get it for me. He would also bring me mail. If mail comes through the system, you can be assured that it's read and photocopied. But if it came through the lawyer, it was still secure. I received lots of mail from concerned parties over the years and there was always something uplifting in a letter.

I saw the good bloke, the one whose name I can't mention, after the visit and told him that I would pay him for the hash I'd ordered after the legal visit the following week. He was fine with that. There are two types of currency and power in a prison, one being muscle or the association with muscle, and the other being cash or its equivalent, tobacco.

Fred and the other members of the Thomas More Institute turned up the next day, and I was keen to attend. We would congregate in the prison chapel, and I would make gourmet sandwiches for them which were very well received, and we would sit, eat and discuss wonderful topics.

On this particular day there was a lecture on forgiveness. It started with a reading of *The Sunflower*, a book on moral ethics and the Holocaust by Simon Wiesenthal, in which he reminisces about his experience with a terminally wounded Nazi.

The young Nazi confesses to Wiesenthal that he gunned down 300 Jews as they were trying to flee a burning house. On his death bed, he asks for Wiesenthal to forgive him. The second half of the book records the responses of leading intellectuals when asked what they would have done in Wiesenthal's place. Would they have forgiven the Nazi? It's a great read, and it certainly set my mind on a process to see if I had the ability to forgive.

So, can you imagine six intellectuals, a murderer, two bank robbers, a car thief, a rapist (still in denial), a con man, two stoned Rastafarians and myself. Now that's entertainment!

The next day I got a call to the visit section for a legal visit. Jack had not turned up and had sent an associate, Valentine Bouchard, a lawyer from his office. She was in her mid-twenties, and she was sultry with a flirtatious manner that she could use to distract from the issue at hand, if necessary.

Waissman had put an envelope in my file with the $1,000 in cash inside. I chatted with Valentine for half an hour and left the visit section to return to the block. Unexpectedly, I was stopped for a search. It was not uncommon to be searched after a visit, but it was unheard of to be searched after a legal visit, and I objected to being searched after leaving.

The guard went directly for my legal papers, grabbed the envelope and without even looking inside, he smiled at his partner. They *knew*. Someone had told them I was receiving cash from the lawyer. Now, many an inmate before me had been given cash on a normal visit, and if searched, and the money found on him, it would be taken off him and placed in his prison account. There is no real value having cash within the confines of the prison; it usually gets passed back to visitors during visits, and commonly to wives or girlfriends by inmates who are doing something dodgy inside. But they were going to throw the book at me. You would have thought they'd won the bloody lottery.

Valentine was arrested at the front gates, and I was taken to the Hole (otherwise known as segregation).

The warden came to see me. 'You've done it now, Staunton. The police will be here to see you tomorrow.'

I calmly pleaded ignorance and said it must have been a mistake, and he smiled. He left, and I had the night to think about what was going to happen. The good bloke would never have given me up – that would make no sense. It had to be George, a dodgy character who turned up everywhere. He was a junkie type, a French-Canadian in his early thirties who'd been hanging around our block for the past month, and already seemed to know everyone's business.

It was a long, cold night. The segregation unit was an eight by six-feet cement room, lacking windows. The light burned 24 hours a day. Certainly, no Egyptian cotton sheets and goose-down pillows. During the night, I was given paperwork that stated that I would be criminally charged with possessing a prohibited article within the confines of the prison.

They had me now, and all the grief that I had given them was about to be paid back tenfold.

My first concern was for Valentine. She was a lawyer, and if she were convicted of smuggling a prohibited article into a prison, she would at the very least be disbarred.

My second concern was that if I were convicted, then I would no longer be a first-time offender and that might mean that I would not be eligible for parole after serving one-third of my sentence. And the bastards knew that.

Finally, how long would they keep me locked up in the Hole? The Prisons Act states that upon receiving an application from an inmate in segregation the warden must see that inmate within 24 hours. Well, the big fellow was definitely coming to see me the next day. However, there was no sign of the warden the next afternoon. Instead, he sent his representative – a French-Canadian lady in her early thirties, who was going to do what the boys wouldn't, and that was to screw me.

She knew the law, and was going to adhere to the letter of it. The discussion began with me trying to sweet-talk her. My mistake. That lasted not two minutes, and the gloves came off, and we were into it.

She let slip that I was being held under administrative segregation. That was her mistake, and rather than bore you with the whole act, suffice it to say that the administrative segregation conditions of confinement, subsection 83(2), says, 'Inmates will on admission be provided with their personal property items – subject to safety and security concerns'. The act continues, but it only got better for me. I had my TV, stereo, CDs and personal items delivered immediately, and the staff in the Hole were livid.

No one had ever had anything in the Hole, and that's the way they liked it. They sent an inmate from the canteen to see me regarding my food, as they said it was a security issue if I were to cook in the cell. I copped this, but the inmate slipped me a note inside a Spam sandwich.

The note said that George was the rat, and that he had been found out. George was now also in segregation for his own protection, and was going to be transferred to another gaol. The note told me to pay attention to the lunchtime sandwiches that would be delivered to me. From that, I deduced that this problem wasn't going to go away any time soon.

Jack Waissman came to see me the next day, and he was furious. He said that Valentine was going to be charged by the Surete du Quebec (the provincial police). She had been detained the previous day, but when she was cautioned, she refused to answer and they were now making further inquiries. I was definitely going to be charged, and they would do it by subpoena. I had no comeback when speaking to Jack. He took the high ground, and I just had to endure his endless berating.

I told Jack that he should contact the Surete du Quebec, and tell them that if they dropped any further action against Valentine, then I would plead guilty to the charge. It would have been a relatively simple charge to beat, even if they had charged the both of us. But I could not possibly put Valentine through the ordeal.

The warden and his motley crew were over the moon when they heard the news, as it gave them numerous options – all of which were seriously going to fuck me. It was war, and I was going to lose this particular battle. I had made up my mind that I would plead guilty in order to save Valentine the grief. That said, there was no way I was going down without a fight

So, it really meant sticking it to the system, and making the most of a truly shitful situation. I had my TV and stereo, and with the stereo came a Louis Armstrong CD, *Satchmo*. I put it on and played the song, 'What a Wonderful World'. With the volume pushed slightly past bearable, I played that song over and over again. I sang the lyrics as it played, and it drove the guards mad and there was nothing that they could do about it. I kept it going every day, at times in the early hours of the morning. Just belting it out it was therapy for me, but it had the effect of annoying them senseless.

After lodging an appeal against the administrative segregation, they had to divulge why they had kept me in the Hole for so many weeks. They wanted me out of the general population, and they came up with the perfect answer to keep me locked in the Hole. The warden said that I had received the money from my lawyer to bribe a guard in order to assist me to escape. What a lot of bullshit that was! I pointed out to him that if it only cost $1,000 to escape, I would have been gone a year ago, as would most of the prison's population.

So, it was mainly for security reasons that I was placed in segregation, and that decision was nigh-on impossible to fight. Messages flowed almost daily via my lunchtime sandwiches, along with the occasional piece of hash embedded inside the sandwich meat.

It was over a month before I attended court in relation to the $1,000 and when I did, I pleaded guilty and was given a further sentence of 15 days, to be added to the nine and a half years. That was bad enough, but then because they kept on about my 'conspiracy to escape', I was reclassified as a maximum-security prisoner. Not a good look at all.

I was to be transported to Donnacona Prison in Quebec City. Donnacona is arguably the hardest, most violent institution in Canada. More than half the inmates are never to be released, and there are more than 500 of them held there. Potentially, I had 18 months to serve. It was clear that the system wanted revenge for the grief I had caused, but this seemed a bit over the top. They had let the lifers in Donnacona know that I was once a cop, so I had valid reasons to be concerned.

Finally, after 67 days in the Hole, I was placed on a prison van, glad to see daylight, but extremely worried as to what was going to happen. A surprise was waiting for me. Maurice, my backgammon partner, was also on the prison van. He had a court date in Quebec, and the van would drop him off on the way.

Maurice was to be sentenced on another robbery charge, and it wasn't looking good for him. He sat with me for a while, and then wordlessly produced a key from his mouth. He had made a handcuff key while working at Cowansville.

'I'm gonna escape,' he said, almost sounding confident.

I smiled, pointing out the stupidity of that idea, and the chances of it being successful. He spat out the key, and then took his handcuffs off, asking if I wanted mine off as well. I declined the generous offer, and told him what would happen if he got out of the van without a pair of handcuffs.

He really had not thought at all about what he was going to do; it was more a 'cry for help'. His world, small as it was, was about to become a lot smaller. He would almost certainly get additional time to the seven years he was currently serving, and that would finish what remained of his flagging relationship.

It also meant he was unlikely to see his children again. He had a poor education, no friends and no money and soon, he would have no family either.

I really felt for him. Heroin had ruined his life from an early age, and he had been discarded by society. I convinced him that he should at least wait and see what would happen at his court hearing, and that I would assist him with a program to help sort some of the issues that had caused him to be in this parlous state.

He agreed, and I placed his handcuffs back on him, and he put the key in his shoe. We arrived at the courthouse in Quebec, where he was taken off the van. I wished him good luck, and said that if I did not see him, I would write to him. The doors slammed, and the van continued its journey for the next 40 kilometres to Donnacona.

It was bitterly cold, around minus 20 degrees. There was an ocean of snow as far as the eye could see. It was a brutal winter, and things were about to get much colder for me.

As I disembarked the van, I was frightened, and told myself I must stay alert. The guards ushered me through to reception, where they placed me in a dock. I was greeted by someone I knew, Blue, a member of the hierarchy within the Rock Machine biker gang from Cowansville. He casually walked over to me in full view of the guards and smiled at me. 'Hey, there's a problem, and you can't come into this prison.'

Brilliant, I thought. *Now, if you can just convince the warden of that, then I'll be on my way*.

He went on to explain that every second inmate was doing life without parole and a number of inmates had heard that I was on my way to the prison. Killing another inmate was neither here nor there for them, and killing a cop would elevate them to legend status among the prison population.

With that remark I had a brainstorm. As the on-going war between the Rock Machine and the Hells Angels had been getting worse, there had been an attempt made by the Rock Machine to amalgamate with the Bandido Motorcycle Club in order to equalise the power base between the two gangs.

I asked if it was true that his gang the Rock Machine wanted to amalgamate with the Bandidos, and he asked me what that had to do with me. I told him if that was what they wanted, I had the power to make that happen. He laughed. I assured him that I could, and that if he rang a number that I recited to him there and then, he would be told by the Australian Bandido president that they would pay a heavy price if anything were to happen to me.

The man was taken aback and seriously doubtful of what I had just told him. He said that I had better go into segregation that night, and that he would make enquiries with the leaders of the Rock Machine and get back to me.

Remember way back in the days when I was working at Baron's my substitute when I wanted a day off was a bloke called Felix Lyle? I had eventually handed the job over to Felix, who then followed me over to Springfield's as the doorman. Well, go figure as they say: Felix had become the president of the Bandidos in Australia.

Felix, never the most punctual of employees, was always late for work and I would ring him and find out where he was. It became such a frequent occurrence that I knew his phone number by heart, and it was probably the only number that I could recall. I knew Felix; he owed me nothing, but he was a good bloke (well, at least to me). I also knew that he would have my back.

The next morning Blue returned to the cell door with the guard in charge of the segregation unit. Blue said that someone had spoken to Felix and that they had been told that I was a member of the Bandidos and that if anything happened to me in prison, the Rock Machine would be held directly responsible and the Bandidos would then offer their assistance to the Hells Angels. Meaning the end of the Rock Machine.

Blue then took me from the cell into the general population at Donnacona, and invited me to share a cell with him in order that I would be 100 per cent accepted. Felix had almost certainly saved my life, and in spite of enduring the worst six months of my life, suddenly I wasn't feeling all that bad.

The staff at Donnacona quickly realised that I should not be in a maximum-security prison, and after the mandatory six months, I was sent back to Cowansville. Much to the surprise of the staff of Cowansville, I was not only back, but still very much alive.

In the six months that I had been away, a new chaplain had arrived at Cowansville, and would you believe it? He was an Australian who had lived in Baulkham Hills in the north-western suburbs, just a few kilometres from where I had lived with my family. He had heard about me from inmates and from the Thomas More Institute where he had studied. He was doing a Masters in theology and was an engineer by trade. His name was Peter Huish, a very good bloke, and quickly became a friend to me.

We bonded immediately, and in spite of my atheist views, he would often point out to me that I had 'faith'. He taught me about spirituality, the true quality of being concerned with the human soul as opposed to material or physical things. The shift in priorities allowed me to embrace my spirituality in a more profound way. I am eternally grateful to that wonderful human being. I would attend the chapel every day after meeting Peter. I don't think I had ever met a man that only had one agenda, and that was to help people. Australia lost a good man when he decided to live in Canada.

A decision came through the system affecting our parole cases. Vagn had sued the Canadian Government on the grounds of discrimination as foreigners weren't entitled to work release as we did not have work visas. The result was foreigners were now entitled to day parole instead of work release. I was furious. I had sued arguing that because we were not allowed work release, we should be deported instead. I wanted to be deported in lieu of day parole. It was only a few months until our parole hearings and the decision on Vagn's case negated my argument. And then after all that, Vagn decided that he was not going to take day parole! He was going to stay put as he thought that he would be vulnerable on the outside, and if he breached his day parole then he would not get deported at one-third of his sentence. So he was going to decline day parole and do his second sixth at Cowansville. I was pissed off, but I was going to take day parole.

Not long after, I received word from Marty Clapp that Steve Hands, our mate from Warner Music, had cancer and that it was terminal. I was inconsolable.

I rang his home the night I found out, and spoke with his wife, Von. She told me he did not have long and that he was in constant pain. I fought back the tears as he came to the phone, and we talked for an age. I told him that each night

I would look at the moon and send out all my energy to him and he should look at the moon and know I was thinking of him from the opposite side of the world. I hoped for a miracle.

Each night, I would ring again and try to raise his spirits. I felt terrible that I couldn't be there. The night before he passed his parting words to me: 'Mate! You know how we are practising atheists?'

'Yes,' I said.

He said, 'Well, you know, just in case we're wrong . . . You relax, brother. There will be an AAA pass for you at the pearly gates when you get there.'

Through my tears, I had to laugh. I said goodnight, and my dear friend Steve Hands passed away later that night, but not before leaving me, his friend the atheist, the greatest gift possible.

I received word about my parole hearing. It was scheduled for March, just over three months away. The prison was busy with daily cell searches around that time, as word had got out that the bikies were going to have a big piss-up on New Year's Eve to celebrate the new millennium. Home brews were being found on a daily basis, and the guards thought they had the matter under control. They could not have been more wrong.

I would say a third of inmates drank the home brews that were distilled in and around the prison. Horrible stuff, I thought and potentially very dangerous for your health, but it was strong, and you certainly would get pissed if you got stuck into it.

The bikies had devised a plan that would make the guards think that they were on top of things, but the home brew that was 'discovered' was actually only a diversion from the vast amounts that they had managed to store in the months prior, in anticipation of the millennium celebrations.

Dubravka was back in Sydney for the event, and I was planning a quiet night with a joint in my cell and watching the world's celebrations on my TV.

New Year's Eve came, and as usual, the lights in the block flashed, the indicator that you have 10 minutes to be in your cell. I went to the cell, wished Vagn, Twitch and the rest of the Rastas a happy new year and closed my door. Then it started. The lads in the wings refused to go into the cells. The home brew had been equally divided among them, and the guards went into panic mode, pleading with them to go inside. They all just laughed, and continued to drink.

They knew the ramifications of their actions: the block would be locked down, the guards on duty would inform the acting warden, and he would then contact the prison riot squad. They would come from Montreal, and with teargas or whatever was deemed necessary, storm the block and they would all eventually end up in segregation or their cells.

They also knew that a process like that would take at least two hours. They were loud and getting drunker by the minute. It went on for hours and at the stroke of midnight, an almighty roar erupted at the institution. Around 12.30am, a voice over a loud hailer spoke in English and French directing all the inmates to return to their cells. Five minutes later, they all dispersed, and they went to their cells and closed their doors.

I fell over laughing. They had ruined the parties of all the guards, had a great party themselves, and had gotten away with it. A well-executed, well thought-out plan. I was impressed.

The following days saw a blitz on urine testing. Randomly selected (so they say) inmates were directed to a security block where they are asked to supply a urine sample. The result recorded could affect your parole or your security classification if it was positive for drugs or alcohol. I had been twice before and refused, and once more, I refused.

The result was that I was charged internally with disobeying a lawful direction. I quite enjoyed the challenge, as I would never give them a sample, as it would show that I had been smoking marijuana and that would be then filed, and I would have to explain the results to the parole board.

My defence this time was the same as the two previous times. The internal hearing was set up like a local court, and presided over by a magistrate from Montreal. The facts were tendered, and I was asked how I pleaded. I pleaded 'not guilty', and then the magistrate called the guard who asked me to supply the sample. He gave his evidence and said that I refused to give a sample.

Then I got a chance to cross-examine him. Well, it certainly paid to have worked with Sydney's best criminal lawyers. Firstly, it wasn't that difficult as the guards didn't, or I should say wouldn't, speak English, and so with the assistance of the court's interpreter, it was quickly established that he had asked me in French to supply a sample and it was just as quick to establish that I didn't speak French. Case dismissed, and nothing was recorded on my file.

Vagn fronted the parole board a week before me, and since he was the model prisoner with no priors, sailed through and was granted parole. He was offered a chance at day parole, but refused and was told that he would be deported on his one-third eligibility date. We had many a heated discussion, but he was adamant: nothing was going to stop him being reunited with his son. He did not trust the system and was more than happy after three years to wait another three months and have the certainty.

I rang Dubravka again. She was back in Amsterdam following her trip back to Australia. I wanted to let her know that Vagn had been granted parole and that I had been given a date for my hearing.

When I rang her number, some bloke answered the phone and I asked who he was.

'Poncho,' came the reply.

'Who are you, and why are you answering the phone?'

'I am Dubravka's boyfriend and I live here.'

'Well, Poncho, if you are her boyfriend, then can you tell her that the fucking landlord Charlie just rang.' I hung up the phone. I wasn't heartbroken at all, but I was well pissed off. I had things that I needed doing, and I no longer needed to involve her in anything.

I spoke with her sister Zdenka, who was without a doubt the female equivalent of a very good bloke, and a friend of mine. Zdenka organised all my needs, and I was ready for the parole hearing. Peter Huish the chaplain and Fred Dubee from Thomas More came as character witnesses, just in case there was any opposition from either the RCMP or the prison staff.

The parole board consisted of three people, two lawyers and a magistrate who headed the hearing. The hearing was held in an office within the prison complex. The panel sat on one table, and the applicant sat six feet away from them in a chair. Vagn had prepared me as to how it proceeded, and I was nervous but felt sure that I would be okay, and that there would be no surprises.

Then the lawyer sitting to the right of the magistrate informed me that my parole was not a straightforward matter.

He said that they had received a file from the Wolverine squad (the squad assigned to bikie activities in Montreal), which contained information stating that I was in fact associated with the Rock Machine, and that I was a Bandido MC member.

Apparently when I was sent to Donnacona, and the boys had rung Felix Lyle, the telephone conversation was intercepted by a task force assigned to gather intelligence on the activities of the Rock Machine, and Felix had made out that not only was I a member of the Bandidos, but that I was in the hierarchy. Felix had threatened the Rock Machine, saying that there would be serious ramifications if anything were to happen to me.

I smiled, as I could just imagine the conversation. Felix would have done exactly as the lawyer had stated, I was sure of that. I can still visualise the look on the faces of the three members of the board, many years later. They could see no reason at all for the broad smile on my face. I recited Felix's phone number to them, and said it was the only phone number that I knew by heart. I then relayed the conversation that I had with Blue in the reception area of Donnacona.

I explained the whole story of how Felix was always late for work; how I worked with his brother Daryl, a sergeant in the New Wales Police Force. That I had given Felix every job he had for a decade. I told them that I had not seen Felix for years, and that he had become a bikie only in the past few years.

I was relaxed, and they were amazed at the story, which fitted exactly with the information file that they had been given by the RCMP. When I finished, the three of them gazed at each other and the magistrate looked at me and said,

'Mr Staunton, that is one of the best stories that this board has ever heard and, I can assure you, we have heard some! I actually believe every word that you have told us.'

Peter Huish came forward with a powerful reference, and after a very short deliberation they granted me day parole for the purpose of work release. The Thomas More Institute had said they would take me as a volunteer worker to restore their archives.

Even though Vagn had won his case about the discrimination against foreigners, we still would not be granted a work permit, so a volunteer position was their way of allowing the application. That left me with two more weeks at Cowansville, and three months working at Thomas More while living at a halfway house in Montreal, and then I would be deported to Ireland. That may sound odd, but I am an Irish citizen, having had an Irish passport since I was a child. Before that, though, I still had a few bits and pieces to sort out at Cowansville.

Conrad Austin (aka Twitch), the Rastafarian in the cell next to me needed a hand. He had received nine years for a drive-by shooting. When he had fronted the parole board after three years and still would not acknowledge his guilt, they said that he was unrepentant, and told him to come back when he had repented.

He fronted them after serving six years, and as he would still not repent, they said he had to do the full nine years. He would have been deported to Jamaica had he admitted his guilt after three years. He was never going to admit to a crime he had not committed, on principle. He hadn't shot the victim and had been verballed by the Surete du Quebec. He was a very good bloke, and my friend, and I was going to try to rectify the injustice. I left all my cell possessions to him. I intended to work on his case once I was free.

The fortnight passed quickly and soon it was time to leave. I was finally walking free after more than three years inside. My time behind bars was tough, I won't lie, but I used my street smarts to squeeze every advantage I could from the system. I made it through and I was determined to move on with my life. I said my farewells and at last walked out the door to freedom.

23

OUT OF TIME

Peter Huish the chaplain picked me up from Cowansville, and drove me to the halfway house in Montreal. The weather had turned. Winter was gone, and the spring was upon us and I too had a spring in my step.

Peter told me that the Thomas More Institute only had female staff and that there were about a dozen of them. It was an adult education centre for women. Their archives were in disarray, and the work was more physical than anything else.

The halfway house was two and a half miles from the Thomas More Institute. I was given a room and a very small list of rules regarding what was expected of me while on parole. There was a difference between me and the other parolees, in that as Canadian citizens they had strict conditions relating to them and their work-release programs. Drugs and alcohol were prohibited, and their finances were closely monitored. There was a curfew, and their employers had to submit behavioural reports on them. There were strict rules regarding contact with known criminals and people associated with them.

My list had a curfew; I had to report back at the halfway house no later than 1am, and could not leave until 8am. I had the association with criminals ban, but I was not required to abstain from alcohol, and even though drugs were out of the question, the system did not have the right to ask for drug testing, as I was not a Canadian citizen. That was it. I had cash from Bram, through Jack Waissman and John Ibrahim, and could get more if needed.

I knew Montreal well, and not much had changed in the past four years. It was spring, the weather was warm and the birds were out, the feathered type as well. I had a job of sorts, and with very few limitations, I was a free man.

My first day at Thomas More, I was introduced to the staff, who had all heard of me and were looking forward to having a bad boy among them. I am living proof that good girls like bad boys. I started work on the archives, and the girls were all glad that after years of just stacking paper a structured system was going to be introduced.

I started most mornings at 9am, and I would wander around the institute, charming the girls with stories of prison life. I would attend lectures, as I was still completing my liberal arts BA. The reason I chose liberal arts was because it allows students the opportunity to explore a variety of courses, especially humanities courses that challenge the worldview. I still wanted to save the world, and with a degree in the liberal arts many a career opportunity could arise, and if ever a bloke needed a new career, I was that bloke.

The student population was 90 per cent women, most of them single, so I was never going to be short of a dinner date. I had

78 days left in Montreal before I was to be deported. I attended a number of lectures, and in the first few days I attended a lecture on the interpretation of dreams. The lecturer was a bloke in his early forties and while he was no Robert Redford, he wasn't Quasimodo either. There were 10 women in attendance, all single, and he seemed to interpret every dream as meaning they wanted a man in their life and that he was available.

I could not believe that the girls were falling for it. Gabrielle Kocken, a very attractive Dutch girl in her mid-thirties, asked the lecturer, two other girls and myself back to her house for dinner after the lecture, and we all accepted. The night went well, and while the lecturer had eyes for Gabrielle, sadly for him, Gabrielle had her eyes on me.

He eventually conceded and left, taking the other two girls home. I stayed, and Gabrielle and I had a wonderful evening together and she then drove me back to the halfway house only minutes before the 1am curfew. She was back at the Thomas More institute the next day and took me home again that afternoon. As we were about to leave, she asked how long I had left in Montreal before I would be deported, and I told her, 61 days. She asked if we could be together for each and every one of those 61 days. I said yes.

She drove me back to the halfway house, and I told her that Peter Huish had asked me to attend the Lotto Quebec building the following day, as he needed to hang some paintings in the gallery for Thomas More exhibitors. Each year, Thomas More held an exhibition at the Lotto Quebec building on Rue Sherbrook, Montreal, exhibiting artwork from students, and the paintings needed to be hung in preparation for the vernissage, a private viewing before a formal opening.

I told Gabrielle I would ring her when we were done. The following day, I walked to the Lotto Quebec building from the halfway house, and Peter was already there placing different artworks in front of where they were to be hung. And then looking through the front doors of the building I could see a woman struggling with some paintings. I raced to the door to help her, and as she turned and looked at me, I was struck by a bolt of lightning. Gillian Wallis Johnston, a truly beautiful woman and a contemporary artist in Montreal, a lecturer at Concordia University, was also a divorcee and single mother. Literally, love at first sight. I fumbled around her and finally got inside. Peter came over and said hello, and introduced us. 'Gillian, this is Charlie.'

'So where have they been hiding you?' she asked.

'For the past few years, in prison.'

Gillian smiled and without flinching, said she knew there was something different about me as soon as she saw me. The morning passed as together we hung the paintings in preparation for the following day. It was impossible for either of us to keep our eyes off each other.

'Would you like to go and have some lunch with me?' she asked.

We said our goodbyes to a smiling Peter, and went to a very trendy modern restaurant in the heart of Montreal. We sat for hours, telling each other about our respective pasts and enjoying some excellent food and wine. We left the restaurant, and booked a room at the Novotel in the downtown area. Then just before 1am Gillian dropped me back at the halfway house. I told her that I would have to tell Gabrielle about what had happened, and I saw her the next day, and though she was a very nice lady, she was not happy and could not believe that she was not going to spend the next two months with me.

The girls at Thomas More were pleased. They had liked both Gabrielle and Gillian, and seemed to quite like the fact that there was a sexual *frisson* back at Thomas More. Gillian and I were constant companions for the next two months, behaving like teenagers. I was cracking on with the archives and my studies in the meantime, and all was well.

I still had to help Twitch before I left. I contacted the victim's sister who said that she knew that Twitch was innocent, and that the actual offender had confessed to the shooting and she wanted to help. I contacted the Association in Defence of the Wrongly Convicted (AIDWYC, now known as Innocence Canada). The executive director was Rubin Carter, an American-Canadian middleweight boxer who was wrongly convicted of a triple murder back in 1966 at the Lafayette Bar and Grill in Paterson, New Jersey. He is also the subject of the Bob Dylan song, 'Hurricane'.

I had read Carter's autobiography, *The Sixteenth Round*, and the association was having success upon success. Twitch would love Carter, and they had a lot in common. The AIDWYC agreed to take on Twitch's case, although he would surely have served his sentence and be deported by the time the investigation was completed. Twitch was about to prove his innocence. I tried on numerous occasions to meet with Ruben Carter but alas it never came about. By all reports he was a very good bloke.

Gillian and I had to make plans. I would never be allowed back in Canada, and she had a 16-year-old daughter at school, and an ageing mother that she cared for. She was busy with both and a career as well. Meanwhile, I was to be deported to Ireland, and the only certainty was that I would not be staying there and would move on to London, where I would start a new life, and a new career, whatever that would be. But we were smitten, and there were questions that had to be addressed about our possible future.

The girls at Thomas More could not do enough for me in the last weeks. Gillian and I were spending every spare minute together. I was studying hard with Fred and Peter, and attending as many lectures as was possible. Everyone in Australia knew I would be out of Canada within weeks, and some were even making plans to fly to London.

On 31 May, the girls from Thomas More took me out to lunch at LYS Restaurant, a lovely little Thai restaurant on St Catherine, just around the corner from the institute. It was a very emotional afternoon, and they presented me with a book that they made relating to my time with them over the past year. In it were pictures and handwritten comments and well-wishes. I was extremely emotional. I was very sad to be leaving, and a part of me wished that I could stay in Canada.

I spent my last evening in Montreal with Gillian, and in the morning, Peter and Gillian took me to Mirabel airport. On the way in the car, an announcement over the radio stated that $1,000 bills had been taken out of circulation the day before Vagn and I were to be released and deported, 12 May 2000.

The farewell at the departure gates was very emotional, as I said goodbye to two of the most wonderful people I had met in my life. Then I reported to immigration, and was handed a deportation notice. I boarded the flight and seven hours later, I landed at Dublin airport. I wondered on the flight what, if anything, would happen when I landed. Pleasantly surprised, I walked straight off the plane and through customs, just like anyone else. My mother had organised for me to spend the night at her sister Sheila's place, who lived in Swords, a town close to the airport.

Before I left Montreal, I had received word that I should return to Amsterdam, and was given a phone number. I stopped on the way, and phoned Vagn to let him know that I had been released and that I was in Ireland. He was pleased, and said that he had very much enjoyed the freedom of the past two weeks. He asked if I had plans to return to Amsterdam.

'No,' I said. Vagn wished me a good life. That short conversation was the last time I have ever spoken to anyone involved in the Pacific Mariner Cartel.

Bram, and all the people I had met years before, were never arrested or even mentioned in dispatches. They were all good blokes, but they had lied to me and of course, I understood *why* they had lied. After all, the lies had to do with a product worth hundreds of millions of dollars. But they had lied to me, and it had cost me plenty – and not just financially. As far as I was concerned, we were done. I would no longer have any business with them.

A lie in the normal world happens as often as it does in the criminal world. The difference is that a lie in the criminal world can get you killed.

I stayed the night at Sheila's, and kept her up most of the night with stories of intrigue and millions of dollars. Being a devout Catholic, she was shocked and terrified that the neighbours might hear, so she kept asking me to lower my voice.

She woke me in the morning and cooked me breakfast, and within a few hours, I was on a plane to London. I landed at

Heathrow, and again to my pleasant surprise, passed through customs without a question being asked of me. I took a cab to the home of another aunt, Bridgett, who lived in Greenford, a suburb close to Heathrow.

She was far more accepting of a scallywag, and kindly said that I could stay as long as I liked and that she would assist me in settling in London. I love London, and know my way around, so I bought a phone immediately and started calling people. I had to start from scratch, find a place to live, get a job . . . It was going to be a challenge. But I was up for it, the quiet life and all it entailed. Whatever I did, it was definitely going to be legal.

The first night of my new life I went to the Ifield Hotel in Fulham, a pub just off the Fulham Road. No sooner had I ordered a pint than I got a tap on the shoulder, and I turned to see a tall man with long dark hair, in his mid-fifties with a broad Welsh accent. 'Charlie,' he said. As he shook my hand, he said, 'Howard.'

It was Howard Marks, aka 'Mr Nice', the notorious drug smuggler turned best-selling author and drug-legalisation campaigner. 'Come and join us!'

I was taken aback as I did not know him, though I certainly knew who he was, and had read *Mr Nice,* his warm and funny autobiography. Just as the title of his book suggests, he was a good bloke, and a very nice man. I walked with him to a table, and was introduced to Freddie Foreman, who I also had never met but certainly knew of. as he was often referred to as the Godfather of British crime. Howard introduced me as a good man that had just been released, or escaped, from prison.

I asked Howard how he knew of me, and he said that anyone who was involved in the moving of such large quantities of hash or marijuana was known to others in the business, as that world was not such a big place.

Sitting next to Fred was the very attractive Tabitha Ritchie, whose brother Guy had just married Madonna. It transpired that the pub we were in was owned by Guy's best man. We sat and drank and talked and talked.

I had been in the country less than a day, and here I was having drinks with England's most notorious gangster, the world's biggest and most celebrated smuggler, and Madonna's sister-in-law. All three had job offers for me. Howard was trying eagerly to get me straight back into the smuggling business, Fred wanted to send me off to a Greek Island to recover $500,000 from a con man who had robbed an acquaintance of his, and Tabitha wanted me to sort out a builder who was threatening her. I was weighing up my options.

What price a quiet life?

Epilogue

My life has been a bit more interesting than most. I've met the good, the bad, and the ugly, the famous and the infamous, and for what it's worth, there's good and bad in all of them.

Life has gone on for everyone, as it tends to do. My old friend Marty now lives in Byron Bay with his new wife and son and coaches a local rugby team. John Ibrahim's family are still causing him grief. We catch up in different countries of the world and it always ends up interesting! Bill Bayeh got 16 years and he did the lot. The world's biggest scapegoat, clearly.

Monty moved back to Peru and finally landed a deal with his timber business and paid me back. Poor old Snapper was convicted and I'm quite sure is still inside, while Jolly is still living the dream.

Vagn Larsen was deported to Amsterdam, and other than a call to wish me luck in life, we parted ways.

Maurice Dubois, my backgammon partner in Cowansville, sadly committed suicide. He took a hot shot – a mix of cocaine and heroin – at Cowansville just before I was released.

Bram and Manfred have never been arrested and have now retired.

As for me, I now live in London with a wonderful Yorkshire lady, Louise Gallaher.

I look at the police force in Australia and see a very different force, and one that's much more politically correct, from the one I served in. I see how some of the life and colour has gone from Kings Cross, and I think the heavy-handed policing that is now the norm has a lot to do with it. My mother said the New South Wales Police Force changed me, and for the worse. I say the New South Wales Police Force educated me. It taught me loyalty, and it certainly lowered my moral code with regard to the law. It taught me that respect is not a given in life, but it is earned. It taught me that we all fuck up at some stage; some just fuck up bigger than others and you will find out how good a bloke you really are when you see who is there for you when you have.

My biggest fuck-up has nothing to do with the importation of 25 tonnes of hashish. It's that I was not there for my two sons through their teenage years. That is surely the crime that I still pay for to this day. Sorry just doesn't cut it. Now that I have four grandchildren I hope I get the chance to be a teacher again.

I am still a good bloke, and I still want to save the world. To this day, I get calls from people in trouble who are looking for advice, and I do everything I can for them. At the end of the day, my decisions and my actions have always been based on truth, and doing what I think is right.

Crimes are relative to history, and as I write this story Canada has just legalised the sale of marijuana, as have nearly a dozen states in the US. It still grates that the felony for which I was given 10 years' gaol, not to mention years of wasted time and uncertainty, is now no longer a felony in those countries.

And I'm a criminal?

Acknowledgements

Mum and Dad, thank you for everything.

There are people who need to be thanked, but sadly some cannot be named as they hold positions that just really do not need the scrutiny that an acknowledgement would bring their way. We shall have a drink and keep it quiet.

I must thank Angus Fontaine from Pan Macmillan for tracking me down and convincing me to write this story. I thank Karen Soich, an extraordinary barrister in New Zealand, for securing me the deal. I am forever grateful to Howard Marks and Freddie Foreman for coming up with the title *The Good Bloke*.

Peter Huish, the chaplain and friend who helped me and introduced me to Fred Dubee and Thomas More. To my mates, both criminal and police, who have all stood tall and are still there, in the world of good blokes. Thank you.

To Bruce Hardin, my friend, you amaze me.

Danial and Timothy, my sons, I apologise for my absence. Thank you to their grandfather, Bernie Harris, for taking my place in that absence. To Kim, their mother, you are the best.

And to Marty Clapp, my friend, meeting you changed my life. No regrets, eternally grateful, thank you.